DEDICATION

This novel is dedicated to my remarkable therapist, Cynthia, who continues to help me find my path.

CONTENTS

ACKNOWLEDGMENTS

So many people have helped, inspired, and supported me. Once again, I'd like to thank the folks at National Novel Writing Month (NaNoWriMo) for all their encouragement and their pep talks. This is the third year I have participated in NaNoWriMo, and it has resulted in my third novel. I just love November! I completed the first draft of *Dragon Magic* in November 2013.

Next, I'd like to thank the members of my Wednesday bridge class, who have been unfailing in their support of my efforts. I would also like to thank my students, both past and present, at Student Link, Vashon's alternative high school, who continue to inspire me with their drive, determination, maturity, and insight in the face of major adversities.

A special thanks to some special people in no particular order: Cynthia Zheutlin, for her gentle wisdom and insight; Nan Hammet, for her friendship and collegial support; Nell Coffman and everyone at Fair Isle Animal Clinic for keeping my family happy and healthy; Lydia Schock, for her empathy and encouragement; Peter Scott, for his interest and encouragement; Anja Moritz, for her wisdom, kind support, and wonderful lunches; Kelly Wright for her gentle support; Amber Starcher for her kindness and enthusiasm; Trevor Tuma, for his continued interest and wholehearted support; Blythe Bartlett for her support and eager reading of my novels; and Alex Witherspoon, for his desire to learn Latin as well as his support and encouragement.

MAP OF THE
FOUR NATIONS

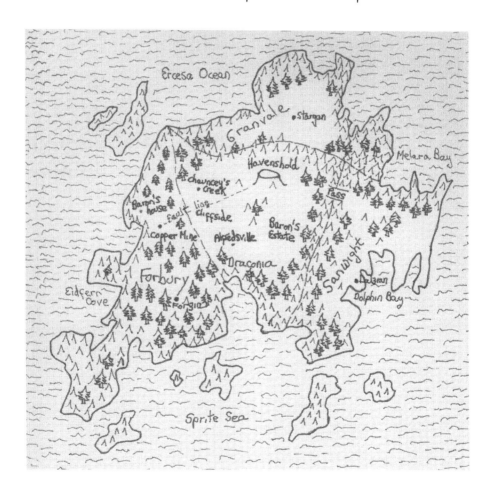

— 1 —
NOTIFYING THE CANDIDATES

Emily sat across from her brother Hans in his office. Hans, a tall, willowy man with brown hair and eyes, was the leader of the dragon riders, and Emily was his assistant. Actually, she was scheduled to take over as the leader of the dragon riders right after this year's egg hatching at the winter solstice. Hans had stepped in to take over after Clotilda, along with her purple dragon, Matilda, succeeded King Jacob as monarchs of Draconia. By tradition, since the riders were always lead by a purple dragon and its rider, Emily and Esmeralda should have replaced Clotilda and Matilda as head of the dragon riders, but Emily was only twenty-one, so everyone agreed that Hans, who was ten years older, and Fire Dancer, his orange dragon, would serve until Emily was old enough to take the reins. Dragon riders were always led by purple dragons whenever possible.

Emily twirled her long brown braids as she wondered what it would be like to sit in Hans's chair with all his responsibilities. *Am I—or rather, are* we *really ready for this? Is thirty-four old enough?* she wondered and was pleased to hear Esmeralda's immediate answer: *"Of course we are!"* Emily smiled and then sat up more attentively as Hans spoke.

"So, you want to notify the candidates for this year's hatching?" asked Hans.

"Yes," answered Emily. "I'd like to get to know them a bit right away, since we are starting the school for the candidates who aren't chosen by dragon hatchlings. I've always felt it must be devastating to prepare for an entire month, fully expecting that you will be chosen, only to find out that you aren't."

Hans said, "They all know the odds from the start."

"Oh, sure, they know there is a chance since there are always more candidates than eggs, and I know there are some who are selected who really don't want to become dragon riders, but still, for those who are hoping and then walk away without a dragon bonding, well, it must be the worst thing imaginable."

"I know you've been pushing for this school for a long time, and I do think it is an excellent idea. The dragons select the candidates because each one has special talents and abilities, and Draconia needs those candidates, no matter what. Will Gregory be doing most of the headmaster duties? You know, I'm retiring from this job after the hatching and your load will really increase."

"Yes, Gregory is just as eager as I am for this school to get off to a good start, and he is the perfect person to run it; I would say that even if he weren't my husband, because he went through the entire candidate process not once but twice, thanks to the insistence of his father, and just because he was one of those who really didn't want to be picked doesn't mean that he doesn't understand the disappointment of those who do."

"OK," said Hans, holding up his hands. "And it is only fair that you should get to take a trip around Draconia notifying the candidates so you and Esmeralda can have some fun before you have to knuckle down behind this desk. Once you are the one drowning in paperwork, you'll really appreciate your few breaks, so get out of here and have fun bringing the good news to the twelve candidates."

"Thanks, Hans!" said Emily as she stood up and headed for the door. "There are three candidates who don't live within Havenshold, so we'll bring them back here as soon as we notify them. Then we'll notify those who live within Havenshold."

"Sounds like a good plan," answered Hans, and Emily left his office.

Emily headed to the cave she shared with Esmeralda and was not surprised to see Esmeralda, a gorgeous fifteen-foot purple dragon with iridescent purple wings, waiting for her. After grabbing her pack containing a few changes of clothes and the list of names, she and Esmeralda headed out to the commons and then flew off to the first candidate: George, a twelve-year-old boy who lived in Chauncey's Creek, where his family had a sheep ranch.

It was a lovely day, cool, crisp, and sunny. *Just the way an autumn day should be,* thought Emily. Emily and Esmeralda enjoyed the flight, stopping for lunch along the way, before arriving at George's home. George's entire family rushed outside to see them—thrilled that a dragon and rider had come for a visit. Emily noticed that George seemed to be bouncing on his feet anxiously, so she suspected that he had already guessed why they were there.

Emily called to George and his parents and announced, "George, you have been selected as a candidate for the next dragon egg hatching. Do you accept?"

"Do I?" yelled George before his parents could say anything. "Yes, oh, yes, I do!"

Emily smiled, and Esmeralda chuckled. She looked at the boy's parents and said, "We can take George back to Havenshold with us today, if that would be all right with you, or you can bring him yourself, but he needs to be present Monday for the beginning of the candidate training."

George looked at both parents with large, pleading eyes, and his parents burst out laughing. "I think George would love to return with you, if that is OK and if you can give me about an hour to get his things packed," said his mother.

Emily said, "Of course! We're happy to wait."

George spent the hour talking with Emily and Esmeralda. He couldn't hear Esmeralda telepathically but was very pleased to learn that dragons could speak out loud also. Soon, Esmeralda had George laughing, and it was obvious that he would make a fine candidate.

George's mother arrived with a backpack for him. Emily vaulted up onto Esmeralda's back, and George's father lifted him so that she could swing him up with her. Off they flew, George waving to his parents.

The next two stops—another in Chauncey's Creek for a fourteen-year-old girl named Patty, and one in the capital, Alfredsville, for a thirteen-year-old boy named Steven—went just as smoothly. Emily, Esmeralda, and the three candidates spent the night at the palace so Emily and Esmeralda could meet with Clotilda and Matilda, but early the next morning, they flew back to Havenshold.

Emily introduced the three candidates to Gregory, who took them off to the candidates' quarters, and then Emily and Esmeralda set off to notify the other nine candidates who lived within Havenshold.

By the end of the day, both Emily and Esmeralda were getting tired, but they had one candidate left to notify. It had been a wonderful day, and Emily remembered just how happy she had been twenty-two years ago when she had been selected.

They landed in a large, grassy yard in front of a white farmhouse. As soon as they landed, a young girl came racing out of the front door saying, "I knew it! I'm a candidate! Oh, I'm so happy!"

Just then, a tall, heavyset woman with gray-streaked brown hair came walking out, a big smile on her face. She said, "Oh, I knew this would be Zelda's year!"

Emily quickly asked Esmeralda, *"We're here for Chloe, right? Not Zelda. This will be tricky."*

"No kidding," replied Esmeralda as Emily jumped down.

"Are you Mrs. Winsong?" asked Emily.

"Yes, and this is my daughter Zelda. She is so thrilled to be a candidate. I know she'll be just as wonderful a dragon rider as her great-grandmother Esme!"

"I'm afraid there has been some confusion here," began Emily. "We're here for Chloe, not Zelda."

"What?" said both Mrs. Winsong and Zelda. Mrs. Winsong continued, "I'm afraid you must be wrong. Chloe is a complete klutz and only an average student with no skills at all. She can't hold a candle to Zelda, even if she is two years older. Zelda is better at everything. It is Zelda you want."

"Mrs. Winsong—" began Emily, but the woman interrupted.

"Please, call me Hazel. You may not know it, but our family is descended from Martha Winsong, a blue dragon rider who came here with King Alfred. Each generation for the next ten generations, we had a woman dragon rider. My mother and I weren't picked, but we knew that Zelda would be. We are born to be dragon riders."

"That is certainly a proud heritage, and I'm sure Chloe will serve just as wonderfully," said Emily. She noticed a quiet, shy girl with dark-red hair standing on the porch. Emily called out, "Chloe?" The girl barely nodded. Emily went on, "Chloe, could you please come over here so we can let you know why we've come?"

"You stay right where you are, girl," snapped her mother, but Esmeralda thought, *"It's just fine, Chloe. Please come meet me."*

Emily smiled as she noticed Chloe give a start at hearing Esmeralda in her head. Chloe walked determinately right down the front steps and over to Esmeralda.

Hazel started to grab Chloe's arm, but Esmeralda snapped her head around so fast that Hazel stepped back a few paces. "You can't have Chloe. The girls are only two years apart. Chloe is fifteen, and as you know, that is the upper end of the age range. Zelda is already thirteen so if she isn't chosen this year, she will be too old for the next hatching in three years. If you wanted Chloe so badly, why didn't you take her at the last hatching? She was old enough then, and she's missed her chance."

Emily noticed that all the time Hazel was ranting on, Chloe kept her head down, staring at the ground, but Emily was also pleased to see that the girl had moved her left hand onto Esmeralda's side.

"Hazel, I don't understand your reaction. You have a daughter who has been chosen; that should cause you joy."

"Not when it is that one," she said pointing at Chloe. "She's never fit in this family at all. You can ask anyone. Ask her teachers. Ask our friends. Zelda is the bright, pretty child, and Chloe is just a misfit."

By this time, an older man had appeared on the porch. Emily assumed him to be Chloe's father, so she called to him. "Mr. Winsong, do you want to say anything?"

"Nope," he answered quietly. "What my wife says goes."

Hazel smirked and said, "So it is all settled then." She put her arm around Zelda. "Go get your things, honey, so you can go back with Emily."

Emily put up a hand. "Yes, things are settled, but not your way." Emily turned to Chloe and said, "Esmeralda and I are here to offer you a spot as a candidate for the upcoming hatching. Do you want to accept?"

Hazel started to say something, but Emily's glare caused her to stop. Emily then turned and looked at Chloe, smiled, and said, "What would you like to do?"

Chloe hesitated. "I'm not really good enough," she finally answered.

Hazel said, "See, even the girl knows the truth."

Esmeralda roared, and everyone except Emily and Chloe backed away. Then Esmeralda said in a very loud voice, "Dragons do *not* make mistakes. We choose our candidates with the very greatest care. It is true that not all candidates are chosen by dragons, but each and every candidate has outstanding qualifications. They each have something that makes them very special and unique. Chloe is such a candidate, and if you can't see that, then I truly pity you. You don't deserve her!"

There was absolute silence after Esmeralda's speech. Finally, Chloe said, in a very quiet voice, "Do you really want me? No one ever wants me."

Esmeralda lowered herself to the ground so that her head was closer to Chloe and said both aloud and telepathically, "I do want you! The dragon riders want you! You are already showing how special you are because you can hear me telepathically and not all humans can do that. Now you need to learn to believe in yourself."

Chloe had tears running down her checks as she turned to Emily and said, "I would very much like to be a candidate, then."

Emily smiled and lifted Chloe onto Esmeralda's back before saying, "Do you need to take anything with you?"

"I'd like my stuffed bear, if that's OK," said Chloe.

Emily turned to Hazel and said, "Will you please pack a bag for Chloe with some clothes and her bear?"

Hazel turned to her husband and said, "Harvey, go do it. Make yourself useful for once."

Hazel then turned back to Emily and said, "You'll see what a big mistake you've made, mark my words. You should have taken Zelda. I bet Chloe won't even be chosen. How could she be? She's nothing but a loser!"

This last remark was too much for Emily. She snapped back, "Just getting Chloe away from you is more than enough. You won't be able to damage her anymore. And if she isn't one of the eight who is selected by a hatchling, then she will find that she is destined for something even greater. That has been true for all of the candidates from the beginning of time."

Just then, Harvey came over to Esmeralda and handed a backpack and a very large stuffed bear up to his daughter. Emily noticed that he clasped her hand and gave her as much of a hug as he could as she sat on Esmeralda. Emily was glad that at least someone seemed to care for Chloe.

With that, Esmeralda stood, and Emily vaulted up onto her back in front of Chloe. "How about we fly back?" she said. "We'll take a long, scenic route first so that you can have a nice dragon ride before we settle you into the candidates' quarters. I think you will enjoy meeting your fellow candidates."

Chloe looked down at her father and waved as her mother and Zelda stomped into the house. Then she answered, "That would be wonderful!" and off they flew.

— 2 —
CANDIDATE TRAINING

After Emily had Chloe settled, she went to report to Hans. "You wouldn't believe Hazel Winsong!" she said.

Hans chuckled and said, "Oh yes, I would. I was eleven when her grandmother Esme died, and trust me, right up to the end, she was not one to cross. But in fairness to Esme, she had a wonderful heart to go with her quick temper. Her daughter Julia, Hazel's mother, is still alive. She's in her nineties, and she was always bitter about not being chosen. She was the first in a long line going all the way back to King Alfred's time not to be chosen, and it hit hard. And then her daughter, Hazel, also was passed over, so that family has turned very bitter."

Emily said, "I should have looked up the family history of our candidates, I guess. Every other candidate was eager, and their families all seemed very happy."

"We'll have to keep an eye on Chloe. From what you have reported, she is going to have a lot of trouble believing in herself."

"I'll alert Jake. I'm so glad he is in charge of the candidates' training," answered Emily.

"Yes, I've been really lucky with both you and Jake. Younger siblings can be such a pain," he teased.

"I'm going to ask Hannah to be Jake's second. She's twenty-seven now and ready to take more command, and she idolizes both of her older brothers," Emily said with a smile.

"What about you?" asked Hans. "Have you thought about an assistant? I can honestly say that you'll want one once you take over my position."

"Yes, actually," said Emily. "I talked with Clotilda when I was in the capital and also stopped in to see Jacob and Marigold. I must say, they look much happier now that he isn't the king anymore. Anyway, I wanted to get their feedback on Rupert. He's Hannah's age, and as a purple dragon rider, not to mention the son of our beloved former king, he is the logical choice. Clotilda agrees, and Rupert's parents were obviously as pleased as could be. I'll let him know after the solstice, and I'll talk with Hannah and Jake today."

"I have to admit, I'm glad you are taking over in four weeks! Be sure you ask all the questions you want now."

"What! You aren't going anywhere, are you?" Emily said with a bit of a tremor in her voice.

"Relax! I'll always be your oldest big brother. But I think I'll spend the winter in the capital. You will need some space to settle in to the position and to make it your own without having me watching over you. Now get out of here and see to the candidates. You have a lot to do this month, and so do I."

Emily grinned and headed for the door. "Thanks!"

Emily walked over to the candidates' quarters and found both Jake and Hannah. "How are they settling in?" asked Emily.

"Great," said Jake, and Hannah agreed.

Emily filled them in on what she knew about each one. She took extra time to explain about Chloe.

"That's horrible!" said Hannah. "We are so lucky to have our family. Mom and Dad never played favorites, and they are so proud of all of us, not just Hans, Jake, you, and me, who are riders, but also Robert the architect and Michael the biologist."

"I know, and our family also dates back to King Alfred. It was horrible to see how Zelda was praised while Chloe was demeaned. Please keep a special watch on her, will you both?"

Jake and Hannah readily agreed.

The month-long training of the candidates was intense. They were rousted out of bed at 6:00 a.m. for calisthenics and breakfast. Then they were taken to the hatching grounds where they gently turned the eggs. There were eight eggs this year and twelve candidates, so they each took turns. The eggs needed to be turned three times a day, and the candidates were given a different egg each time in rotation so that by the end of the month, the dragons inside the eggs would be familiar with each candidate. This was a very important step in the process, as once the dragon hatched, it would want to find its rider as quickly as possible so it could feed on the special meal he or she had prepared.

After the morning egg visit, the candidates went to classes, learning dragon history, feeding, and care. Lunch was served, and they quickly learned that dragon riders ate well. After another egg turning, they spent the afternoon cleaning various pieces of dragon-rider equipment. Usually, each rider took care of his/her own equipment, but during this month of training, the riders got a break so that the candidates could learn about all the equipment a dragon and his/her rider used. After dinner, there was one last egg turning and then the candidates crashed happily in their bunks by 8:30 p.m.

Chloe was hesitant at first as she tried to settle into her new quarters. She shared a room with Patty, and she was glad to have someone she didn't already know. Patty seemed nice, and Chloe learned a lot from her. Patty had grown up in Cliffside, but then after the horrible earthquake two years earlier, she and her family, along with everyone else from Cliffside, relocated to Chauncey's Creek. Patty knew Gretchen, who was now riding a red dragon named Ruby, and her partner, Lucy, who rode a blue dragon named Harriet.

One evening as they climbed into bed, Patty asked her, "Say, tomorrow's Sunday and we have the day off. Would you like to come with me to visit Gretchen and Lucy?"

"I don't know," said Chloe. "I wouldn't want to be in the way."

"Silly," said Patty. "I wouldn't have asked you if I didn't mean it. They're a lot of fun. We can ask them all our questions, and they won't laugh, I promise. They just graduated three years ago, so they know all about the training and the hatching and everything."

Chloe thought, *Patty is so confident and fun. What would it be like to be like that?* After a few minutes, Chloe answered, "Sure, if you're sure it's OK."

The next day, the girls slept in. On Sunday, breakfast was served until 9:00 a.m., and they took advantage of that. After they helped turn the eggs, Chloe followed Patty to Gretchen and Lucy's cave.

Chloe looked around, trying not to stare. The cave was actually two caves with the wall between removed. There were two large alcoves and two big pits lined with colorful quilts and pillows. The walls were covered with various hangings, including some geologic maps of the entire world, not just Draconia. Patty took her by the hand and introduced her to Gretchen and Lucy.

Chloe was shy at first, but both Gretchen and Lucy were so friendly that soon the four of them were laughing and having a great time. Chloe asked after a while, "So what's the hatching like?"

Gretchen and Lucy started laughing, and Chloe wondered what she'd said that was so funny. Patty just smiled and said, "I guess you haven't heard the story about their particular hatching, have you?"

"No," said Chloe in a puzzled voice.

"Let me tell!" demanded Gretchen, giving Lucy a hug. "Usually, the hatching goes just as you'll be taught. The candidates sit in a circle around the eggs and wait. One by one, the eggs hatch and the new dragons stagger over to the rider they've chosen. That's how Ruby and I bonded. But that year, one egg simply refused to hatch."

"What?" said Chloe, raising her eyebrows in surprise.

"That's right," said Gretchen. "Finally, Hans and Fire Dancer—you know, his orange dragon—went down from the stands and into the pit to check on the egg, and the dragon inside was just fine. Meanwhile, Lucy was watching from up in the stands, and, well, you tell it from here, honey."

"Yes, I was in the stands, and I kept hearing this voice in my head calling to me. I hadn't been picked as a candidate because I had lost my right hand—well, as you can see; later, I lost the whole arm, but that's for another day. Anyway, all I ever wanted to be was a dragon rider. I figured that wouldn't happen, but the voice kept calling to me, and finally, I walked down onto the hot sands (and believe me, they are hot so be sure you sit on your robes), the egg hatched immediately, and Harriet ran over to me. Of course, there were a lot of protests—"

"You can say that again!" cut in Gretchen. "The candidates who hadn't been chosen and their parents were all up in arms. I didn't see it, as Ruby and I were already in the new rider caves, but I heard about it. Hans and all the other leaders, from all four countries, met, and finally, they realized that it is always the dragon who picks the rider and that is just what Harriet did," concluded Gretchen, and she smiled at Lucy.

"Wow! That must have been something!" said Patty.

"I bet that's what my mom is hoping will happen again this year," mumbled Chloe.

"What?" said Gretchen, looking puzzled.

"My mom wanted my sister Zelda to be chosen, not me. She's thirteen, so she won't get another try. But if an egg did what Harriet did, then Zelda could still be picked."

"Listen here, Chloe. You are the candidate, and while it is true that once in over five hundred years, a dragon selected a non-candidate, that was a special deal—Lucy is special, and it wasn't her fault that the dragons didn't find her in time to make her a candidate. Your sister was definitely not chosen; she was rejected, in fact, if what I've heard is true."

Chloe felt a lot better; just being with Patty, Gretchen, and Lucy helped. They obviously believed in her. Now if she could only believe in herself. Well, just maybe, if she had a dragon to bond with, she'd get the strength and courage she needed. *Oh, I hope so!* she thought.

— 3 —
THE HATCHING

Chloe woke early on the morning of the winter solstice. She was just too excited and too anxious to sleep. She got out of bed quietly so as not to bother Patty, but Patty opened her eyes and said, "I can't sleep either! What do you think will happen? Will either of us get chosen?"

"I sure hope so," said Chloe. "You will be for sure! You'll make a perfect rider. Any dragon would be lucky to have you."

"Thanks," said Patty, "and I think the same about you! Come on; let's get going. There's lots to do before the ceremony at noon!"

The girls dressed quickly and then headed to the kitchens. All the candidates had to make a meal for a baby dragon, and they had to do it by themselves as part of the test to be sure they'd learned all they'd need to know to take care of a new baby dragon. Of course, there would always be people to help them, but it was an important part of the bonding process that each rider prepared his/her dragon's first meal all by him- or herself.

Patty and Chloe worked at neighboring tables and chatted as they went about their task. They were the first candidates to start, but soon, the other candidates began arriving in small groups. George and Steven found work stations on either side of the girls, and the four of them were busily at work when three other girls walked in.

Chloe groaned inwardly. She had hoped to be finished before Beulah, Imogene, and Clarissa arrived. The three also lived in Havenshold, and they had never liked Chloe. Even as candidates, they took every opportunity to tease her or bully her. Chloe thought candidates were picked because they were good and strong, but these three seemed never to be able to let go of the history they had had with her in school.

As the three girls started to work, Imogene looked around to be sure that none of the older riders were around, and then she looked at Chloe and said, "Surely, *you* don't need to be doing that! You realize that no dragon would ever pick you!"

Chloe kept her head down and continued chopping the meat into one-inch cubes. Soon Beulah and Clarissa had joined in with the taunting. After a couple minutes, George said, "Enough! You are making fools of yourselves and showing everyone that you don't have what it takes to be a rider."

"Yeah," chimed in Steven. "Or haven't you learned the rider code of honor yet? Haven't you noticed that riders don't taunt and bully?"

Imogene looked at them both and said, "What makes you such a hotshot, goody-two-shoes? You come from some hick village. What do you know?"

Steven said, "So you think the capital is a hick village? Queen Clotilda would be most interested to know that, I'm sure."

Imogene said, "Oh, not you. I meant George there. Anyway, we know we will be picked, so there."

Patty, Chloe, George, and Steven just smiled and got on with their preparations.

"All set?" asked Patty.

"Yep," said Chloe. "Let's go get changed into our robes."

George looked up from his work and said, "See you in the hatching grounds."

All too soon, it was time to line up for the start of the ceremony. Chloe made sure she was with Patty, George, and Steven as they walked into the arena. She hardly noticed the circular rows of seats rising up around the hot sandpit, but the noise of the cheers was overwhelming. The candidates formed a ring around the outside edge of the sandpit, spaced evenly around the circle.

Chloe looked up at the dignitaries' box as Queen Clotilda began by welcoming everyone to the one hundred seventy-seventh hatching since King Alfred brought his riders and dragons to Draconia. *Wow,* Chloe thought, *this is a really big deal.* She felt overcome by the majesty of the occasion.

Clotilda was just finishing her opening remarks when the audience gasped. The first egg had begun to hatch. Clotilda sat down, and all eyes focused on the hatching area. Chloe felt as if she had stopped breathing. She looked over at Patty, and Patty turned toward her. They smiled and looked back at the hatching egg.

After a few loud cracks, a scraggly looking wet blue dragon staggered away from its shell, wobbling and heading with determination straight to George. George nearly forgot his part in this, but after Steven whispered, "Food," he grabbed the meal he had prepared and handed a bite to his dragon.

Then George looked up at the stands and said, "His name is Egbert!"

The arena burst into cheers and applause, but George concentrated on Egbert. Once Egbert had eaten the meal, Hannah walked in to escort George and Egbert to the new riders' quarters.

Everyone's attention then turned back to the seven remaining eggs. The hatchings continued, and Chloe was amazed that only one egg was hatching at any particular moment. *It's as if they are taking turns!* she thought. She was beginning to see just why the hatching ceremony was such an important ritual in the lives of everyone in Draconia but especially the riders.

Chloe was thrilled to see Patty bond with a gorgeous green female dragon named Emerald, and shortly after that, Steven was chosen by a red female dragon named Winifred. Chloe was happy that all three of her new friends had been chosen. But now, she was sitting alone with a big space on either side of her. Patty and Steven had left just as George had.

Chloe looked around the hatching pit and realized that there were just five candidates left and only one egg. Besides her, Jerome, a boy who was in her sister Zelda's class at school, and then Imogene, Beulah, and Clarissa remained. Chloe smiled and thought, *Well, they can't all be picked after they were so confident.*

Just then, the last egg began to crack, and before she knew it, a small orange dragon staggered over to Jerome, who announced, "Her name is Stella!"

As the applause died down, the spectators, family, and friends began leaving the hatching arena. Chloe just sat there, wondering what she was supposed to do now. Imogene, Beulah, and Clarissa stood up, and as they walked by her, Beulah said, "Well, at least you didn't get picked." Soon, they were with their families, being hugged and told that it was OK.

Chloe started to stand up just as her family reached her. Her mother was shouting already. "See! You *are* worthless! Why did you have to steal Zelda's chance? She would have been picked. All you had to do was say no when you were asked, and the invitation would have been given to Zelda."

Chloe just stared down at the sand. What could she say? She was sure her mother was right. And now, the only friends she'd ever made were off with their dragons.

Hazel went on, not even noticing her daughter's tears. "Well, they say they are starting a school for the candidates who aren't chosen, so you can just go there. You are no longer part of our family. You are a complete failure, and we don't want you around."

Chloe turned ashen pale and said very softly, "I can't come home?"

"No, not ever!" yelled her mother, and she turned away, grabbing Zelda by the hand and motioning to Harvey to follow.

Chloe looked shocked. She couldn't think. As her father walked past her, he slipped something into her hand and then hurried after the rest of his family.

Chloe started sobbing hysterically. *Where can I go?* she wondered. Suddenly, she was running—out of the arena, out of the riders' complex. She just kept running, trying to get as far away as she could. She hadn't even seen Emily and Jake standing behind her, obviously hearing everything her mother said. *I don't have anyone. I've got to get away somewhere, somewhere where no one knows me.* And on she ran.

Meanwhile, Emily and Jake confronted Hazel. "How could you be so cruel?" said Emily.

"Get out of my way!" screamed Hazel.

Jake stood in front of her, barring her way. "Do you really mean that you are disowning your own daughter?"

"Yes," snarled Hazel. "She's been nothing but a disappointment ever since she was born, and now she has ruined this generation's chance to redeem our family by having a rider once again. For that, she will pay the price."

Emily realized that Hazel was much too angry to hear reason. Maybe another day Emily could talk to her, but for now, she just said quietly and calmly, "You know, it isn't everyone's path to be a rider, but every single person has worth, and everyone has a path to follow that is just as rewarding and fulfilling."

Jake continued, "We'll see to Chloe. She is a wonderful person. It is a real shame that you can't see that. I truly pity you for your warped view of yourself and your world."

Jake and Emily turned, and as they did, Emily noticed the stunned look on Hazel's face.

Emily said, "Where did Chloe go? Can you see her?"

Jake, who was well over six feet tall, surveyed the crowds before answering, "I can't see her anywhere. You'd think that even in this mob of people, we'd be able to spot a white candidate's robe."

"Yeah, unless she took it off. We've got to alert Hans and figure out where she might have gone, poor kid."

Emily and Jake found Hans and let him know what had transpired. "It's going to be hard to find anyone in this crush of people," he said. "Let's spread out and ask as many folks as we can."

However, as the day wore on, it was clear that Chloe was no longer in the rider complex. Emily found Hannah, who was exhausted from settling all the new riders into their caves, and said, "Do you know if Chloe had any special place she liked to go?"

Hannah said, "No, not really. She and Patty did hang out on Sundays with Lucy and Gretchen. They might know something."

"Thanks," said Emily, and she left to try to find Lucy and Gretchen. *"How can there be so many people in such a relatively small space? Esmeralda, have you been able to spot anything?"*

"No, I haven't," answered Esmeralda. *"From the sky, it just looks like a mass of people. Oh, Lucy and Gretchen are over to your right."*

"Thanks!" Emily soon caught up with them. "Have you seen Chloe?" she asked.

"No," said Lucy. "Not recently. She ran right past us and out of the arena, sobbing loudly. We called to her, but she just kept on running."

"I sure hope she's OK," chimed in Gretchen. "She is a wonderful young lady; it is such a shame that her mother doesn't see that."

There wasn't anything more anyone could do until the celebrations were over. All the riders had been alerted, and they did keep patrolling through the various festival booths, asking after Chloe. As darkness fell, the crowds gathered on the hillside to watch the solstice fireworks display, but Emily and the riders kept looking.

Finally, as the crowds departed, Emily, Hans, Jake, and Hannah met in Hans's office.

Soon to be my office, thought Emily. with a feeling of both apprehension and excitement.

Hans said, "Any ideas?"

"We've done all we can for now," said Jake. "It is too dark to search, and we have no idea where to begin."

"Tomorrow, we can go up on our dragons and try an aerial search," said Hans.

"It is starting to snow," said Hannah quietly. "If she's outside, she'll be really cold."

"I know," said Emily, putting her arm around her little sister's shoulder. "But Hans and Jake are right. There is nothing more we can do for now. I checked her room, and she hadn't been back to get anything, but maybe she'll return in the night."

"Let's get to bed so we can start at first light," said Hans, and the other three nodded as they headed off to their separate caves.

Where is she? wondered Emily as she drifted off to sleep next to Esmeralda.

— 4 —

THE FOREST

Finally, Chloe could run no further. She bent over, gasping for breath with a stitch in her side. After a few minutes, she looked around, wondering where she was. *I've run all the way outside the town!* She realized she was on the edge of Havenshold near the entrance to the forest, which marked the border with both Granvale and Sanwight.

She headed into the forest with no particular direction in mind. *I'm just going to go wherever I feel drawn, and hopefully, I'll end up somewhere where I can make my own way.*

She'd taken off her candidate's robe because it was too hard to run in, but she'd held on to it as she realized it was going to get even colder when the sun went down. Onwards she trudged, trying not to trip too many times. After what seemed like hours, she found herself near a small stream. She wondered which way she should go and whether she should try crossing the stream, but first, she needed to rest. Finding a nearby rock, she sat down and began reviewing the day's events.

Everything started out so well! And I really am happy for Patty, George, and Steven. I don't think I would have minded so much about not being chosen if it hadn't been for those girls first of all. Who do they think they are anyway? They weren't chosen either. But Mother was really the last straw. I've always tried so hard to please her, but she has only cared about Zelda. I love my sister, but why can't Mom love us both?

Then she remembered that her father had stuffed something into her hands. She'd just jammed it into the pocket of her robes, but now she fished it all out. There was some money, not a lot, but then, they didn't have a lot and her mother kept the books so he wouldn't be able to give her much. And there was also a note. It said:

Dear Chloe,

I'm writing this before we get to the hatching ceremony, just in case. I'm sure you'll be picked, but the odds aren't great, so just in case, I wanted to let you know how much I love you and how proud I have always been of you. Your mother has vowed that if you aren't picked, she will disown you, so I won't get a chance to say what I want to. I know your mother and her mother before her have this obsession with the family becoming dragon riders again, but I'm not so blind that I can't see that there are many happy, fulfilled people who have never been even a candidate, much less a rider.

Everyone has to find their own path in life, but unfortunately your grandmother, after she wasn't picked, decided that the only path was to bear a daughter to carry on the tradition. And when your mother "failed" at that, both women became horribly embittered. I love your mother, but as the years have gone by, I've lost my way. It is much easier, as you know, not to buck her. I've often wondered why she picked me to marry, but I suspect it is only because my family had riders many generations ago.

If you are reading this, it is because you weren't chosen by a dragon hatchling. But I want you to know that, as Emily said on the day she told us that you were a candidate, everyone chosen by a dragon to be a candidate is a special person with very special talents that are meant to serve the dragon rider community. I have no idea how you are meant to serve the community, but I know that you will figure it out, and that your life will be full and rich.

I love you, and I wish I were stronger so that I could have protected you better. But you have an inner strength and radiance that will shine through and take you far. All my love, Dad

Chloe read the letter several times, with tears pouring down her cheeks. "I love you too, Dad, and thanks," she whispered as she carefully folded the letter and put it into the front pocket of her pants.

She thought over what her father had said. There was something special about her that she could use to help the dragons. How was that possible? Did that mean that she needed to return to Havenshold?

Just then, Chloe heard a gunshot. She looked around and saw a mother bear and her twin cubs pushing through the undergrowth toward her. Then she saw the hunter chasing them with his rifle raised. Just as he stopped to take aim, Chloe raised her own hands and said, "No."

The rifle fired, but to Chloe's great amazement, the bullet bounced off a nearly invisible shield surrounding the bears. The hunter looked past the bears at her and said, "What do you think you're doing?"

"Stopping you from killing these bears!" yelled Chloe.

"Why?" said the hunter. "My family will starve without this meat."

"Don't you know that bears are a protected species?" she asked.

"Oh, that is just some dragon rider nonsense."

"And even if they weren't, it is wrong to kill a mother with cubs," continued Chloe.

"Better that than seeing my family go hungry this winter."

"Look, your family won't go hungry if you go into Havenshold. You can winter there and then make plans in the spring," said Chloe.

"How did you make my bullet stop?" he asked.

"I have no idea. I've had a horrible day myself, and I was just angry and sad, and so I said, 'No,' and your bullet stopped. Now please, go back to your family and take them to Havens hold."

"I'll think about it," he said, but he did turn around to leave.

Chloe looked at the bears and was surprised to see what could only be called a smile on the mother bear's face. And then she was even more surprised when she heard the bear speaking telepathically to her.

"Thank you, young mage. You have saved us! And I have been waiting for you to seek me out."

"You must be mistaken," said Chloe. "I am not a mage, and I wasn't seeking you. I just couldn't let him hurt you or your cubs."

"Well, you were sent, whether you knew it or not, and you are a mage, although untrained. It is my path to help train you. Snow is starting to fall. Will you come with us to our cave and I'll explain more?"

"Sure, thanks. I don't really have anywhere else I can go," said Chloe and then, realizing how ungracious that sounded, added, "I would be honored to follow you."

Chloe accompanied the bears, and as they walked, the mother bear kept talking with her.

"My name is Bertha, and I come from a long line of seers. As you will learn in more detail, there is a reason why the dragons and riders protect all bears. And now we are coming to a point in history where this world will be attacked in ways that are not yet clear to me. But what I know is that there is a prophecy that when the world is threatened from without, a powerful mage will appear."

"But I can't be that mage," protested Chloe. "I'm not good at anything."

"You were chosen as a candidate, were you not? That means that you are special to the dragons, and if you weren't selected by a hatchling, then it is clear that you are meant to serve and help the dragons in other ways."

"That's what my dad said in his letter, but I don't have any talents."

Bertha appeared to laugh as she said, *"My babies and I would certainly disagree with that! Is this the first time that you have conjured magic? Has nothing strange ever happened to you before?"*

Chloe thought for a bit, and then she said, "There was that time my sister was falling from a broken tree branch and I just wished that she would fall more slowly since she surely would have been killed otherwise, and she did seem to slow down. At least she landed with only a broken arm."

"See, I told you. That was your magic. You haven't been trained yet, but if you can stop a bullet without any training, then it is certain that you are not only a mage, but a very powerful one at that."

Chloe was very quiet then as they approached Bertha's cave. She had a lot to think over. This day had been filled with too much, and she needed time to ponder it all.

Bertha showed her into the cave, which was a great deal larger than it had appeared from the outside. Chloe was amazed at how well-appointed it was. There were cozy nests for the twins and a much larger nest for Bertha. But what amazed Chloe even more, was that there was a ledge with a pillow and a gorgeous pink and purple comforter on it that seemed made just for her.

"So you really did know I was coming!" Chloe said in amazement.

"Yes. As you are a mage, I am a seer. I knew that this round of hatchings would also bring the mage to me. That is because I see a great catastrophe in the near future, which only you can stop."

"How can that be?" said Chloe. "And how could you know I'd find you when I had no idea where I was running. Did you know my mother would disown me and cast me out?"

Bertha chuckled again, and Chloe realized that she'd never thought of a bear as a chuckling sort of animal, but then she also realized that Bertha was no ordinary bear.

"No, I didn't know how you would come to me or what would cause you to seek me out. I only knew that it would happen. Now, it is getting late, and I'm sure we are all tired and hungry. Let's eat and then sleep on it all, and I know things will become clearer in the morning."

"That sounds good," admitted Chloe. "I got up early this morning, so excited, and then the day didn't go as I thought. My good friends are now all riders, and that is wonderful, but then after my mother exploded, I just ran and ran. I am very tired, and food would be nice if you're sure you have enough. And the bed looks wonderful!"

With that, Chloe tucked into a lovely dinner of vegetables and roots with some fish, and then after hugging each of the twins and Bertha, she cuddled up with the comforter and was asleep almost before her head touched the pillow.

Bertha smiled and thought, *I'll enjoy working with this one. She really is special.*

— 5 —

BERTHA'S PLAN

Chloe woke up the next morning to find one of the twins licking her face. She sat up and looked around. Bertha was busy making breakfast, and the cubs were trying to climb up onto her bed. Chloe laughed, and Bertha looked over at the sound. *"Boris and Berla, are you bothering her?"*

The cubs turned to look at their mother, and Chloe realized they also could communicate telepathically, just not with her—at least not yet. *Wow! There's sure a lot more going on here than I ever thought about.*

"They're fine, Bertha. Maybe we can play until breakfast."

"They love playing catch, or at least trying to catch their big red ball."

Chloe got out from under the covers and walked across the cave until she found the twins' ball. "OK, get ready to catch!" Both bears sat down and held out their front paws. Soon, Chloe and the cubs were romping and playing and Chloe was laughing at their efforts to catch the ball. Boris succeeded a couple more times than Berla, but for the most part, their timing was really off. They had a wonderful time tumbling around anyway, so it didn't really seem to matter.

Bertha called them all to breakfast. As Chloe ate, the bear said, *"I think we will have company soon."*

Chloe put her spoon down, looking worried. "Who?" she asked in a very quiet voice.

Bertha went on. *"No need to get all worried. I signaled to Fire Dancer, you know, Hans's dragon, to let her know where you are. They were pretty worried back at the complex."*

Chloe looked down at the table and muttered, "I'm sorry. I really didn't think anyone would even notice."

"Well, they did, and Hans and Fire Dancer will be here shortly. But, honey, don't worry. It will all be fine. Now finish up that breakfast. Boris and Berla want to go outside and play, and I think that would be fine if you'll watch them."

Chloe said, "Of course I will," and quickly ate the last of her porridge.

It wasn't long before Chloe saw a beautiful orange dragon overhead. There was just enough room in the clearing in front of the cave for Fire Dancer to land, and as soon as she was down, Hans bounced to the ground and ran over to her, giving her a big hug.

"We were all so worried about you! Why did you run off? Oh, never mind, you're safe. We were so relieved when Fire Dancer heard from Bertha just after dawn. Emily and Esmeralda wanted to come too. Heck, the entire family wanted to rush here, but I convinced them that one of us was more than enough, and I wanted to talk with you and Bertha by myself. Fire Dancer seems to think she has cooked something up. Bertha! Where are you?" called Hans.

"Right here, you old rider!" she answered as she lumbered out of the cave. *"How come you haven't been by to see me in years?"*

Chloe was amazed to see Hans blush as he said, "Sorry, Bertha. Got busy, I guess. But Emily is taking over as leader so I'll have lots more time."

"That's good. You've got talent, you know, for more than just being a leader. Time you got back to your own studies. But enough of that. We need to discuss this young one," she concluded, looking at Chloe.

Chloe was just stunned to realize that Bertha could communicate with both Hans and her at the same time so everyone was included in the discussion. All of a sudden, she realized that both Hans and Bertha were staring at her.

"What?" she asked, thinking she'd missed something. "I am sorry I ran away yesterday. If you'd heard my mother...well, it was horrible."

Hans smiled. "Yes, the whole arena heard Hazel. She does have a voice and a temper. But please, there are a lot of folks who care about you now. Your family includes all the riders, and we were worried. Please, please, know that you have a spot at the complex for as long as you want, which we hope will be a long time!"

Chloe nodded a bit tentatively, but then Bertha got right to the point. *"Hans, do you remember the ancient prophecy, the one that says when the dragons are threatened, a mage will appear?"*

"Yes, but you don't really believe that, do you?"

"Yes, I do. I have been sensing a long-range danger approaching us. Oh, I don't mean today or tomorrow. It feels as if it is several years, maybe even five or six, away. But it is coming from somewhere out there," she concluded, waving her paw toward the sky.

"And yesterday, Chloe stopped a bullet that was aimed at me. She just covered me and my twins with a protective shield. Now what do you think about that? Is that the work of a mage or not?" She sat down on a nearby rock, looking toward the cubs, who were happily rolling in the snow.

"*What*?" exclaimed Hans. "You did that?" he asked, turning to Chloe.

"I was so angry and upset and tired," began Chloe as she then recounted the events for Hans and when she was done, she asked, "Aren't bears protected?".

Fire Dancer spoke for the first time. "They certainly are! Bears are the protectors of dragon lore and hence are sacred to all dragons. This is the first I've heard of anyone violating that."

"This was just one incident by a very hungry man trying to keep his family together and thinking that he could feed them for the winter. Don't worry; Chloe set him straight, and you should be seeing him in Havenshold. Who knows if the fates didn't set up that scene entirely to prove that Chloe has magical powers?" said Bertha.

"OK, let's get back to Chloe. You really think that she is the mage in the prophecy?" asked Hans.

"Yes, I do. And I think that we need to set up a plan to get her the training she needs so that when the time comes, she will be ready to save the dragons and in fact this entire world!"

"I can't do that," said Chloe. "I've never been good at anything. I'm clumsy and not all that smart. How can I save a world?"

Bertha just laughed, and when a bear laughed, she really shook all over. *"Honey, you've got more power in your little finger than anyone else I've ever seen has in a whole body. I don't know who's been stringing you that line, but I'm here to tell you, it is balderdash!"*

Hans looked at Chloe and said, "You'll find out more about the relationship between dragons and bears later, but trust me, if Bertha says you are a mage with strong magical powers, then that is just what you are."

Chloe quickly shut her mouth as she realized it was hanging open. This was just too much to process.

Hans turned to Bertha and said, "So what is your plan, O sly and wonderful seer? You know you have one and are just dying to tell us what to do!"

Bertha chuckled and rubbed a paw through Hans's hair. *"You got that right. Well, my cubs and I are just getting ready for our long winter nap, so I propose that you take Chloe back and get her settled in a good home—Say, don't your parents keep taking in strays?"*

Now it was Hans's turn to laugh. "You're right there. I'm sure my parents would be very happy to foster another student. They haven't had anyone since Lucy and Gretchen got married."

Chloe just kept turning her head from Hans to Bertha and back again, with a most bewildered look on her face. She really couldn't believe any of this.

"Well, Amy and Todd will be perfect for Chloe, and I suspect they will really enjoy having some young blood around again. So that's settled. You take her there and let your mother spread her wonderful love magic, and then get Chloe set up in that new school of yours that Gregory is starting up—it's called Pathfinder Academy, isn't it?"

Hans stared at the bear in amazement. "How do you manage to keep up with all the rider news? Gregory and Emily just finalized the plans and the name right before the hatching!"

Bertha chuckled and said, *"Oh, I have my sources. Remember, I am not only a seer, but like all bears, I am bonded to the dragons as their protector, and I take that responsibility very seriously. Now back to Chloe. Since I am sure this threat is coming from out in space, I think Chloe needs to study astronomy. And if my old memory isn't failing—"*

Hans interrupted with a big splutter saying, "Old? Failing? You can run circles around all of us, and you know it!"

Bertha came as close to blushing as a bear could; she smiled slyly as she continued, *"As I was saying, I believe there is an ancient manuscript in the riders' library detailing how a telescope is made."*

"A what?" said Chloe, feeling that somehow this discussion of her future was getting way beyond her.

"Before King Alfred and his fellow riders arrived here on this world, they had lived in a world with a lot of different technologies. Alfred felt that his people would be better off without that, especially as this world had three other nations who believed in a simpler life. But he was smart enough to store a lot of that information in a secret cave, and he put my grandmother in charge of guarding that cave with its store of knowledge. My mother became the guardian after her, and now I have followed in that role. I admit that I hunted through the cave for some information, and when I came across the directions for this telescope, I made sure (and I'm not saying how) that the manuscript was transferred to the riders' library—"

"OK!" Hans interrupted. "Let's save all this secret-cave stuff for another day. I'm a bit overwhelmed at the moment, and Chloe is looking positively shell-shocked. But, as Chloe asked, what is a telescope?"

"You're right. I'll cut to the chase. A telescope is an instrument that allows someone to look further into the heavens and see things that are really far away. So Chloe needs to spend the winter and spring settling into her new life, studying astronomy, trying to make a telescope, and that sort of thing," Bertha concluded vaguely, waving a paw rather randomly.

Hans laughed again. "In other words, it is your nap time. OK, I get all that, and we'll keep Chloe busy on this path. Anything else?"

"Yes," continued Bertha. *"I want you, Chloe, back up here with me at the summer solstice. I'll see what you've learned, and then we'll start on the magic part of this, unless you figure some of that out on your own. Don't be afraid to experiment in the meantime and see if you can awaken more of your powers."* Then Bertha rounded up Boris and Berla, and they headed back toward their cave. She gave her parting remarks on the way. *"And don't think that I won't know what's going on. I can sleep with one eye open!"*

Chloe called after her, "Thanks so much, Bertha, and I'll see you in the summer!"

Hans shook his head as he said, "That old bear! She is a true seer and also loves to keep the air of mystery about her."

"I heard that!"

Hans and Chloe laughed. Then Hans said, "Let's head back to Havenshold. There are a lot of folks who want to see that you really are fine, and we need to get you settled with my mom and dad."

Hans vaulted onto Fire Dancer and then reached down to give Chloe a hand up as the dragon bent her front left leg to make a step. Once Chloe had settled in behind Hans, she said, "Are you sure your parents will want me? I don't want to be a bother."

Hans turned to look at her and said, "Just wait until you meet my parents and see our home. Then you'll realize that you are just what they need, and I know they are just what you need as well."

Chloe couldn't imagine what he was talking about, but she was too overwhelmed even to think about it. She just relaxed, holding on to Hans, and enjoyed the view as they flew back to Havenshold.

— 6 —
A NEW HOME

It was a short flight to Havenshold. Chloe thought that this was much better than running and crashing through the forest. But she was anxious about how she would be received after her failure to be selected by a dragon and then the angry outburst by her mother. It was all so embarrassing.

As Chloe looked down into the courtyard at the riders' complex, she was amazed to see so many people waiting for them. As soon as Fire Dancer landed and Hans helped her down, she was engulfed in hugs. It took a while to sort everyone out. Emily, Jake, and Hannah were there, along with Lucy and Gretchen and a few others Chloe didn't even know. Everyone was talking a mile a minute. Finally, Hans held up his hands for silence.

"We have some absolutely amazing news," he began, and Chloe thought that was a great way to distract people from her running away.

Hans continued, "As you already know, Chloe found her way to Bertha in the woods and spent the night with her and her adorable twin cubs in their cave. What you don't know is that Chloe is a mage! She actually saved Bertha's life by putting up a shield to stop a hunter's bullet."

Jake interrupted. "Someone tried to shoot a *bear*?"

Hans held up a hand to stop him and said, "Yes, a very hungry man with a family to feed, which is no excuse, but Bertha told him to come here to winter. So, Jake, spread the word so we find this man and his family and make sure they are OK. But to get back to the main news—Bertha thinks that the fates made the man try to shoot her so that Chloe's skills as a mage would be revealed."

"Wow," said Hannah.

"Yes, wow indeed. There is an ancient prophecy, which I won't go into now, but Chloe may be part of its fulfillment. Bertha and her cubs were eager for their winter nap, but she told me what she wants Chloe to study at your new academy," he said, turning to a tall man with light-brown hair and twinkling green eyes standing next to Emily.

That must be her husband, Gregory, Chloe thought.

"Excellent," said Gregory.

"Yes, I'll give you the full information later, but for the moment, just know that she will be studying the stars. Chloe will go back to work with Bertha in the summer, but for now, we need to get her a home and start her in school when your academy begins after the New Year."

As Emily began to ask a question, Hans forestalled her by saying, "And those of you who know Bertha will not be surprised that she has that all worked out as well. Bertha suggests—or more accurately *told* me—that Chloe should be fostered by Amy and Todd."

Lucy whooped with joy and said, "Oh, Chloe, you are so lucky. I was their last foster, and let me tell you, they are wonderful!"

"Why, thank you," said Hans with a big smile on his face. "We sure think so. Anyway, Hannah, could you check with Mom, and then provided they are game—and I know they will be— could you settle Chloe in with them?"

"Sure," said Hannah. "Can Rupert help?"

"I guess," said Hans with a mock sigh. "But remember, Rupert," he continued, looking at the tall, lanky, towheaded young man standing next to Hannah, "you will begin your training as Emily's assistant right after the new year, so don't think you can be running around all the time."

"Yes, sir—I mean no, sir," stammered Rupert.

"OK, that's it for now. Emily, Gregory, I'd like to meet with you after lunch, if that works."

"Sure," said Emily.

The gathering broke up, and as folks left, they told Chloe again just how glad they were that she was safe and how wonderful it was that she'd discovered her gift. Finally, it was just Hannah and Rupert left. Hannah said, "I don't know that you and Rupert have actually met. Well, Chloe, this is Rupert, and Rupert, this is Chloe."

Both Rupert and Chloe laughed, and Rupert said, as he ruffled Hannah's shaggy brown hair, "We figured that out, but thanks!" He turned to Chloe and said, "So glad to meet you."

"OK, enough!" said Hannah. "Emily will have prepared Mom and Dad, so let's just walk over there. Did you have any more things you wanted, Chloe, from your room in the candidates' quarters. The barracks have been emptied out except for your things, which Patty said should be left for you to get."

"I don't have much. It will all fit in my duffel," answered Chloe.

"Why don't you girls head over and pack Chloe's things and I'll grab us some snacks for the walk?" suggested Rupert.

Soon, the three of them were walking out of the rider complex and into Havenshold proper. "My parents live out on the west edge of town," said Hannah.

"I've never been out that way," remarked Chloe. "My parents have a home that has always been in my family, and it is north of the town proper."

"That must be nice," said Hannah. "My parents built their home when they got married, and it was a very small one. Then, as I'm sure my folks will tell you, the house just grew. Every time my mom was pregnant, my dad knocked a hole in a wall and added another room rather randomly. So there's not much order to it, but we love it."

"It sounds wonderful," said Chloe.

They walked along companionably for about twenty minutes, munching on the snack bars Rupert had brought. Soon, a very large blue house came into view.

"Wow!" said Chloe. "Who lives there?"

"We do," said Hannah, running around to the back. "Come on! Let's see if we can surprise them."

They ran around the side of the house and smack into a tall, thin, gray-haired man, who said, "Surprise! Guess who surprised whom?" and he laughed. He hugged Hannah and shook Rupert's hand before giving him a hug. Then, looking up, he said, "You must be Chloe! Welcome!"

"Thanks," said Chloe, shaking his outstretched hand.

"Come on into the house. Amy is waiting for us," said Todd.

Soon, the five of them were settled around a large kitchen table that looked as if it had seen a lot of wear. Amy sat next to her husband, and Chloe thought she'd never seen anyone who looked more content. Amy's hair was gray like her husband's, and it was done in braids, reminding Chloe of Emily. Hannah sat next to her mother, and Rupert and Chloe sat across on the other side of the table.

"So, Chloe, I hear you will be attending Pathfinder Academy at the first of the year," began Amy.

"Yes," answered Chloe. "I'm not exactly sure what happened since yesterday's hatching, but my life has sort of turned around."

Todd laughed. "Welcome to the family! That's how life is around here."

Chloe looked a bit puzzled, and Amy stepped in. "We've never seemed to do things the way others do, and life keeps twisting and turning in interesting patterns. That's what Todd meant, and he also meant that you'll fit right in!"

"Oh, thanks," said Chloe a bit hesitantly.

"You'll get used to him." Hannah laughed, giving her dad a big smile. "Just ask him about Lucy and the moles."

Todd's big, booming laugh filled the room. "Yes, Lucy really started something without even realizing it when she first got here. Do you know Lucy?"

"Yes," answered Chloe. "My friend Patty introduced me to Lucy and Gretchen, and we used to hang out with them on our Sundays during candidate orientation."

"Then you know she's learned to communicate with moles, right?" Todd asked.

"Yes," said Chloe with a very puzzled look on her face.

"Well, I'll save all the details for another day, but suffice it to say that Lucy gave me the idea for that big sandpit out in the backyard! See," said Todd, standing up and moving to the kitchen window.

Chloe went over to the window and looked out. She saw an enormous sandpit, and resting in it were two gorgeous green dragons.

"That's Jupiter on your left and Fern on your right. Jupiter and I are bonded, as are Fern and Amy. We're retired now, actually retired soon after Hans was born, but thanks to Lucy, we now have a heated sandpit big enough for all our family. After all, we have four dragon riders, and Jake is married to William— have you met him yet?"

Chloe shook her head as Todd went right on, "And he's a rider too, and then both Lucy and Gretchen are riders—and once you are fostered, you're family forever—and now this young man seems to be courting Hannah..." At this, both Rupert and

Hannah turned bright red. "…And he's a rider too. So you can see, we really needed this big sandpit, and we have it all thanks to Lucy!"

He finally stopped to take a breath. Amy gently patted his arm and said, "Enough, Todd. Let Chloe settle in at her own pace. Now, Chloe, could I show you to your room?"

"That would be nice," said Chloe, and she grabbed her duffel and followed Amy down a long and winding hallway.

"Have you heard about this house?" asked Amy.

Chloe nodded and said, "Hannah told me a bit."

"Well, you may need a map or a guide for the first day or so. There are rooms in the strangest arrangement, but there it is. Todd always said that if I could grow a baby, he could grow a room, and he did. Six children and they all got their own room and bathroom. Here we are," she added as they turned yet another corner. She opened a door.

"This was Emily's room growing up, but of course, now she and Gregory have their own place. We have a perfectly good guest room. Todd saw to that also. But everyone seems to find this room friendlier. Lucy had it until she and Gretchen were married last summer. And now it is yours."

Chloe looked around the room and was amazed at how warm and cozy it looked. The walls were a lovely purple, and there was a purple quilt on the bed. Stuffed animals and books lined the shelves on one wall, with a purple dresser on another. There were two doors, which Amy quickly showed her went into a closet and a bathroom.

"So what do you think? Will this work for you?" asked Amy.

"Oh, yes!" exclaimed Chloe. "It is wonderful! You're sure it is OK if I stay?"

Amy walked over and wrapped Chloe in her arms. She said, "It is more than OK. It is fantastic!" She released her and said,

"Now, settle your things wherever you like, and then we'll head back to the kitchen for lunch."

"Oh, Rupert got us snack bars for our walk over. I'm sure I'm fine," said Chloe.

"A snack bar, phooey!" Amy snorted. "Might be all right for a walk, but it isn't a meal, and I've a feeling you've been through a lot in the last twenty-four hours."

Chloe looked shocked. Was it just twenty-four hours ago that she had been watching the hatching? Suddenly, she was both tired and overwhelmed, and she nearly fell onto the bed.

Amy took Chloe's duffel and put it inside the closet. She said, "How about you sort that later? It looks to me as if you need a hot lunch and then a good rest. Come on, and let's head back to the kitchen."

Chloe was very grateful for Amy's understanding. She was soon seated at the table with a big bowl of steaming hot stew and a plate of bread slathered with butter. She ate quietly and just enjoyed the chatter at the table. *This is a wonderful family!* And then she got even quieter as she thought about her own. A laugh from Todd shook her out of her sorrow, and she turned to listen to yet another tale of joy and fun.

— 7 —

THE NEW YEAR

Chloe climbed into bed and pulled the wonderful purple comforter over her. *What a wonderful two weeks it has been,* she thought. She never knew a family could be this supportive and loving. And tomorrow was New Year's Day. Amy and Todd were celebrating with all their family there. Chloe was nervous and realized that she didn't even know everybody yet.

She ticked off the names as she tried to relax. There were Amy and Todd, of course, with their green dragons, Fern and Jupiter. Then there were six children: Hans, forty-six years old, and his orange dragon, Fire Dancer; Jake, forty-one years old, and his brown dragon, Harmony; Emily, thirty-six years old, and of course the beautiful purple Esmeralda; then Robert, thirty-one years old—she hadn't met him yet, but he was an architect/designer working in the capital; Michael, twenty-nine years old, and she also hadn't met him, but knew he was a biologist and was usually out in the field; and finally, Hannah, twenty-seven years old, and her orange dragon, Firebolt, who was sired by Fire Dancer.

OK, she continued. *That's the immediate family.* Then there was Lucy, fostered by Amy and Todd, and she was now twenty-five years old and bonded to Harriet, a blue dragon. And then there were all the spouses: first, William, thirty-six years old, Jake's husband, and his brown dragon, Thunder; Gregory, thirty-nine years old, Emily's husband, a volcanologist, and also the head of Pathfinder Academy; Gretchen, twenty-five years old, married to Lucy, and her red dragon, Ruby; and finally, Rupert, twenty-seven years old, Hannah's boyfriend, son of the former king and queen of Draconia, and his purple dragon, Whipper.

Gads! That means counting me, there will be fourteen of us with ten dragons! Oh my! Fortunately, just as she really started to worry, sleep overtook her.

The next morning dawned bright, clear, and cold. There was still nearly a foot of snow on the ground, except, of course, in the sandpit where the hot sand kept the snow away. Chloe looked out her window and smiled as she saw not only Fern and Jupiter enjoying the hot sands, but also Esmeralda, Ruby, Harriet, and Firebolt. That meant that at least Emily, Lucy, Gretchen, and Hannah were there to help get ready.

Chloe quickly showered and dressed and then headed to the kitchen. Sure enough, Amy was in full swing, and Emily, Lucy, Gretchen, and Hannah were helping peel potatoes, slice veggies, knead bread dough, and whatever else Amy asked for.

"Hi, Chloe," said Amy. "Have a seat, and I'll bring you your breakfast."

"I can fix something," said Chloe, not wanting to be a bother.

"Nonsense," said Amy. "In my kitchen, I always feed my family, and I'm betting that before you start, more folks will be walking in looking for their breakfasts as well. Now tuck in," she concluded as she put a large bowl of steaming oatmeal and a plate of toast in front of Chloe.

"Thanks," said Chloe and sure enough, before she could even get her spoon to her mouth, in walked Todd and Gregory.

"I was just talking with Gregory about this school of his," said Todd as he sat down at the table.

Gregory smiled at Chloe and said, "Good morning." Soon, both men had joined Chloe in a delicious breakfast, and the banter around the table was high-spirited and inclusive.

As the morning sped by, there were more arrivals, first Hans, followed closely by Jake and William. Chloe knew Hans and Jake, of course, but she'd only seen William, so they were introduced. Chloe thought William seemed very nice—serious, but nice.

When Robert and Michael arrived, everyone cheered.

"I wasn't sure you boys would make it with the snow in the mountains," said Todd.

"Oh, Dad," complained Michael, "you'd think we'd never seen snow before. I stopped at the capital for Robert, and we rode together. The pass was pretty well tramped down. No worries. Do you think we'd miss Mom's great feast?"

Everyone laughed, and soon, Amy chased most of the family out of the kitchen so she could finish the preparations. Just then, Rupert arrived, carrying a large pecan pie. "My mother insisted that I bring this, Amy," said Rupert. "I told her that you'd been baking for days, but Mom says that there is always room for another pie."

Amy laughed and said, "Thanks, Rupert, and please thank your mom."

"Both Mom and Dad send their best wishes for a happy New Year to you all," concluded Rupert as he went to give Hannah a peck on the cheek.

Chloe wasn't sure how Amy managed, but soon, all fourteen of them were seated around a very large table in the dining room. The table was laden with enough food for a small regiment, thought Chloe, before realizing that that was just what they were.

Robert had managed to seat himself next to her, and as they were enjoying the wonderful meal, he asked her about her plans. "I've heard rumors that you plan to study astronomy and that you are going to build something to look at the stars—a telescope, I think it was called."

"Yes, that's what Bertha the ursine seer recommended. She said that she'd sent plans to the riders' library. I've never built anything in my life, so I'm not too sure," said Chloe.

"Well, that's what I wanted to ask. Would you let me help? I am, as you probably already know, an architect and a designer. I designed the dragon sandpit in our backyard, and I managed all the heating and framing, even with Dad trying to help," he said and then quickly looked up at the head of the table to be sure his father hadn't overheard.

Robert continued, "Dad is wonderful, and you've no doubt heard how he built our home, but he is very enthusiastic and doesn't always think about the consequences. When we were working with the volcano vents, Gregory and I really had to rein him in!"

Chloe laughed and said, "I can only imagine."

"Anyway, I only mentioned that to show you that I don't just do houses and buildings. I can do unusual things too. I'd love to see the plans for the telescope and see if I could help. I don't have a project at the moment. Winter is our slow season. So if you'd like and I wouldn't be encroaching on your work, I'd love to see how it all works."

Chloe looked carefully at this young man. He was tall and thin, like his father, but he seemed much more serious, much more earnest. She thought he'd be a real help and at the same time not overwhelm her, as some of the other members of this family tended to do.

"I'd like that, Robert, if you're sure it won't keep you from something more important," said Chloe.

"From what I've heard—and I know we're not supposed to talk about it—what you're going to be doing is probably more important than anything else. But even if it weren't, I am always looking for new inventions, and I'd just love to get my hands on these plans."

Chloe blushed and looked down at her plate. She got really nervous when folks talked about how important her magic was, but Robert was nice and she didn't think he'd keep bringing it up.

"Thank you," she said quietly. "I start at Pathfinder Academy tomorrow, but I don't know what the schedule will be like. However, I think this telescope is pretty high on the priority list. Maybe we can ask Gregory before the day ends."

"Sounds like a plan," said Robert, and they both finished up the main course.

The rest of the afternoon and evening passed in warm, loving company. After the sumptuous feast, most of the family collapsed onto the couches and easy chairs in the very large family room. Chloe noticed that Hannah and Rupert left for a bit to take a walk, and she thought Jake and William did also. Amy and Todd sat together on a love seat, and Chloe thought that they looked just about as happy as any two people could look. Chloe couldn't help comparing them to her parents, and then she felt sad.

Amy must have noticed something, because a few minutes later, she came over and asked Chloe for a hand in the kitchen.

Once they were alone, Amy said, "Are you OK?"

Chloe started to cry. "Why can't my family be like this?"

Amy wrapped her arms around Chloe and just hugged her tight and let her cry.

When Chloe was able to dry her tears, Amy said, "I don't know either your mom or your grandmother, but I've heard things through the years. I know your heritage is a long and proud one, and I do remember hearing that Julia had a really hard time with the fact that she wasn't picked as a candidate.

That was the first time since King Alfred and his dragons arrived that there hadn't been a rider in your family."

"I know," said Chloe miserably. "She still harps on about it, and then when her daughter, my mom, wasn't picked either, the two of them really got bitter."

"It is hard when a pattern is broken, and it is especially hard when you are the one who breaks it. I really feel for Julia and Hazel. My family also came over with King Alfred, as did Todd's. But our families have tended to be larger." She chuckled as she looked through the kitchen door into the family room.

"And we haven't always had a rider in each generation. We do seem to make up for it down the road, as you can see." She pointed toward the backyard. "We now not only have four of our own six as riders, but we have a foster daughter and then two spouses and a boyfriend, also all riders."

"Yeah," said Chloe. "My family is really small. Mom was the first to have two children for generations."

"And that puts a lot more pressure on that only child or children. Thankfully, Todd and I never worried about what our children would do or what path they would pick. We left that up to them and the fates. Robert and Michael are just as precious to us as the others, and it doesn't matter in the least that they aren't riders. And face it, without Robert and Gregory helping Todd, heaven knows what would have happened with that pit out there!" She chuckled, trying to lighten the mood.

"I just wish my family could be different. I love Zelda, but I have to admit, she is spoiled and a snob. Mom has always liked her better ever since she was born. Zelda is prettier and more talented than I'll ever be, so she has always been pampered and doted on. However, I'm sure she is having a very hard time now since she wasn't chosen. And my dad—I love him, and I know he loves me. I showed you the letter he gave me," she said, looking at Amy. Amy nodded.

"But he is miserable. I saw you and Todd sitting there, and you two are so much in love and have such a warm, happy home. I thought of my family—my father just hides away in his workroom and my mother makes life miserable for everyone. She only married him because he came from one of the original rider families, one that had lots of riders over the generations, so she was sure that they would have rider children."

"Each of us must find our own path. That's why Gregory is so excited about his school. He was forced by his father, and it was hard for Gregory to make his own way. It has all worked out really well in the end, and Gregory's father has totally changed, but Gregory now wants to make it easier for young people who aren't chosen at a hatching or who don't get accepted into the apprenticeship they want or who simply don't have any idea what they want to do with their lives. That is your job now, to find your path. You can't do anything for your parents except show them your strength and just maybe that will make a difference," said Amy.

Chloe tried a tentative smile and said, "I guess."

"Listen, if you want, I'll ask around and see if I can find a way to get a message through to your dad, OK?" said Amy.

"Thanks," said Chloe, and she gave Amy a hug.

"Now, let's see what games are going in the next room. Have you seen the marble game Michael designed? It is fun and not at all hard. Let's join in the festivities."

"Sounds great, and, Amy, thanks," said Chloe.

— 8 —
FIRST DAY

Chloe was up early the next day, apprehensive about her first day at Pathfinder Academy. Yesterday had turned into the most wonderful day she'd ever had, and it was late when everyone finally headed home or to bed. Both Michael and Robert were staying over with their parents, but everyone else had gone back to his or her own home.

Chloe dressed with extra care. She'd never cared about fashion or clothes, and her mother had refused to spend anything on her clothes because, as she had said repeatedly, "What is the point? You have no sense of what to wear or how to match and you never stay neat for any length of time anyway."

Well, Chloe was going to dress the way she wanted. Amy had taken her to some of the resale shops in Havenshold. That was something Chloe really liked, that folks would turn in their good clothes that they no longer wanted or didn't fit into and then swap them for something that did work. Her mother and her grandmother insisted on sewing all of Zelda's clothes, as they thought it was horrible to wear something someone else had worn before. To Chloe, it just made sense, especially since her family didn't have a lot of money (although she suspected her mother had a real hoard hidden away), but then, she'd never be able to figure out her mother.

Chloe had had a lot of fun in the shops with Amy, and Amy let her pick whatever she wanted. So Chloe had found some bright-purple pants and a soft orange sweater and that was what she was going to wear today.

After breakfast, Amy and Chloe walked into Havenshold. Amy said she had shopping to do, and she probably did after her family had eaten everything in the house, but Chloe also thought that Amy wanted her to have company on the first day. It felt good to have someone who cared.

Amy wished her luck as she reached the riders' complex and gave her a hug. As Chloe entered through the big gates, she noticed Imogene, Beulah, and Clarissa coming around the corner. Chloe thought they were going to start in with their usual taunts as Beulah had her mouth open ready to speak, but just then, Gregory arrived with three other students, saying, "Hi, ladies. I see you are all ready to begin. Let me introduce you to your fellow students, Bruce, Linda, and Priscilla."

After Gregory made sure everyone had been introduced, he said, "Let's head up to the riders' library, shall we?"

When they reached the library, Chloe noticed that both Lucy and Gretchen were already there, sitting at a table off to the side in the main reading room. Chloe smiled when both of them waved to her.

"OK, everyone take a seat at this main table," instructed Gregory, and Chloe was surprised when he sat down with them.

"This isn't going to be like any school you have ever been to," began Gregory. "We named it Pathfinder Academy for a reason. You are all pathfinders, and we and the resources in this library and the rider complex are only here to help you as you search for your passion, what you truly want to do."

Chloe felt as puzzled as the other students—at least she assumed they were also confused by the expressions on their faces.

Gregory continued, "Recently, each of you has suffered a major disappointment." He turned toward Chloe, Beulah, Imogene, and Clarissa as he said, "You four are candidates, but you weren't picked by a dragon. I suspect that has hit you hard. I was in your position not once, but twice, because of my age. My father, who was the most powerful baron in the land, made sure I was a candidate when I was twelve and again when I was fifteen. Thankfully, I wasn't chosen either time." He smiled at the surprised looks on their faces.

"My father wanted me to be a rider, but I wanted to be a volcanologist. The dragons knew that so I wasn't selected, but even though I knew what I wanted to do, what my path was, I had to buck a very powerful father. Some of you know what that kind of pressure is like."

Gregory paused for a moment to let that sink in before he continued, "But I know that wasn't the case for the four of you. You wanted to be chosen, and yet you weren't. That is a bitter pill to have to swallow. How will you pick yourselves up? Where will you go now? What will you do?"

Again, he paused, and Chloe thought that he must be the kindest, wisest teacher she had ever had. He allowed things to begin to sink in and didn't just keep racing on.

"For you four candidates, you must first realize that the dragons only pick those whom they know have a talent or gift that can serve the dragon community. Dragons are wonderful beings! I know that from my experience with them. But they are also a bit vain and self-centered, at least at times, and they feel, as many of us do also, that their own well-being comes above all else. So while you weren't chosen to bond with a particular dragon, you have been chosen to serve this community."

Chloe noticed the looks of shock and incredulity on the faces of her three fellow candidates, and she could almost hear them thinking that they certainly wouldn't serve dragons who had rejected them.

Gregory continued, "There are many very diverse ways to serve the dragons, and we will look at them as time progresses, but I just wanted to remind you of why you were chosen and that the reality is you weren't rejected at the hatching. You were just being saved for another path."

"As for you three," he said, nodding at Bruce, Linda, and Priscilla, "you finished your schooling but weren't selected for any apprenticeships. Or maybe you turned down an apprenticeship that your family wanted you to take. Either way, you now also need to find something that you can feel passionate about, something that you'd like to do for a career and a way to serve whatever community you become a part of.

"Each of us has to face disappointments in our lives," he continued. "How we face those disappointments and what we make of them determines how happy and successful we will be."

Again, he paused for them to reflect on his words. "Enough of me for today. I have brought in two visitors to our school, and I want them to be able to share some of their choices and how they got to where they now are. Lucy?" Lucy came over to the table. "And Gretchen?" She picked a seat next to her. "They are both dragon riders, so you might wonder why they are here. But they came to their present position in unique ways, suffering hardships and disappointments in the process. And remember, just because someone is a rider doesn't mean that they don't also have to find their niche, just where they fit in the big picture. So, let's hear their stories. Lucy, would you like to start?"

"Thanks, Gregory, and hi, everyone," began Lucy.

Beulah leaned over to Clarissa and Imogene and whispered, "What could we learn from a cripple?"

"What do you mean 'cripple'?" shouted a voice inside Beulah's head. Beulah looked around and said, "Did you hear that?"

"What?" said her friends. "Be quiet, or we'll get into trouble."

"I said it," came the answer as a brown tabby jumped up on the table.

Lucy laughed and said, "OK, I'm being upstaged. This is Sage, and she is a most unusual cat. As Gregory said, I became a dragon rider in a unique way. I was never a candidate. As some of you already know, I lost my right hand when I was a small girl. But Harriet, my gorgeous blue dragon, didn't care. She refused to come out of her egg until I came to the hatching pit. And then, through another tragedy, I lost the rest of my arm, as you can see. I thought that would be the end of me. I assumed that Harriet wouldn't be allowed to stay with me. How wrong I was! And I learned that my talent is my ability to communicate with a wide variety of life forms, such as the lovely Sage here."

"See, smarty pants! She may be missing an arm, but she is no cripple, so listen up and you might learn something."

Beulah kept looking around. She couldn't believe that she was hearing a cat talk to her and that no one else was hearing it.

"I can talk to whomever I want, but honestly, most folks can't hear me. You might want to think on that. Now pay attention!"

Beulah looked back at Lucy, and Lucy continued, "I've learned through much harder struggles than I hope any of you ever have that I have a gift and a talent that is unique. I have been able to work with the moles and set up an earthquake early warning system, which can save lives. I just want to encourage each of you to look within your hearts and then ask a ton of questions of anyone you want, and you too will find your path."

"Thanks, Lucy, for sharing that. Let's hear from Gretchen, and then we'll open things up for discussion and comments," said Gregory.

"Thanks, Gregory. Well, my story wasn't as unique a Lucy's. I was a candidate, and Ruby did choose me at the hatching. I thought everything was perfect. But then, as Gregory said earlier, I ran into a wall because unlike all the other riders, or so it seemed to me, I couldn't find a place where I could make a difference. I was shunted from department to department, and usually, I managed to make a horrible blunder or two before I was moved again. I think Hans really despaired of ever getting me placed. But then Lucy came up with her idea about the mole warning system, and while I can't talk to anyone but Ruby, Harriet, Esmeralda, and Sage and I couldn't hear the moles at all, I could lug equipment, set up camp, and make meals so Lucy could get on with her work. So that's where I started, but soon, I realized that Lucy had a horrible sense of direction." Lucy laughed. "To make a long story short, it turns out that I am a natural-born cartographer. What's that? you ask," she said when she noticed all the puzzled looks. "I make maps! I make about the best maps that this world has ever seen. There weren't any true maps for the volcano vents or indeed much of the land. I now make them, checking and rechecking and then distributing them to travelers, scientists, anyone who needs a good map. Since mapmaking hadn't existed as a real career until me, I had no role models. I had no one to teach me. But I figured it out, and I love making maps."

She nodded to Gregory, who took over. "So you can see just in this one morning that finding your path can be one of the biggest challenges you will face. And even when you do find it, you may have to be your own guide and teacher. But we will be here to support you along the way. Now, I don't have anything else for today, and as I say, this isn't a regular school with a schedule. Please, stay if you want to talk with any one of us or feel free to browse in the library. Any of the riders will be happy to help if you have questions. Just ask them for an appointment. And starting tomorrow, I'll be meeting with each one of you individually to help you get started on your particular quest."

With that, everyone stood up, and Imogene and Clarissa grabbed onto Beulah as Imogene said, "Cool, we're done. Let's get out of here."

But Beulah didn't move. She said, "You guys go on. I want to ask Lucy some questions."

"*What*!" exclaimed Clarissa. Then lowering her voice, she added, "You want to meet with the cripple?"

"Don't call her that," snapped Beulah. "Didn't you hear what she can do?"

"You've got a problem," Imogene said. "See you later, maybe." The two of them left.

Beulah looked around and saw that Priscilla was talking with Gregory, Bruce and Linda were leaving, and Chloe was with Lucy and Gretchen. Quietly, not sure of her reception, Beulah went over to stand behind Chloe.

"So, you two both had to teach yourselves," Chloe was saying, "and, Lucy, you had to learn a new telepathic skill. What was that like?"

Lucy laughed. "You wouldn't believe me if I told you. All my life, I could understand what an animal was feeling. My dad ran a dairy, and he ridiculed me when I said I could tell if one of our cows was sick or hurting, so I quickly learned not to share that. But still, I'd let him know if I thought an animal needed treatment. Then I worked in a vet clinic while I was in school, and again, I never told anyone, but I could calm the patients or mention that I thought they were hurting in a particular spot. It wasn't until I started working with Sylvester at the Dragon Riders' Animal Clinic that I was taken seriously. And then William, you met him yesterday, well, he went crazy. Telepathic communication is his thing, and he is really a geek about it. Before I knew it, I had two assistantships, one with William and one with Sylvester, and both of them just kept encouraging me to stretch my senses. That's what I was doing when I found the moles in Amy and Todd's backyard."

"So do you think I could find someone to help me with my magic?" asked Chloe.

"For sure," said Lucy.

Gretchen then added, "You'll have volunteers lining up!"

"Thanks," said Chloe, and she moved over to the book-shelves.

Lucy looked up at Beulah and said, "Did you have a question?"

"Your cat talked to me in my head!" Beulah blurted out.

Both Lucy and Gretchen burst out laughing. "And I bet she wasn't very polite."

"Well, I'm afraid I wasn't very polite first, and your cat defended you."

"That's Sage, all right. So what was your question?" asked Lucy.

"My parents have a chicken farm on the edge of town, and they supply all the dragon riders' eggs. I've been tending chickens for as long as I can remember, and it was like you said with your cows. They don't actually speak to me, and in fact I didn't even know that was possible until Sage got in my head, but I just know what they are feeling, and the hens that I'm in charge of lay more eggs than any of the others. No one can figure out why."

"That's wonderful," said Lucy.

"So do you think that's my talent or at least a hint toward my talent?" asked Beulah.

"Sounds like an excellent place to start," said Lucy.

Beulah shifted from one foot to another nervously before saying, "I know I was rude, whispering with my friends at the start of your talk, and your cat was right to yell at me, but I'm sorry. I'd really like to have your help, if that's all right with you."

Lucy smiled and picked up Sage. "What do you think, Sage, my friend? Should we give her a try?"

Sage looked straight into Beulah's eyes, and Beulah blushed and looked at her feet. *"I think so,"* replied Sage so that Lucy, Gretchen, and Beulah could hear her. *"She's just not been in the best company, but her heart is in the right place for sure. And maybe she'll bring me some chicken!"*

"You rascal," said Lucy, rubbing Sage affectionately. Then looking back to Beulah, she continued, "Yes, let's set up a schedule. I'd be happy to work with you. If you can sense what chickens are feeling and you can hear Sage, you might be able to understand more species. Who knows where you will go, but I'll be happy to help you start!"

With that, Beulah left. She caught up to Priscilla to chat as they returned to town.

Gregory thanked both Lucy and Gretchen. "I think we're off to a good start." Then he looked over at the library shelves where Chloe was pulling books down. "Are you coming for lunch?" he asked.

"In a bit," answered Chloe. "I've found some beginning astronomy books that I want to check out, and then I think I'll head home and spend the afternoon reading. Thanks!"

Gregory chuckled as he, Lucy, and Gretchen left.

— 9 —

MENTORS

Chloe sat in a comfy chair in an alcove in the library across from the small study room, which Gregory was using as his office when he was acting as Pathfinder Academy's principal. She was a little nervous, not really sure what the meeting would be like. Gregory was conferring with each of the seven students to set them up with their mentors and devise a course of study, but Chloe really couldn't see what he could set up for her. There weren't any other mages, and according to Bertha, there had never been any mages on this world.

Chloe stared off into space, not even realizing that her fingers were tracing the pattern on the front of the book she'd chosen from the library shelves. It was one of many astronomy books, and the cover showed stars with lines connecting them. Chloe had thought she'd start reading it as she waited but then realized she was not able to concentrate as she anticipated the meeting, so she had closed the book and just sat. As she looked around the library, a thought came to her. *The library seems happier today.* And then she realized that such a thought was absurd. How could a library be happy or sad? It was just a place after all. Gregory had told them that he picked the library as the headquarters for Pathfinder Academy because the library was not used much. It was primarily a storage place for all the ancient rider books, but since it was a lovely space and since they might need to study some of the books, he thought it was an ideal location.

The door to Gregory's office opened, and Beulah came out. Chloe looked down at her book, not wanting to catch Beulah's eye. After all, Beulah and her friends had taunted and bullied her ever since they started school together. Chloe worked hard at staying out of their line of fire.

However, that wasn't going to happen now, Chloe realized as she felt Beulah approaching her. When Beulah reached the alcove, she heard her say in almost a whisper, "Could I talk with you?"

Chloe looked up and noticed a tear at the corner of one of Beulah's eyes. She also saw Gregory standing in his doorway, but he nodded and then turned back into his office. Chloe decided he was letting her know he would wait while she and Beulah talked.

"Sure," said Chloe, rather matter-of-factly. "Have a seat." She pointed to the chair next to her.

Beulah sat but then started wringing her hands, saying nothing, so Chloe decided to try to break the ice. "How was your meeting? What was it like?"

"Oh, it was great," said Beulah, taking advantage of Chloe's question. "Gregory is really nice and understanding. He's set me up with Lucy and someone named Sylvester as mentors. I guess Sylvester runs the animal clinic. Lucy is going to take me to meet him this afternoon. I know it's silly, but I'm so happy I get to work with animals!"

"Why's that silly?" asked Chloe.

"Well…" she said and then stopped, took a deep breath, and raced on, "I've always loved animals and talked to them and sang to them. My family said it was crazy and that I couldn't really know what a chicken was feeling because chickens have no brains, and I always thought that was so cruel, but I learned never to talk about my animals to anyone."

"Oh, that's sad," said Chloe. "I'd think they'd be happy you could help the chickens."

"No, they didn't believe me. That's why it was so great to meet Lucy; she had the same experience until she came to Havenshold. I'm lucky to have her willing to mentor me, especially after I was so nasty about her with Imogene and Clarissa." She bowed her head and stared at her feet.

"I heard you guys muttering, but I couldn't hear what you said, so I'm sure Lucy couldn't either," said Chloe, hoping to alleviate Beulah's remorse.

"Well, Sage sure could! And Sage told me off! That really shook me up, I can tell you."

"I can only imagine!" Chloe chuckled.

"Well, I've been thinking since then. I realize that I've just gone along with what others have said because I wanted to fit in. And Imogene and Clarissa convinced me that we had to avoid anyone who wasn't dressed right or smart or whatever, and they were horrified that they hadn't been chosen as dragon riders, but here was a rider who was missing an arm!"

"I don't see what difference it makes—" began Chloe.

"Don't you see?" Beulah said in a louder voice. Then she lowered her voice again. "I really wanted to fit, and to fit, you have to be like everyone else. People who aren't like everyone else get shunned or worse. That's why we were so horrible to you. Everyone heard when your mother would come to school and yell at you in the playground, and so I just started repeating what your mother said to everyone; then you became the target for us all. But that meant I wasn't being bullied so I just stayed safe."

Tears began to fall onto Beulah's cheek, and Chloe reached out to pat her on the arm. Beulah continued, "I was so afraid they'd find out that I was different that I worked that much harder to keep their focus on you. You were such an easy target, after all."

"I know," said Chloe. "I've tried all my life to fit in also and to do what my mother wanted, or the teachers. I just never could manage it. Maybe I'm a bit like Lucy that way, even if I didn't lose a hand and then the whole arm. I knew I could never fit in, so I gave up trying."

"Well, Sage really made me think, and I'm not going to be like that anymore. I'm going to work hard with Lucy and Sylvester, and if my family or anyone else thinks that my love of animals is weird, well, then that's just too bad," Beulah said with determination in her voice.

"Good for you," said Chloe.

"And is there any chance we could start over? I'd really like to be friends," Beulah asked a bit hesitantly.

Chloe thought for a minute, remembering all the years of taunts and bullying. But would she be any better if she held the grudge? She looked over at Beulah and said, "Yes, that would be nice. Maybe we could have lunch together and start to get to know each other."

Beulah let out a big sigh of relief and said, "I'd like that!"

"It looks as if I'm going to be spending a lot of time here in the library," said Chloe as she pointed to her big, thick astronomy book. "So when you're free, just come on in, and we'll figure something out."

With that, the girls stood and hugged, and then Beulah turned to leave, this time with a smile on her face. Chloe looked over and saw Gregory standing in his office doorway; he too smiled at the girls before beckoning Chloe over to her meeting.

"So," Gregory began once they were both seated, "Beulah looked a lot happier when she left."

"Yes," said Chloe. "She really seems to be changed, and she wanted to apologize for all the years of bullying. I think yesterday, and especially Sage, really helped her to start thinking about the world in a new way."

"I'm going to have to get that cat a special treat," said Gregory with a chuckle. "Now, let's get down to you." He shuffled some papers and picked one out. "To be honest, I saved your meeting for last because it is the hardest. Oh, not in a bad way," he continued quickly when he noticed the alarmed look on her face. "Let me explain.

"Each of the other students has decided to try a field that already exists. For instance, Beulah can understand animals, and Lucy has already started to blaze that trail, along with William and his interest in alternate forms of communication and Sylvester and his animal clinic. So setting Beulah up to start with Lucy and Sylvester was an obvious and easy move."

Chloe nodded, and Gregory went on. "And that has been the case with the other five as well. They each had at least an idea of something they might like to try even if they weren't entirely sure. Some, like Bruce, knew what they wanted. He's always wanted to be a blacksmith, but his parents are sheep farmers and they were insisting he go into the family business. Having Bruce mentored by our blacksmith, Harold, was an obvious selection."

Again, Chloe nodded her understanding.

"I'm not sure yet about the other four girls, but each one was willing to pick something that interested her as a way to start. So I have mentors lined up for everyone, everyone except you, that is. We've never had a mage, at least not in this world. Bertha is unusual enough, but she is a seer and not a mage, as she told you herself. So I'm a bit flummoxed. Do you have any thoughts?"

Chloe hesitated, and then she said, "Well, Bertha did tell me to study astronomy, and I found a book yesterday quite by accident that is an introductory text. In fact, I was quite lucky to find an entire section devoted to astronomy."

"Really," said Gregory. "That's wonderful. To be honest, this lovely old library has really not been used by many. It is a shame, as it is a really beautiful building and I'm sure that there is a ton of knowledge here. Everyone just seems so busy keeping up with their daily lives that no one comes in here much."

"That is a shame," said Chloe, "but I'm really glad that we have all these books. I love to read! And remember Bertha said that somewhere in here we'd find the plans for the telescope that she sent."

"That's right," said Gregory. "I remember Hans mentioning that."

"And Robert also heard about that, and he asked me at the New Year's dinner if he could help me."

"Fantastic," said Gregory, scribbling notes on his sheet of paper. "Robert is really clever, and he loves building things. I'm sure that between you, that telescope will be built."

"Remember yesterday, when Lucy was telling about her efforts to find her path?" said Chloe.

"Yes," said Gregory.

"Well, she said that both William and Sylvester told her just to keep reaching out, trying to feel what was around her and see what she could do. Lucy had no mentor either, and she was blazing a brand-new path, but William and Sylvester encouraged her and directed her to find new contacts."

"That's true," said Gregory, "and look where that led."

"To the moles!" they exclaimed in unison and laughed.

"So," Chloe went on once they were able to resume the discussion. "I was thinking that I need to do something like that.

I'm sure you know how I kept my sister Zelda from killing herself when she fell out of the tree."

Gregory nodded, so Chloe continued, "At the time, I didn't realize that I was the one who had slowed her down, but Bertha showed me that I had used mage powers without knowing it, just as I did when I shielded her and her cubs. So I'm guessing that I need to try to do that deliberately."

"That sounds like a good idea," said Gregory. "Just how do you plan to do that?"

"Well, I was thinking that if I could find folks willing to help, that I could try to stop falling objects, like rocks or what not," she went on quickly lest Gregory think she was going to endanger anyone.

"Excellent! And I am guessing that, among others, Emily's father would just really love to help you!"

Chloe laughed. "I'm sure he would. I don't know what kind of magic I have, but I think it involves being able to move things, so I've already started, without any success, to try to move small objects."

"Well, it will take time, I'm sure," said Gregory. "Maybe you'll find some books in the library to help as well. OK then. Let's see if I have this right." He jotted notes as he talked. "You will study astronomy and get Robert to help you with the telescope. And you'll play games with my father-in-law trying to learn about magic." He looked up from his notes and smiled.

Chloe laughed again. "That's about the long and short of it. I'll also see if there are more books in the library on magic or mages."

"Great! That should keep you moving forward for the next six months until you see Bertha at the summer solstice. And remember, Chloe, that while Bertha put a lot of pressure on you with that prophecy, she also said that whatever the threat is, it won't be here for five or six years. You'll be ready by then; I just know it!" Gregory paused and then went on, "Before we wrap up this meeting, I need to check on the rest of your life outside of the academy. Are you comfortable at my in-laws'? Is that a good place to stay?"

"Oh, yes!" exclaimed Chloe. "They are wonderful."

"Great, and you have everything you need? I gather that your father sneaked you some funds, but remember, as an academy student, you have access to all our resources if you need clothes or anything. You can always have lunch in the rider cafeteria, for instance."

"Yes, Amy explained all that," murmured Chloe, her cheeks turning red with embarrassment.

"OK, then," said Gregory. "At some point, we will have to talk with your parents..." He stopped when he noticed Chloe sit bolt upright. "But not now. We have a plan in place that will keep you very busy and I hope very happy, at least through the summer, and we'll review everything again then. Sound good?"

Chloe relaxed a bit. "Yes, it sounds really good, and I'll work hard, I promise."

"I know you will," Gregory said as the two of them stood.

Chloe started to leave but stopped and turned in the door-way. Looking back, she said, "Thank you so much!"

— 10 —
THE LIBRARY

Chloe woke early the next morning. She was determined to spend the day in the library finding out as much as she could about what was in there. No one seemed to use it on a regular basis, but there it sat—one of the nicest buildings in the complex. Why? What was there?

When Chloe entered the kitchen, Amy and Todd looked up in surprise. They were enjoying their first cups of coffee, and they hadn't even had breakfast.

"Gads, you're up early!" said Todd.

"What would you like for breakfast?" asked Amy and started to stand up.

"I'll just grab a couple of pieces of bread," said Chloe as she sliced the large loaf sitting in the middle of the table. "I really want to get to the library early before anyone else."

Todd looked up at the kitchen clock and said, "You'll sure do that! Not sure the roosters are even up yet."

"Why the big rush?" asked Amy with a note of concern in her voice.

"I'm not sure," admitted Chloe as she wrapped the bread and picked up her backpack. "I felt something odd there yesterday...as if the library is trying to send me a message. I know it sounds weird," she continued, noticing the bewildered looks on their faces. "Buildings don't do that, right? But I just have this feeling that the library wants me there. I won't be able to rest until I check it out. That is OK, isn't it?"

Amy and Todd looked at each other, and then Amy said, "That is totally OK. That is, after all, just what you are supposed to be doing. It is all about trusting your instincts and following your gut. Just be sure you eat something more nourishing than bread and honey. Let us know if you need anything."

"Thanks," said Chloe with a sigh of relief. She thought it was wonderful to be trusted and supported. It was a very new feeling for her, and she found it most surprising and also very comforting.

Chloe ate her bread and honey as she walked quickly into town. Once there, she headed right into the rider complex. As she walked up the library steps, it suddenly occurred to her to wonder if the library was even open. What would she do if the doors were locked? But as she touched the main front door, shivers ran down her arm and the door clicked. She pulled on it, and it swung open easily. *What was that?* she wondered.

She entered the library, and as she walked into the main reading room, she heard the front door shut and click again, as if it had locked itself. She walked back to check, and sure enough, the library was locked again.

Well, that's probably a good idea. I don't need more people asking me why I am here at 5:00 a.m.!

She found the nice alcove that she had used yesterday and put her backpack on the table next to her chair. She pulled out a notebook that she had found on one of the library shelves when she was looking for astronomy books.

I think I'll start by trying to map this place so I know what kinds of books are here. I really need to know where astronomy is, where the plans for the telescope are, and where I might find books on mages and magic. It will be more efficient if I jot everything down now.

She took out a pen, grabbed the notebook, and began walking through the library. The area immediately in front of the main door was a very large open space with a few tables. There were small alcoves opening off the main room, like the one she'd taken over. Directly across from the alcoves on the other side of the room, there were three smaller offices with doors. Gregory was using the one farthest from the front door, but the other two were empty except for a desk and a couple of chairs.

Directly across from the main door on the far side of the room, there were rows of bookshelves. The shelving was perpendicular to the main door, with enough space between so people could walk and browse. Chloe counted and found there were fifteen rows of shelves, each about eight feet tall. *You'd need a step stool to reach the books on the top shelf,* thought Chloe, and sure enough, she saw several of them placed randomly between the rows.

Chloe started walking to the shelves and then thought that she'd better start by drawing her floor plan. She moved to one of the large tables, opened her journal, and gasped. *What! This was empty, I know it was, but now just as I thought about doing it, the floor plan has appeared. How is that possible?*

She sat down in the nearest chair feeling a bit faint. *I really should have had that breakfast Amy offered or at least a cup of coffee. I must be half asleep.* She looked at the journal again and then realized that she could smell coffee. She looked to her right, and sure enough, there was a large mug of steaming hot coffee!

OK, this is really weird now, she thought. She reached over and held the mug. It sure felt solid. Tentatively, she took a sip of the coffee, trying not to burn herself when she found out that it was piping hot. *It tastes wonderful! It tastes just the way Amy's does, just the way I love it.*

She took a few more sips and began to analyze the events of the morning. *I woke up at an outrageously early hour, driven to get to the library. Then the door unlocked itself as soon as I touched the handle, and it locked itself back up again after I walked through it. And this journal. I found it hanging most of the way off a shelf next to the astronomy books, and when I picked it up and looked at it, I just felt somehow drawn to it. I've never had such a nice, beautiful journal before, with its soft purple and pink cover and pale-blue pages. I couldn't have asked for anything better. And now the journal is writing itself with whatever I think I ought to know. Finally, when I come over faint with the shock, something which I will never tell Amy or she won't let me out of the house without breakfast again, I find the most perfect mug of hot steaming coffee right next to me where I know it wasn't before. What is all this?*

Chloe drank more of her coffee, trying to piece all the data together. She remembered that she had felt yesterday that the library seemed somehow happier now that it was being used by Gregory and the Pathfinder Academy. Chloe knew that most people never set foot in the library. They were too busy working. Maybe occasionally someone would try to find out information for something he or she was working on, but most of the time, people just taught themselves or learned from apprenticeships and later on-the-job training. Chloe wondered if the library was lonely. *But how can a library or any building be lonely? That's not possible! And why is the most beautiful building in the dragon rider complex a building that isn't used? Who put the building here anyway? And why are all the manuscripts so ancient?*

Chloe went back to her alcove and looked at the astronomy book she had taken off the shelves yesterday. She'd started looking at it but realized that the text was in a very ancient version of today's language, and it was extremely hard for her to read. She'd spent most of her time looking at the drawings, and she was so glad that there were so many of those.

She opened the book again now to confirm what she'd seen yesterday. As she started to turn the pages, she felt again that strange tingling sensation she'd felt when she opened the library door. And now, when she looked at the book, she saw that it had the same writing of an ancient-style manuscript copied by a scribe long ago, but Chloe was astounded to realize that she could read it easily, just as easily as she'd read her school textbooks.

Chloe had more of her coffee and just sat, stunned by all that had happened. *This must be magic,* she thought. *But how does it work and who's doing this?*

She pondered the events again and thought, *I was drawn to the library, and then I needed to open the door. I needed a journal to write in. I needed to map out the library. And then I really needed a cup of coffee to get my brain functioning. Is the magic responding to my needs?*

She sat there, drinking her coffee and tried to remember times in her life when strange things had happened. The only really strange things she could place were first Zelda's falling from the tree and then the hunter trying to shoot Bertha. In both cases, she really felt the need to stop her sister's fall and keep Bertha and her cubs safe.

Maybe I am on to something here! When she'd tried moving small objects last night in her room, absolutely nothing happened, except that she got really frustrated. *But I didn't need those objects to move, not like I needed to slow Zelda's fall. OK, but there was no danger to me this morning. I could have waited until the library opened. I could have drawn the plan all by myself,* although she admitted to herself that it wouldn't have looked half as good as the one that had been drawn magically. *And yes, I really do feel better after that cup of coffee, but I wasn't in any real danger without it.*

She was struggling on the edge of a discovery, she just knew it. But it wouldn't quite come. *OK, let's just keep on going. I wanted to try to figure out what books are here.*

With that thought, Chloe stood up with pen and journal in hand and headed to the leftmost row of books. She wandered down the row, looking to see what kinds of books were on the shelves. It was much easier now that she could read the ancient writings. There seemed to be books on history, very ancient history mostly, but a few more recent volumes that Chloe suspected were current records of kings and so forth. Then there were books about dragon riders. She opened her journal to start recording this and was only mildly surprised to see that the journal had filled in everything she had thought of. *This is really nice, but why? Where are the astronomy books? The books on mages and magic? And where is the best early history of this land and King Alfred? Maybe I should start there to figure out how this library came to be.*

Chloe looked down at her journal and found that sure enough, all the locations of the materials on the topics she'd asked about were now clearly written on the pages of her journal. *This really is rather spooky,* Chloe thought, but then she realized that a sense of calm and warmth had spread through her. Where was it coming from? Chloe walked through the stacks of books. In the very back, she found a door, a door that she was sure hadn't been there earlier.

Chloe went to open the door, and as she touched the handle, she again felt the tingling that she was coming to understand was the activation of magic. She walked into the room and saw a very cozy sitting room with a lovely, soft rug; overstuffed chairs; and a coffee table, which had a plate of hot, steaming scrambled eggs and toast next to a glass of orange juice. Sitting in one of the chairs was a small silver-haired lady. She was calmly knitting. She looked up at Chloe and said, "Please come in, won't you? I'm sure you have lots of questions, and I bet you are hungry. Please, enjoy," she concluded pointing at the wonderful breakfast.

Chloe did as the lady suggested and took a bite of the eggs. They were wonderful, and soon Chloe had finished everything in front of her. She looked up at the smiling lady and said, "Thank you. That was delicious. I'm Chloe, and I'm happy to meet you. This is a wonderful library."

"Oh, do you think so? I am so glad. Not many people come here, and I'm so glad that the academy has decided to use the space. Still, I don't think most of the students will need the knowledge that is stored here. But you, my dear, you certainly will."

"I have no idea what I am going to need," said Chloe, looking down at her lap. "Everyone says I'm a mage and that I'm meant to fulfill some prophecy, but I just can't believe that is true."

"I can assure you that it is definitely true and that is why you have been born now, as a mage. It will be a difficult path, but you are the only one who can walk it."

"I don't mean to be rude, but who are you? I haven't seen you around," asked Chloe.

The old lady laughed, and her laughter sounded like the tinkling of glass. "I'm the library," she said after a few minutes.

"Pardon me," said Chloe, certain that she hadn't heard correctly.

"I'm the library. I thought you'd find it easier to interact if I took on a more human appearance, but I'm the one who called you here and did all those things you were thinking about earlier. I was placed here by King Alfred and the first riders as part of their repository of knowledge from the world they had fled. I believe you have met Bertha?"

Chloe nodded, and the old lady continued, "Well, the bears have always been the protectors of dragons and dragon knowledge, and Bertha is the current seer. When you work with her in the summer, she will lead you to the hidden cave she and her ancestors have been guarding. Between us, we will point you in the right direction and assist you to fill in the gaps in what knowledge we do have that has been handed down through the ages. We will be your mentors. But the difficult work is still yours."

Chloe looked a bit shocked and said, "But how can you be a library? You look so human!"

The old lady laughed again. "I can manifest in a variety of forms as needed. Mostly, I will just help you by leading you to the most informative books, showing you where Bertha hid the plans for the telescope, and maybe giving you a mug of coffee or a plate of scrambled eggs if needed. But no one else will be able to see me. The door you came through is a magic door, one that only you can open. Whenever you are stumped or just want to talk things through, the door will appear, and we can have a cozy chat like this."

"What should I call you?" asked Chloe, totally overwhelmed by what she was hearing.

"Why not call me Libby?" she answered. "It is sort of short for library, don't you think?"

Chloe laughed. She was glad that Libby had such a delightful way about her.

"Now, you need to get back before the library opens for the day. In future, if you have a question during the day, just write it in your journal, and I'll write back with an answer. And then why don't we plan on meeting here each morning before the library opens? I'll be happy to provide the breakfast, if you don't think Amy would mind."

Chloe was amazed. Libby seemed to know everything about her. "But what shall I say? Can I tell people about you?"

Libby smiled and said, "I don't think that would be a good idea for either of us. Why don't you just tell the truth without divulging the magic? Why don't you just say that the library is your mentor? That is true, certainly, but you don't have to tell anyone about me. And as your magical powers grow, you will be able to do what I am now helping you with all by yourself."

Chloe stood up and said, "It is a lot to be getting on with. This morning has certainly given me a ton to think about. Should I start with the book on beginning astronomy?"

Libby laughed again. "Yes, my dear. That is why I had you pick it first. I know you will find it absorbing, and when Robert comes, I'll be sure you have the telescope plans as well."

Chloe opened the door and looked back. "Thank you so much!"

"You are most welcome. You will be a great mage, you'll see."

Chloe shut the door, and as soon as it was shut, the door disappeared. *Wow,* thought Chloe. *This is some library!* And with that, she headed back to her alcove to begin her studies.

— 11 —

A VISIT

Chloe's days started to blend into a routine. Amy was accustomed to her early departure, and Chloe really enjoyed sharing her questions with Libby and having breakfast in her cozy sitting room. Once the library was open, Gregory would usually stop in. He was getting used to the fact that Chloe always beat him and that she was inside even though the doors were locked. He seemed amused when she told him that the library was her mentor, but he asked no questions.

Chloe and Beulah would grab lunch together sometimes, and Chloe was enjoying their new friendship. Beulah was always excited to share her work and what she was learning. She spent a lot of time at the animal clinic working with Sylvester and learning to be a vet tech. And she loved Lucy and appreciated all the help the dragon rider was giving her. Chloe was truly amazed by the change in her new friend.

Chloe spent most of her days studsying in the library, and then in the evenings, she would chat with Amy and Todd. Chloe reveled in the calmness of their home when the rest of their family was off doing their own things. Amy and Todd gave her a feeling of stability and warmth, grounding her in the real world as she learned more and more about her magic.

As February approached, Chloe looked forward to starting on the telescope with Robert. He'd had to return to the capital to finish up some things but promised her that he would have plenty of time beginning sometime in the first week in February. Libby, as she had promised, had revealed the location of the telescope plans, and Chloe had studied them but realized that she really hadn't a clue where to start.

Chloe was reading yet another book on astronomy. She was definitely beginning to get a handle on planets, moons, suns, and stars as well as rotations, seasons, eclipses, and so forth. She heard voices as someone came into the library and went to Gregory's office, but she really didn't pay any attention until suddenly Gregory was walking into her alcove with Zelda and her father behind him.

Chloe jumped up and hugged both her father and Zelda as Gregory said, "Nice to see you both. Chloe is really making amazing progress as a mage, and she is going to be really powerful in a few years. You can be very proud of her. I'll leave you all to catch up."

With that, Gregory gave Chloe a big smile before he returned to his office.

"Wow," said Zelda. "Are you studying all those books?" She pointed to a tall stack on Chloe's table. "Do you really like that?"

Chloe laughed. It was so good to see her sister and father again. She had missed them. "Yes, I do. I'm studying astronomy, you know, about the stars and things, and it is truly fascinating. But how are you two doing? What are you up to?"

Her father hesitated and then said, "We really miss you, Chloe. I know what your mother said and what she is like, but I'm sorry you can't live at home. Are you in a good place?"

Chloe looked at him and noticed a tear in the corner of one eye. "Yes," she said. "I am truly happy with Amy and Todd. They are very good people, and they seem to love to foster. I am their second foster, and they take excellent care of me. But I've missed you too, and I am so glad you stopped by."

Zelda and her father looked at each other before her father continued, "We aren't letting your mother know, and we can't stay long or she will wonder where we are, but we wanted you to know that you have really made us think."

Chloe raised her eyebrows and said, "Me? Why?"

This time, Zelda answered. "You've shown us that there is more to life than being a dragon rider. You know how Mom and Grandma are. They are so bitter, and they have never been able to find anything that they really like to do, well, except make life miserable for everyone around them."

Harvey added, "You've opened our eyes, and we really want to find different paths for ourselves too. We've been hearing so many wonderful things about you. People really like you and want to be around you, and that certainly couldn't be said of me."

"Oh, Dad," said Chloe, "that just isn't true. The truth is that no one wants to be in Mom's path, so they avoid you in order to stay away from her."

"And I want to apologize," said Zelda. "I hadn't realized how badly you'd been hurt, and I just enjoyed all Mom's favors. But you saved my life, remember, and you're my sister."

Chloe noticed tears forming in Zelda's eyes. Suddenly, Zelda began crying. "I don't want to end up like Mom and Grandma!"

Chloe went over and hugged her sister, holding her tightly until Zelda's tears stopped. Then she said, "Listen, you two. If I've learned anything in the last two months, it has been that we each have to find our own way. There are lots of people to help, if you ask, but you have to make the start. Now, do either of you have anything that you do that you enjoy? Zelda, you should be looking for an apprenticeship now that you've finished your required schooling. What would you like to do?"

Zelda hesitated for a minute and then said, "Don't laugh, but I've always wanted to design clothes. I've spent a lot of time drawing my ideas. Of course, Mom and Grandma think that what I draw is rubbish, but my friends are really impressed. I've even sewn a few things for them, which they really liked."

Chloe said, "That's great, but why should I laugh? Just because I don't care about clothes doesn't mean that a lot of others don't. I can do some checking, since I know you won't be out of Mom's sight long enough to do it on your own. I'll see if I can find out whether the garment-makers' guild has anyone looking for an apprentice. If you guys can come back in, say, a week, I should have information."

Zelda said, "Thanks! Dad said you'd help."

"And what about you, Dad? You have your workshop, and you love making toys. Have you ever thought about getting a spot in the Saturday market and selling them, even doing special orders? You'd be great!"

"But your mother—" he started to say before Chloe interrupted.

"Dad, I love you, but you really need to start doing what you want to do. Mom has beaten you to a pulp, at least figuratively, until you are afraid of your own shadow. You need to get out more. Start thinking about it, and I'll ask Amy and Todd if they have any ideas to help you."

Harvey gave Chloe a big hug and said, "I love you, Chloe!"

"OK," said Chloe, "this is the start of Operation New Life. You two start thinking about your possibilities, I'll pull together some resources, and we'll meet here same time next Tuesday! Now stay firm in your hearts. This will work."

Harvey and Zelda each hugged Chloe again, and as they left, Chloe thought there was more of a spring to her father's step than she had ever seen, and she smiled. She'd talk with Amy and Todd tonight to see what could be done for them both. And on that happy, determined note, Chloe got back to her own studies.

Later in the afternoon, Gregory stopped by to see how she was doing. "Did you have a nice visit with your father and sister?" he asked. "They seemed much happier when they left."

"Yes, it was wonderful to see them. I do miss them a lot. Turns out that they've heard people talking about me and what I'm studying and they realized that maybe they could do something positive. It was so sad when my sister sobbed that she didn't want to turn out like my mom and grandma," said Chloe with a sigh.

"Your sister has just finished school, hasn't she? What about her apprenticeship?"

"Hah! In our family, apprenticeships aren't permitted. Zelda is stuck at home now, cleaning and cooking for my mother. She doesn't even get to see her friends now because they all have found apprenticeships."

Gregory thought for a minute before saying, "It sounds as if she'd be a good candidate for Pathfinder Academy."

"Oh, if only," said Chloe. "Actually, maybe you could help. Zelda knows what she wants to do, and I know she'd be great at it. She wants to design clothes. She knows how to sew, as my mother and grandmother taught us both to make our own clothes. They don't believe in the resale shop! Heaven forbid that they wear anything someone else has worn. Would you know of anyone willing to offer her an apprenticeship? We just have to get her out and away from my mother!"

Gregory smiled. "Now that is something I can work on. As head of Pathfinder Academy, I've made contact with a lot of people who might take on apprentices. I'll ask around and see if we can't find just the right spot for her. OK, got it. You've given me enough to run with."

"Thanks so much!"

"But what about your dad?" continued Gregory.

"He's a wonderful toymaker. He's done it for years, as he has a workshop at home where he spends most of his life. I want him to set up a booth at the Saturday market. That at least would get him out of the house and making some of his own money. Any kid would be thrilled to have one of his toys. But..." She paused here. "I just don't know if he's got the gumption to fight my mother, and she'd be horrified at the thought of his selling his toys. Our family doesn't do that, she'd say; we aren't tradespeople."

"Hmmm," said Gregory.

"I thought I'd talk with Amy and Todd tonight and see if they have any suggestions," concluded Chloe.

"If anyone can manage it, they can. I am so happy you were able to connect with Zelda and your dad."

"They'll be back next week, same time, same place, to find out what I've learned," said Chloe.

"Excellent! Now what about your studies? How are they coming along?"

"Really well. Robert is coming here next week to help me with the telescope. He said he could stay for both February and March if need be," answered Chloe.

"You'll enjoy working with him," said Gregory. "He is kind and smart, with a good head on his shoulders, and he won't run over you as, say, Todd might."

Both of them laughed at this. Todd's enthusiasm was legend. "Well, I'm out of here. Emily is fixing something special for dinner so I better not be late. Don't work too hard," said Gregory as he stood to leave.

"I won't! And thanks, Gregory," answered Chloe.

"My pleasure!" And he left the library.

Chloe packed up her things too, thinking that the day had really taken a wonderful turn. She sure hoped things would work out for Zelda and her dad. She couldn't wait to talk with Amy and Todd tonight.

— 12 —
THE LAB

Chloe spent the rest of that week getting ready for Robert's arrival. She was enjoying the morning chats and breakfast with Libby, and as they chatted that week, Chloe mentioned that she needed space in the library for a workroom, complete with tools, so she and Robert would have a place to begin building the telescope.

"So, why don't you make that happen?" Libby laughed.

"Me? But you are the library. I wouldn't know how to do it, and it is you we are talking about. It seems rather brazen of me to rearrange your form!" said Chloe. She still had trouble realizing that Libby really was the library—walls, furniture, books, and all. When she took on the appearance of Libby, she just seemed like any older woman. But her magic convinced Chloe otherwise.

"Don't you realize that your magic has been growing? Some of the things you have decided you needed, you have brought into existence," said Libby softly.

"No, I don't do it," said Chloe a bit stubbornly. "I don't know how."

"Well, I certainly am not making your lunches when you decide you don't have time to go to the cafeteria," said Libby.

Chloe looked at her with wide eyes. "Truly?"

Libby laughed. "Truly! Your powers are starting to blossom in a variety of ways. That last book you read was one the riders had found in their old world; it was written in a language they could never translate. But you read it with ease. So just trust me. I'm a catalyst for you, helping your powers to grow, and yes, some things are beyond you still. You have a lot of learning to become a full mage. But you can do many things for yourself."

Chloe just sat there and couldn't think of a thing to say. *Am I really doing my own magic?*

Libby went on, "So, what do you need. What are your ideas for this space you want to build a telescope in?

Chloe shook her head and regrouped. "Well, there are two empty offices next to Gregory's. I was thinking that if they were combined into one and made a bit larger even, maybe doubling their combined size, that we would have enough space. Then—"

Libby held up a hand. "Whoa, let's stop there for a moment. You'll want the room first, so let's just concentrate on that. Can you visualize those two rooms?"

Chloe nodded. Libby went on, "Now see the wall between them in your mind and simply slide it out of the way."

Chloe laughed. "Simply slide it out of the way? I'm not sure that's possible."

"Well, it won't be if you don't believe in it. Now concentrate. I'll help boost your power, but you have to decide on the direction."

Chloe closed her eyes and thought about the wall, moving it out of the room. She realized she could actually see what was transpiring, but then she was horrified because there was a free-standing wall in the middle of the main reading room. She looked over at Libby, who had a big grin on her face.

"You did that all by yourself," Libby said proudly.

"But now there's a wall in the middle of the main room," moaned Chloe.

"I'll take care of that," said Libby, and Chloe looked again with her mind's eye and saw that the room was now twice its original size and there was no stray wall hanging around.

"Thanks," said Chloe with a sigh of relief.

"Well, you don't have the strength yet to do it all, but I wanted you to realize that you can do some of it," said Libby.

Chloe sank back into her chair exhausted. "I don't know if I can do anymore. I'm really tired."

"Magic takes energy," said Libby. "Don't worry. You'll get stronger, and once this telescope is operational, we will begin magic lessons in earnest. I just wanted to give you a peak at what is in your future."

"Why can't I just build the telescope with magic, then?"

"The knowledge which King Alfred brought to this world and sealed away in Bertha's secret vault is protected so that magic can't be used to create any of the alien technology or machines. That way, no one can use it unless they understand it. Be grateful that you have the plans as well has those who can help you figure them out."

"Of course," said Chloe. "That makes perfect sense."

With that, Libby closed her eyes, and Chloe watched through her own mind as the library shifted walls, sliding things around effortlessly, adding a wonderful work table, stools, a fully out-fitted workbench, several cabinets with various supplies, and a few extras, such as a large window to let in daylight, a skylight, so they would be able to see the stars at night, and even a small area equipped with a coffeemaker and mugs.

When she was done, she looked over at Chloe and said, "So is that what you had in mind?"

Chloe gasped and said, "It's perfect! Thank you so much. Can we go see it for real?"

"You go, and I'll watch you from here," said Libby.

Chloe raced out of the room and found the new lab right next to Gregory's office. It looked as if it had always been there. Chloe noticed that while she was running out to see it, Libby had also added a white board and a bulletin board on the only empty wall, and the telescope plans were neatly pinned to the bulletin board. *This is totally amazing,* Chloe thought as she went back to thank Libby yet again.

When Gregory walked into the library later that morning, he stopped and said, "Wow! Where did all this come from?"

Chloe looked at him a bit sheepishly and said, "The library helped me. I wanted a lab so that Robert and I would have a good place to work when we start next week. Is it OK? I didn't change your office at all."

Gregory laughed. "It is certainly OK," he said, "and you are right. You do need a space to build the telescope. Robert will be so impressed! I just can't get over this. You really are a mage!"

Chloe blushed and then said, "Well, not yet, really. I had a lot of help. The library is truly magical, and she, I mean, *it* did most of the work. I just thought of ideas."

"Well, however you managed it, it is truly spectacular. Maybe down the road, I'll ask you for some upgrades to my office," teased Gregory.

"Sure," said Chloe with a bit of hesitation. *I wonder what he would like. He's been so wonderful with all of his students, me included. He should have something nice.*

"Now don't go thinking on that," said Gregory. "You have your own work to be getting on with, and after all, I have a very nice office in the headquarters building. This is just my satellite office for the academy, and it works just fine. Now I'd better prepare for my next student meeting."

Chloe was glad that she and Libby had fixed up the lab so quickly, because the rest of the week was pretty much a lost cause as far as work went. People kept traipsing into the library on any pretext at all, or even no pretext, just to take a look at the lab, and of course, they had a million questions, which Chloe did her best to answer.

Her favorite moment though was when Zelda and her father came in. The looks on their faces were really remarkable. They stood in the middle of the lab, mouths hanging open in astonishment before Zelda exclaimed, "You really are a mage!" and ran up and hugged her.

Harvey just looked at her with such pride, tears welling in his eyes. "I wish your mother could see this. You are so talented and wonderful."

Chloe turned beet red and said, "Well, I had a lot of help. I couldn't do this all on my own. The library is amazing."

Zelda and Harvey just shook their heads in disbelief before Zelda said, "OK, but we know who really did it."

There was no convincing them, so Chloe didn't even try. They sat down on the stools at the work table, and Chloe got coffee for them all. Then she asked, "How are things going with you two?"

Zelda started right in. "Gregory has found someone who wants me as an apprentice. I've met her, and her fashion designs are incredible. She even has a small apartment that she lets her apprentice use. I can live there, and it is just on the other side of the plaza, so I won't be far away. Dad and I are headed there now to sign the apprenticeship papers."

Chloe looked at her sister, noticing the glow in her cheeks, and said, "That is wonderful! You'll do a great job, I know!"

"When I told Mom, she exploded, but there is nothing she can do about it. She tried to say that no one would sign the papers for me, but when she looked at Dad for confirmation, he simply said he would sign and quietly left. Mom has been yelling ever since, but I have my bag packed, and we're setting me up today."

Chloe looked over at her father and said, "Thanks, Dad!"

"Once I'm all set up, I'll have you over. It is just a studio apartment, but Marjorie, that's my boss, said I could fix it up in my free time outside of work and that would count as part of my design training. Isn't that cool? And I get Sundays off. I will be working Saturdays at the Saturday market, so I'll see people then and everything," she concluded as she ran out of breath.

"Excellent!" said Chloe. "And now what about you, Dad? Life isn't going to be much fun at home now."

"I know, but just knowing you two are out and on your own is enough. And I have my workshop to hide out in. Todd came by the other day, and he is such a nice man. He loves to build and tinker with things so we had a lot to talk about. He is very supportive and seemed to think my toys were something unique and special. I'll be fine," concluded her father.

"Well, we better go, Dad. I don't want to be late," said Zelda, grabbing her duffel.

Harvey laughed and gave Chloe a big hug. "Don't worry, I'll stop by often, and I'll let you know how everything's going. Now, I'd better get Zelda signed off," he said with a chuckle.

Chloe watched them heading out of the library and thought how much happier they both looked.

Chloe lost track of the number of people who stopped by. Amy and Todd came in, of course, and Todd looked at the lab with a gleam in his eye. "Say, could I come work here?" he asked.

Amy playfully smacked his arm and said, "This is for the telescope, not for your latest invention!"

Chloe laughed. "Maybe once the telescope is built, we can open the lab up on a reservation basis. I'll put your name at the top of the list, OK?"

Todd laughed. "That would be wonderful, but you know I was kidding."

The week sped by. Emily, Hannah, Lucy, Gretchen, Jake, William, and Rupert all showed up in their off hours. Chloe began to feel overwhelmed, but Gregory assured her that the novelty of the lab would wear off. Beulah came, and then, much to her surprise, both Imogene and Clarissa stopped by.

"You made this?" asked Imogene with amazement in her voice.

"Well, not by myself. The library did most of it," said Chloe quite truthfully.

"Yeah, right," said Clarissa. "You know, you really are amazing. I had no idea. I guess you have truly found your path."

Chloe thought that was the nicest thing either of those girls had ever said to her. "Thanks so much, and what are you two doing? Have you found apprenticeships that you like?"

"Yes," said Imogene. "I'm now officially an apprentice weaver! It is so awesome! I am learning to warp the loom and dye the yarn, and before long, I'll be weaving my first project!"

"That's wonderful," said Chloe. "You have such an artistic nature that I know you will be a wonderful weaver. And you, Clarissa?"

"Well, you know how I've always loved to paint. Who knew you could make a career out of it? I'm apprenticed now to an awesome painter, and I'm learning all about colors and how to mix my own paints. I am getting real drawing lessons and everything!"

Chloe looked at both girls and thought how happy they looked. Maybe now that they each had found their true callings, they could be friends.

"I am so very happy for both of you, and I hope you'll let me know when you have your first works completed, as I would really love to see them," said Chloe.

Finally, the week came to an end. Chloe was exhausted but very happy. Robert was due to arrive at his parents' later that night. She looked forward to telling him about the plans so far, but first, she wanted to sit by the fire at Amy and Todd's, listening to the conversations, having wonderful meals, and just doing nothing!

— 13 —

THE TELESCOPE

Monday morning, February 1, dawned sunny and very cold. Chloe snuggled deeper into her covers before she realized that today was the day that she and Robert were going to start on the telescope. Cold or not, she was out of bed in a flash. She dressed warmly and grabbed her heavy down coat for the walk to the library, gratefully taking the mug of hot coffee that Amy offered. She walked as briskly and yet carefully as she could since there was some ice on the road. And as she always did, she marveled when the library door unlocked to let her in and locked behind her. Robert wouldn't arrive until the library actually opened, but Chloe didn't want to miss her morning visit with Libby.

"So!" exclaimed Libby as Chloe walked into the lovely sitting room. "Today is the big day. The work begins!"

Chloe nodded and said, "Yes, I am a bit nervous about it all, although I did talk with Robert over the weekend and get to know him better, and I think he will be wonderful to work with."

Libby laughed. "You must remember that you are always a bit apprehensive when something changes, but usually, it all works out."

"And hopefully we won't have quite so many people stopping to take a look," said Chloe.

"I wouldn't count on that," said Libby. "This is a big deal. No one had even heard of a telescope until you started training. You'll have plenty of gawkers, but I suspect you and Robert won't really notice much."

True to Libby's predications, every day that they worked, people stopped by to check on the progress and offer suggestions, but also as Libby predicted, she and Robert weren't really distracted and most people only looked and then returned to whatever they were supposed to be doing.

On the first day, Robert studied the plans, which Chloe had to admit didn't mean much to her. He started jotting down a list of supplies and then said, "I can get everything but the lenses from Dad. Can you go over to the clinic and see Nurse Beatrice. She will know what these numbers mean," he said as he handed her a piece of paper, "and all the lenses are at the clinic ready in case they are needed for a pair of glasses. Tell her that we will cut them ourselves to fit once we have the tube made."

"OK," said Chloe, who felt a bit overwhelmed by it all.

Robert heard the hesitation in her voice and said, "Don't worry. You'll soon see where all this is going. These plans aren't that different from architectural drawings, and I am very familiar with them. So of course this looks easier to me, but trust me, you'll get the hang of it in no time."

"Thanks, Robert. OK, I'll get the lenses, and you can get the rest; then we'll see how it goes together."

"It will probably take me most of the morning to round everything up. I'll be back after lunch. Can I bring you anything?" asked Robert.

"No, I'm fine," said Chloe. "See you after lunch then."

The two of them headed out of the library. Chloe turned down toward the clinic to see Nurse Beatrice as Robert headed back home. *I wonder how he will get everything and still keep Todd at home,* she thought. She knew Todd was really intrigued by the whole concept, and she suspected he would be their most consistent visitor.

Chloe walked into the clinic and saw Nurse Beatrice at the front desk, checking a patient out of the clinic. Once she was done, she looked up at Chloe and said, "Well, hi there. Haven't seen you in the clinic for years. How's the mage training going? What can I do for you?"

Chloe chuckled. Nurse Beatrice could be brusque, but she had a heart of gold. Chloe answered, "It's all a bit overwhelming at times, but I'm learning a lot and I have to admit it is fun. Right now, Robert and I are going to build a telescope to look at the stars."

Beatrice said, "Yes, I've been hearing all about that. Meant to get over before now, but I just haven't found the time. But how can I help?"

Chloe handed her the piece of paper Robert had given her and said, "Robert says we need these lenses and that you'd have them. He doesn't want them cut. Says we'll be doing that."

Looking over the paper, Beatrice said, "This will be really easy. I'll get these for you right now, and if the stock isn't too low, I'll give you two of each, just in case. Lenses can be tricky to cut. Be right back." Beatrice bustled down the hall.

A few minutes later, she returned with a small box. "I packed them securely for you. Good luck!"

"Thanks," said Chloe, "and you are welcome to stop by anytime to see the progress."

Chloe took the box and headed back to the library. She tried studying the plans for the remainder of the morning but wasn't sure she was any more knowledgeable by lunchtime. She headed to her favorite alcove and conjured herself a bowl of piping-hot bean soup and a mug of coffee and relaxed.

Chloe and Robert began work that afternoon. It was slow, and they had to experiment with a number of techniques for each phase. The days rolled into each other as the work progressed. Chloe was right in her guess that Todd would stop by frequently, but she also was most impressed by his restraint. He clearly respected his son, so he didn't offer suggestions unless he was asked. As an inventor, he had made a lot of gadgets of one kind or another, some successfully and others not, giving him a wealth of experience, which she and Robert were happy to tap into. Others stopped by as well, and Chloe was really glad that Libby had put in a glass wall between the lab and the rest of the library. Folks were perfectly willing just to watch the progress from the windows, and soon Chloe noticed a few chairs had been added. At times, she felt as if she were in an aquarium, but still, it allowed them to work without tripping over people.

Near the end of February, word started to spread through the community that the telescope was nearly ready to test. One day, they had many more visitors than usual during the lunch hour. Bruce stopped in after his weekly meeting with Gregory. He watched for a bit and then said, "You know, you are going to need a tripod for that, one with a swivel top. If you like, I bet I could make that in the blacksmith shop."

Robert looked up and said, "Really? That would certainly be nice. How would you do it, and what do you need?"

Soon, Bruce and Robert were talking figures and Bruce was measuring the telescope, which was actually beginning to look like the one drawn in the plans. As they were working, Gregory popped in. He looked at Chloe and said, "I really admire Robert and his way of working with people. He is a natural leader."

Chloe thought about that for a minute and then realized just how true it was. Robert listened. He asked questions that allowed Bruce, in this case, to shine and gain confidence. By the time Bruce left with several pages of notes, there was a real spring in his step. "I'll be back in a couple days with a mock-up," he said as he nearly ran out of the library.

Just then, Beulah, Imogene, and Clarissa came in. They had taken peeks before, but now that things were coming together, they really wanted to see it up close.

"So that is going to be able to show us the stars?" said Beulah, pointing at the telescope.

Chloe answered, "Yes, we sure hope so."

"I'm sure it is impressive," said Clarissa, "but it isn't much to look at, is it?"

Everyone laughed, and Chloe said, "What would you suggest?"

"It needs color and designs, designs of the stars," said Clarissa. "Can it be painted?"

Chloe looked at Robert, and he answered, "Sure thing. The outside can be decorated any way you like. It is just a tube to hold the lenses, and it only needs to keep all the light out except for what comes through the lenses. Otherwise, it can be anything."

"Well, could I decorate it then?" asked Clarissa. "After all, it is the first ever telescope. It should look impressive."

Soon, Clarissa and Robert were discussing kinds of paints and which would last the longest. Finally, Clarissa said, "I'll sketch out some ideas and get back to you."

"And don't you think our telescope should have a name?" said Beulah.

"Yes! That's just what it needs," concurred Imogene.

Robert looked at the two girls, and again Chloe noticed how Robert encouraged them, leading them but not forcing. He never laughed at their ideas; he just added a question of his own every now and then. As they were talking, Emily, Hannah, Lucy, and Gretchen came in and added their two cents to the discussion of colors, designs, and names. The room was filling up with very excited people.

Chloe watched from the sidelines, standing next to Gregory, who was also just observing. Chloe said, "You are right. Robert is really amazing. How does he do it?"

"I think he gets it from his mother. Have you ever noticed how Amy orchestrates everything without ever appearing to do so?"

"I'm beginning to learn that there are different kinds of magic. I can move a wall or make my soup for lunch out of thin air. But I think what Robert is doing here is also magic and in the long run, a much more important and powerful magic. He really understands people."

With that, Chloe and Gregory joined in the conversation, and somehow, without anyone even realizing whose idea it was, they had decided to have a Havenshold contest to name the telescope. The contest would run for the next month, since Robert and Chloe thought it would be that long before the telescope with the tripod Bruce was making and the artwork that Clarissa was providing was completed.

"What's the prize?" asked Beulah.

"And who are the judges?" chimed in Imogene.

This time, Robert looked to Chloe, who said, "First, I think Beulah and Imogene should make the posters and the ballot box. The ballot box should be placed in the library's main reading room."

Everyone nodded in agreement. "Then I think the prize should be the first look through the telescope. Of course, Robert and I will have to test it beforehand, but we will have a public unveiling when it is all finished, and the winner will get the first look."

"That's wonderful, and I can weave a blanket to cover the telescope for the unveiling," added Imogene.

"Finally, for the judges, I think there should be a panel. How about if everyone who helped build, decorate, et cetera, the telescope is on it? That would be Robert, Bruce, Beulah, Imogene, Clarissa, and me, oh, and Gregory, since this is turning into an academy project."

Everyone agreed that Chloe's plans were perfect. Soon, the crowd dispersed as everyone left to start on his or her part of the project or else return to work.

Finally, the room was empty except for Robert and Chloe. Chloe said, "This really is a community project, isn't it?"

Robert nodded, and they got back to work.

— 14 —
THE UNVEILING

Time just seemed to fly by. February became March, and still they worked. Chloe found the project fascinating, and she was learning a lot about lenses and magnification. Bruce kept stopping by with plans for the tripod, and Chloe enjoyed seeing him so engaged in the project. He was certainly never meant to be a sheep farmer. She sure hoped his family respected that.

By the end of March, all the parts had come together, and it was time to dedicate the telescope and begin using it. Emily and Gregory decided that the grand unveiling would be done on the evening of April 1. Queen Clotilda was coming from the capital for the event and would do the actual unveiling.

Emily stopped by one morning the week before the unveiling to talk with Chloe. "Well, it seems as if all of Draconia will be gathering for the unveiling, and even some dignitaries from the other three countries—Forbury, Granvale, and Sanwight—so this will be quite an event."

"But we're going to have the telescope on the library roof," said Chloe. "How will everyone fit up there?"

Emily laughed, shaking her head. "You may have the telescope there after the unveiling. But for that night, you'll have to be in the town square. There isn't anywhere else large enough for the crowd that is sure to appear. Remember, this is a new invention and people are curious. It is also one that we hope will help you to save this planet, so of course, people want to check it out."

Chloe wrung her hands, and Robert patted her on the shoulder. "It will be fine," he said. "Our dads have already figured out a platform with three wide stairs so that Clotilda and the heads of the other three nations can be where everyone will see them; meanwhile, the telescope will be out of the crowd, safe, and also high enough above people's heads so that everyone can see. It will be fine."

Chloe laughed. "I am so excited about the observatory that the library has made on the roof that I guess I didn't think about the realities of the unveiling."

"That's what Gregory and I are here for," said Emily. "Now, has the committee met to decide on the telescope's name? We really should have the winner on the platform as well."

Robert started laughing as Chloe tried to explain. "About that..." she started. "Turns out that the winner isn't just one person."

"What?" asked Emily in a puzzled voice.

"Well, we had tons of entries, but the winner is actually Havenshold's school," said Chloe.

"An entire school? How is that possible?" exclaimed Emily.

Robert had finally stopped laughing and explained, "Miss Murphy thought it would be fun to engage the students in the naming contest. So she ran many smaller contests at school, and eventually, the students, from the youngest to the oldest, worked together to decide on one name to submit. And that name turned out to be the winner."

Emily snorted and then said, "Things were simpler when we were in that school. I can't see Miss Raven doing anything like that."

Chloe smiled and said, "I've heard about her. She's retired now, isn't she?"

"Yes," said Emily with a sigh. "So now we have Miss Murphy to deal with. Who's going to get the first look through the telescope?"

Chloe looked at Robert, who nodded. She said, "All the children."

"*What*?" exclaimed Emily. "There must be nearly fifty children in that school. That would take all night and then some."

"Hang on, Sis," said Robert, who seemed to be quietly enjoying his older sister's discomfort. "We have a plan."

"That's good," said Emily. "I'm all ears."

Chloe smiled, enjoying their banter. "May I explain?"

"Please do," said Emily with arms crossed.

"OK, what we thought was that the very youngest child would be picked for the first look on the unveiling night. Then each of the other students would be given a pass to be redeemed at a mutually convenient time for their own private viewing in the new observatory. Does that sound fair?" asked Chloe with a slight hesitation in her voice.

Emily relaxed, and a big grin spread over her face. "That sounds absolutely brilliant!"

Robert and Chloe saluted themselves, and Emily went on, "So on the platform, we will have Clotilda, Queen Priscilla from Sanwight, King Alfred and Baron Geldsmith from Forbury (no way to keep my father-in-law off the platform), Queen Penelope from Granvale, you two, Gregory, me, and this youngest child. Wait! We better have Miss Murphy to watch the youngest child. Is that everyone?" she asked as she looked up from her notebook where she had been jotting everything down as she spoke.

Robert quipped, "Well, except for the telescope! And don't you think we should also have Bruce, Imogene, and Clarissa, as they helped make the telescope what it has finally become?"

Emily groaned and jotted down the other three names before saying, "You are right. Give me the dimensions of the space you want for the telescope. I obviously need to find Dad and Harvey so that they can figure just how big this platform needs to be."

Robert scribbled some figures onto a piece of paper and handed them to Emily. "Thanks, guys," said Emily as she turned to leave. "Say, what is the name anyway?" she asked from the doorway.

Robert and Chloe looked at each other and then turned to her, making the universal zipping-the-mouth gesture. Emily said, "Spoil sports. OK, keep your secrets," and she left the library.

Thankfully, the day of the unveiling was sunny and bright, a wonderful spring day. Todd and Harvey had built a lovely platform large enough to fit all the dignitaries and the telescope safely and reasonably comfortably.

People seemed to be streaming into Havenshold all day. Chloe had heard that all the heads of state were being entertained in the rider complex, and she was very relieved that she didn't have to participate in that. She and Robert were quite busy enough getting everything prepared.

"I guess we can point the telescope at the moon for tonight," said Chloe tentatively. "Do you think that will be enough for the first viewing? I'm betting after little Joey gets the first turn that many others are going to want a peek."

Gregory walked in just then and said, "If I can butt in. Emily and I talked about that, and we decided that after Joey, the heads of state will get to look, since they don't live around here, beginning with our own Clotilda. And my father will be included because he is not one to be excluded," he said with a chuckle.

"And then what about the large crowd?" asked Chloe.

"Well, we are going to announce that the telescope will be moved to its new observatory tomorrow, and then it will be open to the public each clear night in April and May. That way, everyone should get a chance to take a look if they want to," concluded Gregory.

"But my original question for tonight: do you think that just seeing the moon will be enough?" asked Chloe.

"Are you kidding?" answered Robert. "Remember how excited we were when we saw the moon for the first time? And we were just testing lenses. Now that we've adjusted the magnification, people will be blown away by what they see."

"I agree with Robert," said Gregory. "And from what you've told me, it will be much easier to 'find' the moon in the telescope than say a distant star."

"True," said Chloe. "And do we have a small step for Joey to stand on? I don't think a five-year-old could see through the telescope without one."

Gregory laughed before saying, "Todd and Harvey have already met with Joey at school and measured him! They have made a step customized just for him."

Robert groaned and said, "I should have guessed!"

"So do you two need anything else?" asked Gregory.

"No," said Chloe. "Everything seems to have been done. Thanks for checking, and I think your plan for the viewing is a good one, although it is going to mean I won't get a lot of viewing time before I leave to spend my summer with Bertha. Well," she concluded more positively, "I'll have late nights, and then by the time I return in September, I'm sure opening the observatory one night a month will be plenty."

Gregory said, "I'm sure. Now if you really don't need anything, I'll be off to help Emily entertain the dignitaries. See you at the unveiling."

The unveiling went off without a hitch, although Chloe couldn't remember seeing so many people crammed into the town square before. She was nervous sitting on the platform, but she had Robert on her left and Emily and Gregory on her right, so that helped.

As they were waiting to start, Baron Geldsmith leaned over both Emily and Gregory to greet her and to say, "You have really done something special here. I'd like to get to talk with you one day."

Chloe said, "Uh, thanks, sir," just as Queen Clotilda went to the front of the platform.

"Welcome, my fellow monarchs, dignitaries, riders, ladies, gentlemen, and children—I hope I've included everyone, but if I missed anyone, welcome to you too," and Clotilda paused as folks laughed. The atmosphere became even more festive.

"I guess by now," Clotilda went on, "you all know about this new invention called a telescope, which will allow us to look at the stars. Many thanks to Chloe, our apprentice mage, and Robert for figuring out the ancient plans and building it."

Chloe and Robert stood, and everyone applauded. Clotilda went on to explain what Bruce, Imogene, and Clarissa had added, and they stood for their acknowledgments.

"Finally," said Clotilda, "it is time to name this telescope. As you know, there was a naming contest; what you may *not* know is that Miss Murphy, Havenshold's wonderful teacher, took the contest to heart in her school and all the students participated in choosing one name to submit to the contest. And that name was the winner!"

The audience let out loud cheers and applause, along with lots of laughs.

Clotilda continued, "Obviously, we can't have every student up here for the first look, but each student has received a pass for a private viewing in the observatory once the telescope is put in its permanent location tomorrow. And the youngest student in the class, Joey Samwright, will be the honorary viewer tonight for all the winners."

Everyone applauded as Joey, clutching a piece of paper, walked slowly and hesitantly over to Clotilda, who bent down to greet him.

"Joey has the name that the school picked and which our judging panel voted on as the best," continued Clotilda. "Joey, can you tell me the name?"

Joey shook his head and whispered, "I can't read yet."

Clotilda chuckled and said, "Could I see your paper?"

Joey nodded solemnly and held out the paper to Clotilda.

Clotilda read the paper, smiled, and turned back to the audience to announce, "The name of our very first telescope is…" She paused for a moment before continuing, "Dragonstar!"

Chloe looked across at the crowd as they exploded into cheers and applause, and she realized that she felt warm and happy inside. This was a real community project, and everyone was taking part in it. She looked out to the front of the audience where she could see her father and sister cheering the loudest, and she was very happy. This was a wonderful night. She wished her mother were there, but before she could become sad at that, she was drawn back into the ceremony when Clotilda began to speak again.

"Chloe, would you step over to Dragonstar and help Joey take a look at our moon?" asked the queen.

Chloe positioned the telescope for Joey and helped him up onto the stool, which, no surprise, was the perfect height for him. It took the little boy a few minutes to realize that he needed to close one eye and look with the other, but after Chloe's gentle instructions, he finally could see through the telescope.

After a quick look, Joey turned to find his parents in the crowd and said, "The moon! It is so big!"

Everyone laughed and clapped for Joey. The evening ceremony then ended after the visiting dignitaries got their chance to look and Clotilda explained about the open viewing opportunities for April and May.

Clotilda concluded by saying, "Thanks to everyone for sharing in this most historic moment. There are plenty of refreshments for all, so please, enjoy the evening."

— 15 —
FAMILY

Spring was a blur for Chloe. Every clear evening, she was up in the new observatory, which she and Libby had "built" on the top of the library. Chloe was pleased that her magic skills had become stronger so that she could do more of the work. The circular stairs were all her doing! And the observatory dome looked as if it had always been there. People were amazed, and as Chloe couldn't tell anyone about Libby, they gave her all the credit. She was modest in her acceptance and pointed out quite truthfully that she had had a lot of help. She just didn't explain exactly what that help was.

By early June, the number of visitors to Dragonstar had dropped to only a few on the weekends, so Chloe was able to begin her own more intense studies. She had made large charts of the sky and compared those with her books. She really felt that she was making progress. And she was looking forward to the summer solstice when she would leave to study with Bertha for the summer months.

One evening, three days before the summer solstice, as she prepared to work in the observatory, she noticed her father and Zelda entering the library. She smiled as she welcomed them. The changes in the two of them were remarkable.

"Hi there!" Chloe said as she hugged each of them in turn. "Do you want to look at the stars with me?"

Zelda said, "Not tonight, Sis. I can't stay, but I wanted to show you my new outfit." She twirled around to show off the flow of her skirt.

"Wow!" said Chloe as she looked more closely. The top was a lovely pale-pink flouncy sort of blouse, and the deep-purple skirt really twirled well. "It is gorgeous! Did you design that all yourself?"

"Yes, it is my first solo design, although I did have help and some suggestions from Marjorie," answered Zelda.

"Well, it is wonderful, and thanks so much for showing it to me. You look radiant."

"Marjorie is going to let me enter this in her next show," said Zelda excitedly.

"That is truly fantastic! You are learning so fast!" said Chloe.

"Well, I have to run, but I just wanted to show you. Dad took me out to dinner, but I have to get back to my apartment now, as I still have some sketches to finish up tonight," said Zelda, and she gave Chloe a hug before racing out the library door.

Chloe turned to her father and said, "So what about you, Dad? Would you like to go up to the observatory?"

"Maybe another time. I wanted to talk with you if that's OK."

"Sure," said Chloe. "Let's head over to my cozy alcove."

Once the two of them were seated, her father began, "First, I want to thank you for all you have done for Zelda and me."

"I haven't done anything," said Chloe.

"Oh yes, you have. It was a huge thing when you left home. That opened the door for both of us."

Chloe chuckled and said, "Well, it isn't as if I had any choice."

"But you did," insisted her father. "That's what I mean. You could have done what your mother and grandmother did. You could have turned yourself into some kind of victim and become bitter. But you didn't. You grabbed life by the horns and made a new path for yourself."

"I had a lot of help with that," said Chloe.

"I know, and I know all about that prophecy thing, but don't you see? Once you left and you found a way to start over, that gave both Zelda and me the courage to try as well. And you saw tonight just how well Zelda is succeeding." Harvey paused, taking a big breath before continuing, "I wanted to let you know that I've moved out of the house, and I've found a small cottage. It's just down the road from the town square, so it's very convenient, and it has a small shed that I'm converting into a workshop," he said, talking very fast to get it all out in one breath.

"Oh, Dad," said Chloe, "I'm so sorry, but I'm also so glad, if that makes any sense."

"Yes, I do understand. You know, I loved your mom and I could never figure out why she married me. I know now that she was determined to marry someone from one of the original dragon rider families, and there weren't a lot of choices in our class. I was just thrilled she seemed to want me. She was so pretty and popular, just like Zelda really. But over the years, she changed, and I've just not been able to stand up to her. I feel really badly that I didn't intervene when she abused you. I really wanted to, but I was scared. I'm sorry," he finished softly, staring down at his feet.

"I do understand, Dad, more now than I ever did growing up. And while I was mad when you didn't speak up, I also knew that had I been in your place, I might not have spoken up either. I was never able to talk to Mom at all, so I can't very well fault you. And you know what, Dad? You were there to soften her harsh edges more often than you know. I wouldn't be who I am if it weren't for you," she concluded.

"Thanks, dear, although I'm not sure I deserve it."

"Now, tell me about your new place. When can I come see it?"

"Well, Todd helped me find it. You know the road that leads out of town toward their home?" he asked, and Chloe nodded and smiled.

"Just as you leave town, there is a small cottage on your left—"

"A cute little blue one?" asked Chloe. "I pass that every day, and I've always wondered who lived there, as it is so pretty."

"Well, Todd said that it had been empty for several years. I guess it was a second home for a couple who live in the capital but who had family in Havenshold. They used it as a place to stay when they visited, but now the family has moved away and the place has just been standing empty. Todd arranged for me to rent it from them for a very reasonable rate."

"That's wonderful!"

"And Todd is helping me fix up the shed in the backyard. I packed up the few things I had in the house and then moved out to my workshop several weeks ago. Your mother didn't even seem to notice. Then with the help of Todd, Robert, and Gregory, I moved all of my things, including my workbench and tools, to my new place. We finished over this past weekend. I asked everyone not to say anything until I could tell you myself, but I feel so much happier already."

Chloe gave her father a big hug. "I'm truly happy for you, and it sounds as if you and Todd have become good friends."

"Well, he is an inventor, and I'm a toymaker; those two things have a lot in common, and I think now, especially as his family has grown up, that he enjoys my company as much as I enjoy his. We share ideas and brainstorm off each other. The twenty-year age difference doesn't seem to matter at all. And he lets me use some of his tools when I need to. I've got a lot of ideas for new toys now. I am planning to work really hard over the summer so that by the holiday season, I'll have a ton of new toys to sell."

"Oh, I am so proud of you, Dad! I know it hasn't been easy."

"I have to earn my own way now because you better believe your mother will never part with a bit of her family wealth, not that I'd even want it. And the truth be known, I think that there isn't much left anyway, probably just enough to see her and her mother through. I do feel really sorry for her, but I can't stay in that house any longer."

"And you shouldn't have to. I'm glad you have your own place. But honestly, Dad, how are you going to eat? You can't even boil water, much less cook."

Harvey laughed out loud and said, "You've got that right, but Todd told me about a program here in Havenshold where people can apply for a meal card to the rider cafeteria. At the moment, I'll get free meals, but once I start earning enough to pay for more than my rent, I hope to be able to buy the meal card. For now though, I'm really glad that Havenshold has such a plan."

"Sounds as if you have it all worked out. I know you'll be fine. I'm proud of you, Dad!"

They stood up and hugged. Harvey then headed out of the library, and Chloe climbed up to the observatory.

After lunch the next day, Chloe thought, *I really need to stop at the house and see Mom and Grandma before I leave for the summer. I don't want to, but it is the right thing to do.* And with that thought, she headed to her old home.

Chloe walked up the path to the front door, and just as she was wondering if she should ring the doorbell or not, the door opened. Her mother stood there glaring and said, "So what are you doing here? Have you come to gloat?"

Chloe was taken aback, caught completely off guard. She hesitated for a moment and then said, "No, Mom. I just wanted to stop by and be sure you and Grandma are all right."

"Why wouldn't we be?" snapped her mother.

Chloe thought, *This really was a bad idea*, but she went ahead anyway and said, "Well, I'm leaving Havenshold for the summer, so I just thought I'd stop by and let you know." Chloe felt very funny having this conversation out on the front porch. She continued, "Is Grandma OK? Could I see her?"

"She's napping, and it is no good your coming around here. I meant it when I disowned you. You won't get anything from me ever, especially now that you've taken your father and sister away too." She turned back into the house.

Chloe caught the door just before her mother slammed it in her face and followed her into the house. "I didn't come here to argue, Mom. You know that I did nothing to take Zelda and Dad away from here. I was just worried about you here alone, and I thought I'd stop by. I don't want anything."

"Well, we're fine. You can get out, and stay out!" said her mother.

Chloe looked around and noticed that there were no lights on anywhere. The house was always dark, even in the daytime. She could see dust on the table, and her mother had always kept an immaculate house. Things were far from all right, but Chloe had no idea how to begin. Then she thought about what she'd been taught at Pathfinder Academy. Her mother needed a path as well, so maybe she'd try there.

"Mom, both you and Grandma have been grieving for dragons you never had. You have never been able to accept that being a rider was not the path you were meant to follow."

"What would you know, Miss Apprentice Mage? Hah! Think I didn't know? I was at that telescope unveiling. I heard everything they said. So you think you know better than me now?"

"No, Mom, I don't. What I do know is that both you and Grandma are grieving, and it has turned you both into very bitter women. I was never meant to be a rider—"

"Then why," said her mother interrupting, "didn't you turn Emily down and give your sister a chance? You know our family has only had one child in each generation for centuries. And that child was destined to be a rider. Then your grandmother failed. But she had me and hoped I'd redeem her and the family heritage. But I failed also. I was determined that I would be the one to redeem the heritage so I had not one but two children, even though the doctor advised me not to have another child. But look what happened. You are a failure, and you kept Zelda from saving us also!"

"I'm really sorry, Mom, that you can't see the truth. First, Emily and others have told me that if I'd turned down the candidate offer, they would not have picked Zelda. They would instead have had just eleven candidates. So Zelda was never going to be chosen. If the dragons had wanted her, they could have chosen both of us."

"So you're an expert on candidates now, are you?"

"No, I'm not. But I was so upset after the hatching that Emily and Hans talked to me and explained things. I have a gift. Whether you want to acknowledge it or not, I am the first mage since the riders came to this world. And you know what? I'm not only the first mage, but I'm your daughter. My gift came through you and Dad. Without you, I wouldn't be here."

"So good riddance."

"I'll leave now, since obviously you don't want to hear what I have to say, but truly, is this life of yours what you want? Zelda has a wonderful apprenticeship with Marjorie, and she is learning to design clothes. You've always liked Marjorie's designs. Don't you want to see what Zelda is doing? She is so happy. She showed me her first outfit yesterday and told me that Marjorie is going to let her enter it in the next show. Doesn't that make you proud? You and Grandma taught her to sew."

Her mother just stood in the hall silently glaring at her.

"OK, I'm going since that is obviously what you want. But please..." And here, Chloe started to cry. "Please look around you and see just how far you have fallen. You are unkempt, the house is dusty, and you are in the dark, with nothing to live for. Haven't you been miserable long enough? Don't you think it is time to find out what your path truly is instead of grieving for one that you were never meant to have?"

Her mother started to raise a fist but stopped and instead just said in a low, threatening voice, "Get out of here now, and never come back!"

Chloe walked out the front door, sobbing harder than ever. *I need to get out of here.* With that, she hurried down the path and headed home—to her real home with Amy and Todd.

— 16 —

SOLACE

Chloe staggered into Amy's kitchen, still sobbing. Amy looked up from the sink where she was preparing vegetables for dinner and just dropped everything into the sink and rushed to embrace Chloe.

After holding her long enough so that her sobbing lessened, Amy said, "What's the matter?"

"It's m-my mom," stammered Chloe.

"Come on; let's go sit in the family room. I can get us some hot tea, and you can tell me all about it."

Amy got Chloe settled on the couch and wrapped her up in a cozy quilt before she went to fetch mugs of tea for them. Once they were settled and Chloe was a little calmer, Amy said, "Why don't you tell me what happened?"

Chloe took a sip from her mug and then started, "You know how I told you about Zelda and Dad and how happy they are now?"

Amy nodded, and Chloe continued, "Well, I got to thinking about Mom and how she has lost everything. I mean she still has her house and Grandma, and I know she's OK financially, but she has lost everything that matters—her family. So I thought I'd stop by and check on her before I leave next week for Bertha's."

Amy held her and said, "That was very sweet and definitely the right thing to do."

"But, Amy, it was horrible. She yelled at me, blaming me for everything. The house was dark and dusty, and Mom was unkempt. She even smelled. I tried to say I was sorry. I remembered everything Gregory had told us about finding our path and how that path might be very different from what we expected or what others expected, but she didn't listen. I said that both she and Grandma were still grieving for the dragons they never had. And then I told her about Zelda and how she was Marjorie's apprentice because I thought that would be something Mom would appreciate, but nothing worked. She was hateful, and she threw me out of the house and told me never to come back!"

Chloe collapsed in tears again, and Amy just held her tight. Finally, when Chloe had calmed enough to hear her, Amy said, "You were right to try, Chloe. We can never give up on those we love. But you also have to know that you can't change anyone else."

"But the two of them are so miserable, and they have been for as long as I can remember! It is worse now that all their hopes for a rider have vanished. Can't they see that something needs to change?"

"It is very sad, Chloe, but no, people can't always see their own pain, and even when they do, they sometimes find that the familiarity of that pain or bitterness is better than the threat of a change. Do you remember what your father said to you last evening? You told me that he thanked you because without you, he and Zelda wouldn't have been able to start on their paths. He said that when your mother threw you out, you chose a new path. And that is the operative word—*chose*! You could have become just like your mother, embittered and lonely. But you chose a different route."

"Well, I don't know if I would have without Bertha," admitted Chloe.

"Oh, I am sure you would have, given time," said Amy.

Chloe frowned, but Amy went on, "You have been told all your life that you are a failure and a disappointment, but still, when Emily showed up, you were game to accept the candidacy. If you were going to be an embittered person, you would already be showing that after all you have been through, trust me. And the fact that you chose another path was an inspiration to your sister and father, giving them the courage to follow you."

Chloe said, "But what about my mom?"

Amy took a drink of tea and continued, "Just as you made a choice, so did your mother. She was in nearly the same spot you were in at the hatching. She hadn't been chosen as even a candidate, but still, neither of you were chosen by dragons. The same for your grandmother. The family heritage, so to speak, broke with her. She had a choice to follow another path but didn't. Neither did your mother, and now, for your mother, it was doubly hard. Your grandmother was the first to be accused of failing the family. Your mother was the next generation of so-called failures. Each time, it got harder. If your grandmother had had your strength, then your mother need never have struggled. Are you beginning to see?"

Chloe thought for a minute and then said, "So it was hard for my grandmother, but it was doubly hard for my mother since she not only wasn't chosen; she also would have felt as if she had failed her mother as well as the entire family lineage?"

"Exactly. And then your mother pinned all their hopes on you and Zelda."

"And my mother said today that she'd been the first to have two children in generations and she'd done it against the wishes of the doctor just to double her chances and then failed again. No wonder she is so bitter!"

"But, Chloe, don't you see? You could have felt an even greater failure as the third generation, failing both your mother's and your grandmother's dreams. The fact that you didn't become like them is a tribute to your strength and your heart. All of us face trials and tribulations in this life. And no one understands why those trials will cause some to fall into despair and bitterness, while others, with the same or similar trials, rise above the challenges. Maybe your mother and grandmother just don't have the strength or heart or whatever to manage a different path."

"Why can't I help?" wailed Chloe.

"The reality is that each of us can change only one person and that is ourselves. You can't change your mother, but you can be an example through your own life. You do make a difference that way, and that has already been proven, through the change in your sister and your father, through the way this entire community has bonded over the telescope, through the way Beulah, Imogene, and Clarissa now see the world, and on and on and on. A small pebble can make many ripples, and I have a feeling that your ripples have just begun."

"I guess," said Chloe hesitantly.

"So just keep your mother and grandmother in your heart, but don't be weighed down by their grief and bitterness. Move forth along your path with an open heart and a willing mind, and leave the rest to the fates," said Amy.

Chloe nodded, and Amy said, "Now, do you want to help me with dinner? I think you've had enough for one day!"

Chloe nodded. They stood, and Amy gave her another big hug and said in closing, "You are young to have to face such tough facts, but you are also strong. I'm guessing that this summer will be a wonderful one for you, in the forest with Bertha and her cubs."

The two women chatted companionably as they prepared the evening meal. Once the roast was in the oven, Amy said, "Would you like me to help you pack? Have you figured out what you want to take? And how are you getting there? I assume you aren't running this time?" she said with a chuckle.

"No, for sure. Emily and Esmeralda will take me day after tomorrow, leaving just after first light, so tomorrow is my last full day at the library. I am really going to miss Li—I mean the library," she said, realizing that she had nearly revealed her secret.

"Well, it won't be going anywhere!" Amy laughed. "And it will just feel all the sweeter when you return in September. Now, since you are home earlier than usual, why don't we take advantage of the rest of the afternoon and pack your duffel. That way, you can have a full day at the library tomorrow and even stay to watch the stars if you want, knowing that you are packed. And if you think of anything you've forgotten, well, we can add it tomorrow evening."

Thanks so much," said Chloe. "I think that is a wonderful idea."

"And remember, there are enough of us here who will be wanting progress reports that you'd better send messages. If you need anything, I'm sure Hannah or Rupert would love the chance to play messenger."

They set to work, and before long, they had Chloe's big burgundy duffel all packed except for her last-minute items. As they were heading downstairs, Chloe thought she heard more than just Todd and Robert in the kitchen.

"I thought it was just the four of us tonight," said Chloe to Amy.

"Didn't you think we'd made an awful lot of dinner for just four?" kidded Amy. She then covered Chloe's eyes and marched her into the kitchen.

Chloe opened her eyes and saw Todd and Robert and behind them, Zelda and her dad. Chloe ran over to them and hugged them and then turned around to Amy. "How did you invite them?"

Amy laughed. "You may be a mage, but we are telepaths," she said, linking arms with Todd. "I let him know that you could use some cheering up and also that tonight would probably be your last regular dinner here before you leave, as my guess is that you'll stay at the library watching stars tomorrow, so we just decided to have an impromptu early summer solstice party."

The words were no sooner out of Amy's mouth than Chloe heard shouts coming through the back door. "Did someone say party?" and in walked Emily, Gregory, Hannah, and Rupert.

As they all enjoyed the wonderful meal, Chloe thought just how lucky she really was. She knew she would keep Amy's words of wisdom tucked in her heart and ponder them often over the years ahead. But for tonight, she was content just to enjoy all the love surrounding her as she noticed just how well Zelda and her father fit into this large and wonderful family.

— 17 —

BERTHA

Chloe went off to the library the next morning after saying good-bye to Amy and Todd. "I'm taking my duffel with me," she explained, "because I want to spend as much time at the library as I can. Emily and Esmeralda said they'd pick me up there tomorrow."

Todd nodded, and Amy said, "Well, don't work too hard, and be sure you stay in touch this summer. We want to know how you are doing."

Chloe gave each of them a big hug and said, "I'm going to miss you so much!"

"The summer will fly by," said Todd, "and you'll be back before you know it. I'll watch out for your dad."

"Thanks so much for everything," Chloe said as she grabbed her duffel and headed out the door.

Chloe enjoyed breakfast as usual with Libby, but it was bittersweet. "I don't know how I'll manage without you," she said as she was finishing up. "You have taught me so much, and I really enjoy our talks," said Chloe.

Libby laughed and said, "You are going to have a great time with Bertha and her cubs, and I think there are some wonderful surprises waiting for you. You may find that you aren't as far away as you think."

"What do you mean?" said Chloe.

"Now, now, that would be telling. It is really Bertha's secret to share. But I just don't want you getting yourself into a stew. I know what a worrier you are, and trust me, there is nothing to worry about! Now get out of here. We'll have one more breakfast before you go. Come on in just before it gets light."

Chloe tried to study, but she found that everyone she knew wanted to stop by and wish her well, so she didn't get a lot accomplished. She'd promised Libby that she wouldn't try to take any of the ancient manuscripts out of the library, but she wanted to make more notes.

However, she had to admit that she was really touched by all the folks who stopped by. She realized just how much her life had changed in only six months.

After the library closed, Chloe went up to the observatory and worked on her star charts. She would be taking those along, as she wanted to show them to Bertha and ask for her help. It sounded as if the prophecy was referring to something that would be coming from space to threaten the planet, and Chloe hoped that Bertha could help her understand just what that threat might be. When she had done all she could, she used her magic to form a cozy spot to sleep in. She was so excited and apprehensive that she really didn't think she'd be able to relax, but before she knew it, she was snuggled into the bed she'd conjured, fast asleep.

At breakfast the next morning, Libby gave Chloe a small brass locket with a mirror inside. "If you want to see something, just think about what you want to see and then look into the mirror," explained Libby. "In time, with Bertha's help, you won't need the mirror, but for now, take it as my gift to you to help you begin the next phase of your training."

"Oh, thank you so much," said Chloe. "It is a beautiful locket."

"Now you get along. Emily and Esmeralda will be waiting for you in the courtyard."

Chloe nodded, fastened the locket around her neck, picked up her duffel, and headed for the door. "Thanks again, and I'll see you at the autumnal equinox."

"I'll be here!" Libby laughed.

Sure enough, out in the courtyard, Chloe found Emily and Esmeralda waiting to give her a ride to Bertha's. "All set?" asked Emily as she tied Chloe's duffel onto Esmeralda's back.

"I guess," said Chloe.

Emily laughed and said, "Well then, let's go for a ride." Emily vaulted onto Esmeralda and then reached down to help Chloe. Soon Chloe was sitting atop Esmeralda, holding on to Emily and looking around.

"It all looks somehow different from up here," said Chloe.

"Perspective is everything," agreed Emily, "and it will look even more different as we fly. Here we go!"

And with that, Esmeralda took off, circling over Havenshold slowly so that Chloe could get a look at everything. She spotted her mother's home and then Amy and Todd's. She even caught a glimpse of her father's cottage, and she wasn't sure, but she thought he was outside waving, so she waved back.

It didn't take long to reach Bertha's clearing. "It's sure easier to get here with you, Esmeralda. Last time, I ran and it seemed such a long way away."

Esmeralda snorted and said, "Running isn't my idea of fun. Why run when you can fly? I always say."

Emily patted Esmeralda and said, "Yes, my dear, but remember, not all of us can fly."

As Esmeralda landed in the open area in front of Bertha's cave, Chloe saw the big bear lumbering out, followed by Boris and Berla.

"Wow, you two have really grown!" Chloe exclaimed as Emily helped her jump down from Esmeralda.

Bertha looked at her cubs with a big grin. "That happens," she answered. Chloe was so used to Bertha's telepathic speech that it seemed as if she could hear it out loud as well as in her head. Then she realized that Bertha really was talking out loud! *Wow,* thought Emily, *could she always do that?*

"We have brought Chloe here to you as you requested," said Emily to Bertha, giving her a low bow.

Bertha bowed back, saying, "And I thank you, oh leader of the dragon riders!" "Now is that enough of the formal for you?" She chuckled, and everyone laughed.

When they had all enjoyed the humor, Emily said, "Well, we need to get back. I have a mountain of paperwork to attend to. Have a wonderful summer, Chloe, and remember, if you need anything, just let us know. I have a funny feeling that you will probably get a few visitors along the way."

"Well, not too many," warned Bertha in a tone that was meant to be stern, but somehow, Chloe knew the sentiment behind it really wasn't. "Chloe's got a lot to learn, and we can't be taking time to play around."

Boris and Berla sighed. "Well, except for relaxing with these two," continued Bertha, rubbing each of them on the head.

Emily gave Chloe a big hug, and then before Chloe could even think what to say, the dragon rider was on Esmeralda and they were off into the clouds.

Once they had left, Bertha came over and gave Chloe a hug as well and then grabbed her duffel and said, "Come on inside, and let's get you settled."

"You can talk out loud," exclaimed Chloe.

Bertha chuckled, and then said, "Yes, you've found me out. Not everyone can hear me telepathically in the first place. You and Hans are in that select group. And when you were here before, I wanted you to get used to telepathy, so I didn't let you know that I could have spoken out loud. The twins won't grow into this ability for awhile, but it is important for them to hear me, so I speak out loud more for them as well. Now come on inside."

Chloe was happy to find that the shelf in the cave she had slept on last winter was still to be set aside for her. There was plenty of room for her duffel on one end, and Bertha had a down quilt on the other half of the shelf, with a pillow.

As Chloe shifted things a bit to make it as she wanted, Bertha said, "Now, you two," looking over at the cubs, "remember, anything up there is Chloe's and that means it is out of bounds."

The two cubs nodded solemnly. Chloe got off the shelf, went over to Boris and Berla, and gave each of them a hug. "We'll still play ball and have fun when I'm not studying, I promise."

"It is a beautiful day, so let's take a walk and I'll show you our part of the world. And as we walk, you can tell me what you know about the history of this planet," said Bertha. "Come on, you two," she said to the cubs. "You can come too, but stay out of mischief."

Chloe looked around as they walked, admiring the tall firs and the ferns, the babbling brook they passed, and all the birds singing in the trees. It was just midmorning, and the forest was alive with activity.

Chloe looked around and said, "No one seems alarmed by your presence."

"And why should they worry? We are here to protect not to harm. Now what do you know about our early history?" asked Bertha.

Chloe had to think for a few minutes, and then she said, "Well, Miss Murphy said in history class that this world originally had just three nations, Forbury, Granvale, and Sanwright. Then, over five hundred years ago, well, five hundred thirty-four years ago actually, King Alfred and his riders were teleported here by their dragons because they were being attacked in their own world and the dragon population was dwindling."

Bertha nodded, "So far as that goes, it is accurate. What then?"

"Well, King Alfred met with the other monarchs, and they learned that they had a lot in common. This world already had telepathic beings, and just as the dragons bonded telepathically with their riders, so to this world already had gryphons in Forbury, unicorns in Granvale, and dolphins in Sanwright, all of whom had ways of choosing humans to bond with. So King Alfred and his riders were encouraged to remain in this world, and since the extensive region around the volcano was not claimed by any of the other three nations, King Alfred took it and named it Draconia. Since then, the four nations have lived in nearly complete harmony with only occasional minor disputes."

"Excellent," said Bertha. "Now what about magic?"

"I don't really know anything about magic, except what Libby—I mean, the library has been showing me about transforming things."

"Libby, huh? So that's what she's calling herself now?"

Chloe looked alarmed until she noticed the grin on Bertha's face. "I asked her what I should call her because she takes on human form for me every morning and we share breakfast in her cozy sitting room."

"I know, child, and I am really pleased for both of you. To be honest, I was worried about my old friend. The library has never been much used, and I thought she might just fade away, so I am thrilled that Gregory has moved Pathfinder Academy into the building and even more so, that you are finding it to be a comfortable spot to spend your days."

They walked a bit further into the forest, and Chloe saw a lake off in the distance. "I didn't know there was a lake here," she said.

"Not many folks do," said Bertha. "This forest is protected, and it is rare to find any humans wandering in it. Somehow, the forest just doesn't seem inviting to them. But let's find a spot near the lake to sit and talk while Boris and Berla run off some excess energy, shall we?"

After giving very specific and complete directions to her cubs, Bertha settled comfortably on a log bench at the edge of the lake and Chloe followed her. Bertha then said, "Have you ever wondered why this world has telepathic individuals?"

"No, not really," said Chloe. "I just thought that was how things were meant to be."

"In a way, you are right. Let me tell you the history of the world from a slightly different perspective," said Bertha, and when Chloe nodded, she went on, "You are right in the overall chronology of your account and your explanation that each of our nations has a special bonded system. That was all set up when the world was founded by the gods or fates or whatever you want to use to explain the beginnings. In fact, the beginnings were the result of the conjunction of a planet ripe for life and a swirling mist of magic that surrounded it."

Bertha paused so that Chloe could absorb that much. "We don't need to go into great details now, although down the road, you might want to explore the early history, but let's just say that guardians were commissioned early on to keep a watch on this planet's magic to ensure that the magic stayed good and pure."

"Guardians? I've never heard of them? And what do you mean by good magic. Isn't magic a good thing all by itself?" asked Chloe.

"Let me digress. You know about riders and their telepathy, right?"

Chloe nodded and Bertha went on. "For a while, that telepathy seemed to dwindle so that riders thought they could only communicate with their own dragons. Then along came the Baron's War—that was the year you were born, 518, and Baron Geldsmith went power mad."

Chloe said, "I heard something about that, but not a lot."

"Well, it is all in the past now. It was a good kind of war in that there were no casualties, and the baron learned his lesson. Now he is a changed man with his own bonded mate, Oswald, a gryphon with no wings, but that's not what's important. What is important is that because of the war, the nations all had to come together to work out a solution, and in the process, they learned a lot about communication."

"That's what William's working on, right?" asked Chloe.

"Right, and now many riders can communicate with several dragons, and some non-riders, like Gregory for instance, can communicate telepathically with some dragons; we also have Lucy communicating with moles and setting up an early warning system for earthquakes, and your friend Beulah is able to tell what animals are feeling and so forth."

Chloe nodded, wondering where all this was going.

"Well," continued Bertha, "with all this telepathy, have you ever noticed even once when someone has stuck themselves uninvited into someone else's head? Have you noticed any spying or eavesdropping?"

"No," said Chloe. "That wouldn't be polite. We were warned about that in our candidate training."

"Exactly," said Bertha, who then sat back a bit as if she'd made a really important point.

"But what does that have to do with good magic?" asked Chloe with a puzzled tone in her voice.

"Good question," said Bertha. "The fact is that the guard-ians—remember I told you about them—well, they monitor all forms of magic, including telepathy. In fact, it goes even fur-ther. The guardians watch over all five of the species capable of being telepathic, and they search into the hearts of each individual even before he or she is born, in the case of dragons, gryphons, unicorns, and dolphins, since all of them are tele-pathic and they are the ones who initiate the bondings. If the guardians discover a being who isn't pure in heart, who might corrupt or try to turn magic, well, the guardians simply ensure that the being is never hatched or born."

Chloe thought hard about this. "So is that why some eggs don't hatch?"

"Well, of course that isn't the only reason, but I have to say that it's one of the most common reasons. Remember I told you about Oswald, the gryphon with no wings? Well, he was born with only one wing and that had to be removed surgically to improve his balance. But we didn't stop his birth because it would be hard to find a bigger, softer, more generous heart than Oswald's. We knew that when Oswald was born, he would be cared for until he could find the baron. As a seer, I knew that eventually the baron, who was originally from Forbury anyway, would change, with the help of a lot of folks, including his sons, Gregory and Lance. But what was more important to the guardians was that Oswald would play a major role in what I like to call the softening of the baron so that now, he is one of the biggest philanthropists on the planet, doing a lot of good."

"So the guardians don't stop births or hatchings because of anything except the bad heart. However, some creatures just are damaged and sometimes too damaged to live, so not all eggs that don't hatch or stillbirths are the doings of the guard-ians?" Chloe was starting to get tangled in Bertha's explana-tions. "So, magic stays pure because of the guardians."

"That's it in a nutshell," said Bertha with a big smile.

"But who are the guardians?" asked Chloe, still confused.

"Oh, didn't I say? Why, it is the bears, of course."

Chloe's mouth dropped open, and her eyes widened. "The bears," she finally said.

"Yep," said Bertha with what could only be called a smug look on her face. "OK, I left out a bit at the beginning. When the world was first made, the bears were put in charge of the magical species. Specifically, we looked after the gryphons, unicorns, and dolphins because they in turn watched out for their humans. When the dragons came, we took them on also, and it has worked out really well. There aren't a lot of bears in this world, and we are fine with that. Our society is a matriarchy, and the lead female sets the tone for everyone. I am the current matriarch, and in time, Berla will follow me, just as I followed my mother and she hers before her and so on back to the beginning. And now that this world has a mage, namely you, someone with magic but with no bonded creature to watch over you, well, I now am your guardian as well."

"Wow! That's impressive, Bertha, and at the same time a bit overwhelming. It's going to take me awhile to think all this through."

Bertha laughed. "That's just fine. I've seen your heart, and you also are true and good and kind, so there are no worries. You wouldn't have become a mage if that weren't true. You see, that's why in each of the nations, the magical creatures pick the candidates for the hatching or birthing. Only those who are good and true become candidates. That's not to say that the candidates are the only good and true humans. Thankfully, there are many others. But no one who has, shall we say, ulterior motives is ever chosen to be a candidate. So you are already vetted, so to speak. Now where are those young ones of mine? Let's call the lessons over for the day and head back to the cave for lunch and fun."

Chloe let out a big sigh of relief and said, "Wonderful!"

— 18 —

MAGIC LESSONS

Bertha soon established a routine, which suited Chloe just fine. After breakfast, Bertha sent the twins out to play while she taught Chloe more about magic. After a morning of lessons, they'd have a lovely lunch and then the afternoons were free for wandering, playing with the twins, napping, or whatever else seemed nice. After dinner, Chloe would work on her star charts with Bertha's help before everyone headed to bed. It was a simple but very rewarding life, and the summer was as close to idyllic as Chloe could imagine.

On her first full day with Bertha, Chloe learned her goals for the summer.

"There are three main magical skills that a mage needs. Others may develop, depending on your particular talents, but every mage must be able to transform and conjure. You are going to learn most of that with Libby—I can't believe after more than five hundred years she has picked a name! Good for you! I am pleased even if I can't get over it. I've just always called her "Library." Anyway, where was I?"

Chloe was getting used to Bertha's wandering, discursive style and found that she actually enjoyed it. She'd also come to realize that Bertha's digressions were rarely pointless.

The bear continued, "And that leaves the two I will be helping you learn, namely farseeing and teleporting."

Chloe looked stunned, and she realized her mouth was hanging open. "*What*? Teleporting?"

"Yes," said Bertha calmly, "and farseeing. You need to remember that you aren't just Havenshold's mage or even just Draconia's mage. You are the mage, the one and only ever seen on this planet, and so you are 'The Mage,' in capitals, for all the nations. That being the case, you will have to be able to look at people from a long way off and you will also need to be able to transport yourself there instantly. Dragons are all fine and dandy, I know, and flying sounds fun, but what if you are needed in, say, a mine in Forbury, right now, this minute?"

"I can't do that!" complained Chloe.

"Of course you can't now, but you will in a number of years. Didn't Libby explain the steps to becoming a mage? Well, I'll review them anyway," she continued after Chloe gave a tentative nod. "Now you are an apprentice mage. When Libby and I think you are ready and you pass our tests in about four years, you will become a journeyman mage. And then after another indeterminate period of time, depending on your progress and abilities, we will grant you the rank of mage—"

"But that means," said Chloe, interrupting in her anxiety, "that means that when I have to fulfill the prophecy, I will only be a journeyman mage! How will I do it?"

"You'll do it because you must," said Bertha with exasperating calmness and certainty. "Now, let's begin with farseeing. You've already done a little of this when Libby had you start on the building of your lab."

"Wait a minute," said Chloe. "Do you know everything that I've been doing? You didn't say you were a farseer."

Bertha laughed. "I'm not, but the library and I, pardon me, Libby and I are close, and we can talk back and forth. Yes, she has kept me abreast of your progress. Now, can we proceed?"

Chloe nodded, and Bertha said, "Anyway, as I was explaining, you and Libby built the lab while you were in her cozy sitting room, which is nowhere near the lab. You did it by visualizing what was there, thinking about what you wanted, and then using magic to make it so. Well, the first part of that, the visualizing what is there and then watching it transform, well, that is farseeing. Farseeing is the ability to see something when you aren't really there in person. Got it?"

Chloe nodded again. Bertha said, "Good, so now we are going to use that locket Libby gave you, and we are going to see if you can talk with her. You'd like that, I'm guessing?"

"Oh, yes," said Chloe. "I really would. She said when I left yesterday that you'd have a surprise for me. Thank you so much!"

"Well, don't thank me until you actually do it. I'm not going to do it for you, after all. Now, concentrate on what Libby's cozy sitting room looks like, and picture her sitting in her chair. When you have your mind fully focused, then open the locket, look into the mirror, and call her."

Chloe was excited. She did just what Bertha said, but when she opened the locket, she couldn't see or hear Libby at all. She closed the locket and looked down at her feet, trying not to cry.

"Come on now," comforted Bertha. "You didn't think it was going to be so easy that you'd do it on the first try, did you? You are going to need a lot of practice. Now let's sit in the sunshine so I can keep an eye on the twins, and you just keep trying."

Chloe concentrated as hard as she could, but she kept failing. She wouldn't give up though, even when Bertha suggested they take a break. Over and over, she went through the steps. And over and over, there was nothing in the mirror. Finally, on what felt like her millionth try, Chloe remembered the very first time she'd seen Libby. She thought back to that morning and pictured the room as she had first seen it. She thought about the steaming hot mug of coffee so hard that she thought she could smell it. She saw the breakfast on the table. She remembered every single detail and held it firm in her mind as she opened the locket and said, "Libby?"

She nearly dropped the locket when she heard, "Is that you, Chloe?" Chloe looked into the mirror. She didn't know how it worked, but that tiny mirror in her locket showed her Libby, sitting in her chair, knitting a scarf.

"Oh, Libby!" Chloe exclaimed. "I can talk to you! This is wonderful!"

"And you are pretty wonderful yourself, to manage your first farseeing so quickly," answered Libby.

Just then, Bertha looked over Chloe's shoulder and said, "Maybe it's because she has such a good teacher, *Libby*," and she emphasized the name.

Libby's cheeks turned pink, and she said, "How are you, Bertha? Are you treating Chloe well?"

"Of course I am, silly. Anyway, I'll let you two chat for a few minutes, and then Chloe needs her lunch. She did manage quite well, thanks to the wonderful instructions, but it has taken her four hours!" finished Bertha, and she turned and walked into the cave.

"Has it really been that long?" asked Chloe, but by then, Bertha was out of hearing range, or at least she didn't answer.

Chloe looked back at Libby, "I tried and tried and tried, and nothing worked. But then I finally thought to picture the very first day I met you and I saw everything. I even thought I smelled the coffee! And then I heard you and you were there!"

Libby looked at her and said, "You have learned a valuable lesson today. Bertha could have told you more, but she gave you just enough so that you would be able to figure the rest on your own. Especially at first, you will need the fullest, most complete picture in your mind before you try the mirror. And you will, as I mentioned when I gave you the locket, need the mirror. Soon, you will be able to use any mirror or reflective surface, and eventually, after a lot of hard work, you will be able to see and hear in your own mind without any aids at all. That is your ultimate goal."

Chloe looked downcast as she said, "That sounds so hard."

"Now listen to me, young lady," commanded Libby. "It is hard work, and there is no denying it. But anything worth doing usually is. The thing to remember right now is that you managed your first farseeing in just one morning. And even if it seemed frustrating and impossible, you didn't give up. You also succeeded really quickly, and believe me, I know. One day, Bertha may show you the hidden library. I believe there are journals from mages in the world the riders came from. Just read some of those, and you'll see just how well you are doing."

Chloe gave a small smile and said, "Thanks, Libby."

"Now this is enough for today. You are going to be exhausted, even if I have kept the link open for you. In future, the link will depend half on you and then finally all on you because there will be times you will need to farsee something where there is no one on the other end able to do magic."

Chloe just nodded, thinking that there sure was a lot to being a mage, a lot more than reading books and building telescopes.

Libby said, "Good-bye for now. Go find your lunch. Oh and thank Bertha for me, will you? She is really a wonderful friend."

As Libby's face faded out and the mirror turned back into a regular mirror, Chloe closed the locket and nearly fell as she tried to stand. She remembered back to when she moved her first wall and how tired that had made her. She could do more now, for sure, but this morning's activities had really drained her.

Bertha stuck her head out of the cave just as Chloe got her balance and started to move toward it. Bertha came over and put an arm around her, helping her into a chair at the table. Chloe noticed that the twins had already come in, probably while she was talking to Libby. They were digging into their lunches, and Bertha put a bowl of soup and a sandwich in front of her. "Now you just eat that and then take a nap. You'll feel a lot better after that," said Bertha.

"Does magic always take so much energy?" asked Chloe.

"Well, you don't get something for nothing," quipped Bertha. "But really, you did do a fantastic job, as I know Libby told you. I deliberately gave you just enough information so that it was possible to succeed. Honestly, I didn't expect anything on your first day. I figured I'd give more hints tomorrow and so on until you did it. The fact that you figured most of it out on your own is proof, if you still need it, that you are an amazing apprentice mage and one day you will be the greatest mage this world has ever seen."

Chloe laughed. "Thanks, Bertha, but really that isn't hard since I'm the only mage this world has seen. Still, I do appreciate your encouragement. And it was great to talk with Libby. She says to thank you as well, and she also said that you are a wonderful friend."

Bertha looked as if she might be blushing, although with her brown fur, it was really impossible to tell. She started bustling around the kitchen area cleaning things up, and then she told the twins that she would be taking them out foraging for a while. "And you," she said, looking at Chloe with a smile on her face, "you take advantage of the quiet cave and get a good nap. We won't have any more lessons today."

Chloe climbed up onto her ledge and slid beneath the quilt. *Farseeing and teleporting*, she thought. *Who ever knew?* and she drifted off to sleep.

— 19 —

TELEPORTING

Bertha is relentless in her teaching, thought Chloe as she climbed into bed a week later. The entire week had been spent on farseeing. Bertha had said, "You will really need this, and I am even thinking it could help with the telescope. I'm not sure, but I think if you master farseeing, you will be able to improve on what the telescope can do."

Chloe realized just how important that possibility was, so she kept right on working. She could now contact Libby on the first try nearly every time. Next week, she'd see if she could contact someone else with the locket and Libby without the locket.

Chloe hadn't had any success with teleporting, even over short distances, and nothing Bertha said helped. Finally, as her second week with Bertha came to an end, Bertha said, "Don't be discouraged. The farseeing is much more important at the moment. I know! Let's take the weekend off and take the twins camping. A change of pace will do you a world of good, and the twins will love it."

As Chloe fell asleep, she wondered if camping with bears was going to be fun.

The next day was sunny and warm. Boris and Berla were so excited about the camping trip that they would hardly sit still long enough to eat their breakfast. Chloe laughed as Berla asked for about the fiftieth time, *"Is it time to go?"* The twins had really developed their telepathy over the past months, and Chloe could now hear them clear as a bell. She helped Bertha clean up the cave as the twins chased each other around in circles just outside the cave entrance.

Chloe was glad she'd thrown her backpack into her duffel, as she decided to use it now, putting in a few notebooks, some sun lotion, and a change of clothes.

Finally, they were on their way, and Bertha led them up a trail higher into the wooded mountains. They hiked all morning before coming to an open meadow where sheep were grazing.

Bertha said, "We won't stay here, as the farmer who owns these sheep is not very friendly, but we can certainly skirt around his meadow to enter the forest over there to the north. Now, children, you stay really close to Mom and Chloe."

The twins agreed, and Bertha picked up her pace, obviously anxious to get to the other side of the meadow. Chloe wondered why anyone would object because they were barely on the meadow. The meadow abutted a steep, rocky slope, and it would have been nearly impossible for the twins especially to cross there. Chloe watched Berla carefully as Bertha kept a paw on Boris. They were nearly to the forest when Chloe sensed danger. "Hurry," she said just as a dog came charging at them. Chloe picked up Berla and ran, but Boris couldn't keep up, and the dog charged right at him, knocking him down.

Chloe had reached the forest, and she put Berla down and told her to get into the forest. Then she went back, seeing Bertha up on her hind legs trying to scare the dog away from her son. Chloe watched as Boris started to roll down the steep, rocky slope, and without even pausing to think, she reached out her mind to Boris, snatching him up and all but flinging him into the forest with his sister.

That would have been that, except that the farmer had heard his dog barking and was now running across the field with his rifle held up. He stopped to take aim at Bertha, even though the bear was now on all fours, moving quickly toward the forest. Again without thinking, Chloe reached for the rifle with her mind and snatched it out of the farmer's hands, and this time, she twisted it into a knot, totally destroying it, before throwing it back across the meadow.

She started to stagger from the effort, which had cost her, but not before she shouted, "Bears are a protected species. We were only on the edge of your meadow and never bothered your sheep. We will report you." She wasn't sure to whom she would report it, but certainly to Emily, who would know what action to take.

Chloe then moved into the forest and found Bertha and the twins waiting for her just a little ways in. Chloe nearly collapsed, but Bertha reached her first and just hugged her as tears fell from her eyes into her brown fur. Chloe thought, *Now I truly know what a bear hug is!*

Bertha all but carried Chloe further into the forest as the twins, shaken but unhurt, followed. Chloe smiled when she heard Boris saying, *"Did you see how I flew through the air? And I landed right beside you! Didn't I do well?"*

And then Chloe really laughed when Berla said, *"Chloe rescued you. You can't fly."* It was good to hear them chattering, and soon, Bertha found a wonderful campsite near a tiny brook.

Bertha insisted that Chloe just sit and rest while she and the cubs foraged for greens and berries to supplement the dinner she had packed. As soon as everything was ready, they ate. Chloe thought that food had never tasted so good. *Do danger and camping make things taste better?* she wondered.

Bertha tucked the twins into the lean-to shelter she had put up earlier and then came to sit beside Chloe. She had two mugs of tea and handed one to Chloe.

"I really can't thank you enough for what you did today, Chloe," said Bertha.

"You're welcome, but honestly, I don't think that farmer could hit the broad side of a barn, and Boris had enough sense to catch onto a boulder and stay very still. Nevertheless, I'm glad we didn't have to test my assumptions."

"You've been struggling so hard with the teleporting all week, but do you realize that you teleported both Boris and that rifle?" said Bertha.

"*What*? No!" said Chloe. "That's not teleporting."

"Well, actually it is if you think about it. You transported Boris at least twenty-five feet, maybe more, through the air just with the power of your mind."

"Maybe," said Chloe doubtfully.

"And the rifle was both teleporting and transforming. You yanked it out of the farmer's hands, then twisted it into a pretzel, and finally threw it across the meadow. That seems like pretty impressive magic to me!" finished Bertha.

Chloe started to smile. "Yeah, it was, wasn't it?"

"Now, you did that the same way you put up the shield for us last winter and the same way you say you saved your sister. You did it with an adrenalin rush when someone was in danger. And while that is certainly a wonderful time to manage it, I want to work on seeing if we can get you to do that without the danger."

"That would be nice, because then it would also, I'd guess, be more reliable," said Chloe.

"And let's take this one step further. If you can transport other things and people, well, it is just another perspective to transport yourself. So think on that. How would you move yourself if you, say, pretended to step outside yourself and see yourself as you saw Boris today?"

Chloe shook her head and said, "That is an amazing change in perspective. OK, I'll try to wrap my head around that thought, but maybe not tonight."

Bertha laughed and said, "Definitely not tonight. Let's go join those twins. You know they will be up early raring to go, and we'd better be ready for them."

The two of them walked over to where the twins were sleeping, and Bertha gave Chloe another hug, this time not nearly as tight. "Thanks again," said Bertha. "I'm really lucky you were here today. Sweet dreams."

"You're welcome, and sweet dreams to you also," said Chloe.

As Bertha had predicted, the twins were up with the sun. After they all had some breakfast, they made their plans. They were determined to take another route back to the cave. "No way do I want to tangle with that farmer again," said Chloe and Bertha agreed.

"I know an alternate route, but it is longer, so let's just say this is a three-day weekend," said Bertha, and the twins clapped their paws and cheered.

"This tiny brook will meet up with the brook by the cave, so let's just follow it and see what we find."

It was a wonderful day. The twins kept running into the woods and then coming back to Chloe and Bertha with yet another treasure. They found special rocks and twigs, berries and branches, and lots of other things that were just too special to leave behind. The twins kept begging Chloe to put yet another item into her backpack, and Chloe was glad that she had brought so few things of her own.

As the twins were romping back and forth, covering at least three times the distance that Bertha and Chloe did, Bertha and Chloe got a chance to chat and get to know each other a bit better. Chloe was sure that Bertha had had gotten most of her story from Libby, but Bertha seemed happy to hear it directly from Chloe. When Chloe was done, Bertha said, "It is funny what grief can do to a body. Remember I told you a bit about Baron Geldsmith? Well, his is also a tale of grief, but luckily for him, it didn't end there. He lost his parents when he was young, and he was then raised by an uncle who really didn't want him. The uncle sold precious gems from his mines. They went to a fair in Draconia and the baron—well, he wasn't a baron obviously, but I don't know his real name so we'll just call him the baron—met a young lady whom he immediately fell in love with and she with him. They were only twelve years old, but the baron always did know his own mind, so he begged his uncle to let him be apprenticed to the girl's family. The uncle was just happy to be freed of the responsibilities of a twelve-year-old, and the girl's parents were happy to have help. No one ever thought the love would last, but the baron then came to Havenshold, finished his schooling, and fulfilled his apprenticeship, or so I'm given to understand. As the years passed, the baron and the young lady fell more deeply in love, and eventually, they were married. The baron has always been a smart man, and he soon turned the land he earned from his apprenticeship into the largest cattle and sheep ranch in Draconia. His wife bore him a son, Gregory, and the three were very happy. But the wife knew the baron would like a bigger family, so without letting the baron know that the doctor had told her she shouldn't ever get pregnant again, she bore a second son, Lance. However, she died giving birth to him."

"How horrible," said Chloe.

"Yes, and the baron became very bitter, paying little or no attention to either son, just working to get more and more wealth. He tried to have Gregory picked as a dragon rider because he had always felt that he'd missed out on a bonding and that it was the riders who had the real power. Gregory's age allowed him to be a candidate twice, and the dragons were perfectly happy to choose him as a candidate because he is a good and kind soul, but no dragon selected him because they also knew he didn't want to be a rider. Finally, the baron kidnapped former King Jacob's son, Rupert, in order to put pressure on Jacob to give the throne to the baron—"

"Is that Hannah's Rupert?" interrupted Chloe.

Bertha laughed and said, "Yep. Anyway, the war didn't last long, and the baron was reunited with his sons as they really are. Lance now runs the baron's estate in Draconia as he always wanted to do. The baron inherited his uncle's mines in Forbury, and he also met Oswald. Those two are one of the happiest bonded pairs I've heard of. They live on the baron's Forbury estate, and the baron has really made his uncle's holding pay well. He has more money and power than he could ever have imagined when he was orphaned at twelve. But the thing that makes his story so wonderful is that he is now our world's greatest philanthropist, and he is always ready to help any in need. His heart was always a big and generous one. It just took a wrong detour for over fifteen years. If you have a chance to stay with him and Oswald as you learn about our world, be sure to grab it."

"I'll remember that, and thanks for sharing his story. I don't know if anything like that could happen with my mother, but I guess you never know."

Just then, the twins came back with more things and also whimpering that they were tired and hungry. As Chloe stuck the new treasures into her pack, she said, "Well, no wonder. You've walked much farther than we have."

Bertha laughed, and she told the twins they could ride on her. They set off to find a good spot to have dinner and spend the night.

The walk the next morning wasn't long at all, and the twins soon spotted familiar landmarks. *"We'll beat you home!"* they said as they raced off.

"I'm sure you will," called Bertha.

Soon, the clearing in front of the cave was in sight, and Chloe thought it never looked better.

"It was a fun camping trip," said Chloe, "but my bed will feel so good!"

And with that, they chased the twins into the cave.

— 20 —

SUMMER'S END

Chloe worked very hard for the rest of the summer. She was determined to have a lot to show Libby when she got back to the library. She finally managed to farsee Libby without using the locket early in September. It was such a wonderful feeling, and Libby was obviously very pleased.

Libby then suggested she try to reach someone else using the locket, and Chloe immediately thought of her dad. Libby left a note on Gregory's desk asking him to contact Harvey and let Harvey know that Chloe wanted to try farseeing him the next evening.

And that's tonight, thought Chloe. *I don't know. Will it work? Will Dad be disappointed if it doesn't?*

As she was calming her mind in preparation to begin, Libby spoke to her instead. "Gregory got my note, and you know, for a non-magic person, he's pretty smart. Maybe he is soaking up something from me just by having his office here."

Chloe laughed as Libby continued, "Gregory talked with Amy and Todd, and it was decided that Harvey should come to your alcove at the library. They all thought that would make it much easier for you, and I agree. Gregory left me a note just as if he knew that whoever this Libby was who left him a note would find it. Well, I mean, I would, but you know what I mean."

Chloe really laughed now. "Watch out! You are starting to sound like Bertha!"

"I heard that!" said Bertha as she walked into the clearing. "I think Gregory's idea is perfect, Libby. Are they all there now?"

"Yes, everything is set on our end. Your father is sitting in your favorite chair, Chloe, so give it a whirl."

Chloe concentrated harder than she ever had. She wanted this so much. She pictured her father sitting in her chair, maybe with a mug of tea beside him. She opened the locket and looked. "Dad?" she said when she saw him in the chair. "Can you hear me?"

"Yes, Chloe," he said, looking around, trying to see her. Then all of a sudden, he looked straight at her. "I can see you too!"

"That's wonderful! I can see you too, just as I pictured you. You even have a mug of tea as I imagined you would."

Harvey looked startled and then glanced at the table as Amy came into view. She said, "Hi, Chloe. The mug of tea just popped onto the table, but I'll be sure he gets it." She smiled and waved as she let Harvey talk.

It was absolutely the most marvelous visit. "Gregory told me something about farseeing, and I don't know what that is, but it is just so wonderful that you can speak to me. Oh, and Amy and Todd are here too and Gregory and Emily and Zelda. No one wanted to miss out on this."

One by one, each person stuck his or her head in front of Harvey long enough to say hi. Emily also asked, "Now are you ready for me to return on the equinox to pick you up?"

Chloe looked over at Bertha, who nodded. "Yes, I'll be ready. I can't wait to get back and see you all in person and tell you about my incredible summer, but I'll also be sad to leave Bertha and the twins. You should see how they've grown—the twins that is."

"We'll be waiting and eager to hear it all," said Harvey.

"I've got to go now, Dad, but soon I'll be there to hear all about your summer too."

With that, everyone said good-bye, and Chloe closed the locket. Then she contacted Libby. "Thank you so much! I know you boosted that so everyone could see me and I could talk with them all. Thanks!"

"You are most welcome, but you made the contact. Remember I talked about the sharing of energy in the farseeing? Well, I only boosted a little. You have really grown strong in magic this summer. Now get some sleep and learn all you can from Bertha in the next two weeks. Take care, and I'll be seeing you soon."

The next morning after breakfast, Bertha said, "Do you have any idea what you managed last evening?"

Chloe looked puzzled and said, "Well, yes, I managed to far-see someone other than a magic user."

Bertha laughed. "You really are something, Chloe. Yes, you certainly did do that, and yes, that is a big achievement in your magic learning. But what about that mug of tea? Did you hear Amy?"

Chloe thought for a minute, and then her face lit up as the light bulb went off. "I made the mug of tea? Did I?"

"Well, just to be sure, I checked with Libby after you crawled into bed, and yes, you did!" said Bertha as she did a mock twirl. "We couldn't have been prouder if you'd talked to the moon! You conjured a hot, steaming mug of tea, and my guess is that when you get home, Amy will tell you that it was even your father's favorite flavor. Furthermore, you sent it all the way from here to the library, and then not just anywhere in the library, but right onto the table next to your father, setting it down carefully enough that no one except Amy seemed even to notice."

Chloe's mouth fell open. "I did that without even trying. I mean I was wishing so hard that I'd be able to see and talk with my dad, but I didn't wish for the tea. I just saw it sitting there on the table."

"And it was!" Bertha laughed. "Right where you visualized it to be. That is some fancy magic. I can farsee with Libby as she can with me, but neither of us could conjure at that distance. I did manage to send the telescope plans, but that requires a lot less skill. Congratulations! Your summer's work has been outstanding!"

"But I still can't teleport myself," moaned Chloe.

"Enough! Your farseeing is more advanced than a journeyman mage, so rest on those laurels. The teleporting will happen when it is ready, and even so, under pressure, when someone is in danger, you can teleport others."

"I guess," said Chloe.

"And now, we have just two weeks left. It is time that I showed you the secret library, the one King Alfred placed under the sole protection of the guardians. Come with me," she said as she turned back into the cave.

Chloe followed Bertha into the cave, wondering how there could be anything in the cave that she hadn't already seen. Bertha walked up to the left-hand corner of the back wall. Then she placed her hand on the stone, and suddenly, the wall shimmered and disappeared.

Bertha turned around and said, "Bet you weren't expecting that!"

Chloe shook her head and said, "That is amazing."

"The guardians have always lived here. My great-grandmother set this up for King Alfred, and no one has seen the inside except the guardians since then."

"Your great-grandmother? So how old are you?" wondered Chloe.

"Just never you mind. It isn't polite to ask a woman her age," she said with a chuckle. "Dragon riders are long-lived, and guardians live even longer. But I'm certainly not as old as Libby. Now come on; let me show you what's here."

Chloe couldn't believe it. She was the first human to see these archives since King Alfred had them sealed away. She followed Bertha into the space and stared. The space was not much bigger than her special alcove at the library, and all the walls were lined with shelves, shelves that were crammed with very old and fragile-looking manuscripts.

"Why is all this hidden here?" asked Chloe.

"King Alfred and his companions came from another world, a world which he said was filled with lots of gadgets and what he called 'technology.' But he didn't want that knowledge to be used here. He said that it had only made wars nastier and the rich richer and really damaged the planet. While he didn't want to destroy the knowledge in case some of it might be needed, he also didn't want it to be readily accessible. He and my great-grandmother decided on this solution."

"But how do you know what is in here?" asked Chloe.

"Each guardian, during her apprenticeship—"

"You have apprenticeships?"

"Well, of course. How else would we be trained? Anyway, as I was saying, during our apprenticeships, we have to become familiar with the general overview of the entire contents of this room. That way, should the need arise for any of this informa-tion, we'll know it is here and be able to release it."

"So that's how you knew about the telescope plans," said Chloe with awe in her voice.

"Right in one! Now you can be thankful that you don't have to learn the contents as I did. But what I do want you to study in these last two weeks is this manuscript," she said as she lifted one off the shelf and handed it to Chloe.

Chloe took it. It seemed to be a thick journal with a leather cover, and as she opened it, she was surprised to see that it was in such good shape. "How have these manuscripts lasted for so long?" asked Chloe.

"That is the job of the guardian and our magic. And it is why I can't let anything leave this space for more than a short time. Libby has already sent back the original telescope drawings. She sent those as soon as you and Robert had copied them. Now you may keep this on the shelf in the main cave for the remainder of your stay, and then I will put it back in this vault."

With that, she motioned Chloe out into the main cave. The minute Bertha walked through the archway, it disappeared, and the cave was back to just the way it always was. No one would ever suspect that there was anything different about that wall.

Bertha watched as Chloe ran her hands over the wall and then said, "Only the guardian can activate the vault. I couldn't even do it when I was training. There is just one guardian at a time who can access this. King Alfred and my grandmother were determined that nothing from his old world would come into this world, at least until the society was ready for it."

Chloe climbed up onto her shelf and opened the book. "*The Rules of Magic*," she read. "So this is a rule book?"

Bertha laughed. "Of a sort. I want you to study this, not because I think you need it, but just so that you will understand the nature of your power. It is too easy to use magic when you don't really need to. It can become a crutch. Oh, I'm not saying that it is wrong to conjure up a mug of tea or the like. But don't abuse that. There is nothing wrong with making the tea in the kitchen. You get the idea, I'm sure."

"Yes." She chuckled. "A few times at Amy's, especially when she was running around trying to get a big meal ready, I've thought about helping with a bit of conjuring. But then I watched her and saw how much joy it brings her to fix food with love for her family. And I've seen the interaction in the kitchen when others help her. That is a different kind of magic, isn't it?"

"For sure! And this book will also explain about telepathy, teleporting, farseeing, and the like. We've talked about it a bit already, but the most important thing to remember is never invade someone else's mind or space without asking."

Chloe nodded, and Bertha went on, "There will be exceptions, of course, and you've already had a few of those. You didn't need to ask Boris before you saved him from falling off the cliff. And I doubt that asking would have stopped the farmer. But those situations should be the exception. Listening in on every conversation going on around you is rude, and it will also make you crazy. Learning to shield yourself and to respect the shields of others is vital."

"Got it," said Chloe, and she curled up in her quilt and began reading. She took out one of her journals so that she could make notes on anything she wanted to be sure to remember or which she found confusing.

Over the next two weeks, she and Bertha discussed the finer points concerning the use of magic. "It seems to me," said Chloe on her last day with Bertha, "that it all comes down to using some common sense and showing respect for yourself and others."

Bertha smiled and said, "Yep, that pretty much sums it up. Now let me put this safely away in the vault," she continued as she took the book, "and I bet Boris and Berla would love to play ball with you. Why don't you just have fun on your last afternoon, and I'll make a special dinner?"

Chloe had a wonderful time romping in the clearing with Boris and Berla. They were actually pretty good at catching the ball, and she even taught them some of the rules for kickball, although they had to be modified a bit. It was more like head-ball, but they had a lot of fun, and Chloe reveled in how much their skills had improved since she first met them.

Chloe enjoyed the evening and thought just how much she was going to miss this cave and Bertha and the twins. She knew she'd be spending summers here for a number of years, and she knew she could now farsee with Bertha in between, well except when Bertha and the twins were hibernating, of course, but she also knew she'd miss the warmth and love she felt in this cave.

Early the next morning, she packed her things into her duffel and then sat down to breakfast with Bertha and the cubs. They'd just finished when Emily and Esmeralda landed in the clearing.

There were hugs all around, and soon, Chloe was flying off with Emily, waving for as long as she could to the bears in the clearing.

— 21 —

BACK HOME

Chloe was very glad to be back home again. Emily and Esmeralda dropped her off at Amy and Todd's so she could unpack her things. "But I want to see you in my office as soon as you get settled," said Emily. "I think you have things you want to tell me."

Amy came out in the yard, waved at Emily as she took off on Esmeralda, and then gave Chloe a big hug. "It is so good to see you!"

They walked into the kitchen, and Amy offered Chloe a mug of fresh coffee. "I have missed your coffee," said Chloe, dropping her duffel and taking the mug. Then thinking that might have sounded odd, she added, "but I've missed you more!"

Amy laughed. "I hope so!"

Chloe picked up her duffel and took it to her room, just dropping it in the corner to be unpacked later. After returning to the kitchen, she sat for a few minutes with Amy as they enjoyed their coffee. "So is everyone here doing well?" asked Chloe.

"Oh, for sure," said Amy. "I think you will be surprised by all that has happened while you were away, but it is all good."

"Wish I could stay now and catch up, but Emily said she wanted to see me right away in her office, so I'm going to have to run," Chloe said. She stood and rinsed her mug in the kitchen sink. "Thanks so much for the coffee. It is sure good to be home. I'll be back for dinner; I promise."

And with another hug from Amy, she was out the door heading to the rider complex. When she reached Emily's office, she knocked on the door and entered at Emily's request.

"Have a seat," said Emily.

Once Chloe was settled, Emily said, "I've heard rumors that you ran into trouble up in the mountains above Bertha's cave. Can you tell me about that?"

Chloe gave her the complete story of the farmer's attempt on Bertha and the cubs, including her role in stopping him.

Emily roared with laughter. "You tied his rifle into a knot! I would have liked to see that! But seriously," she continued, "I know that farmer, Harry Wartle, and he has always been a loner. I don't think he has any family left. We only see him once a year when he brings his wool down to sell and to pick up his supplies. He does have a temper, but that's no excuse. Anyway, I have noted everything down, and I'll be getting with Clotilda to decide what action needs to be taken. That is the second attempt on Bertha in less than a year. Thankfully, the hunter you stopped last winter did move his family out of the forest, and they wintered on the outskirts of Havenshold. I think he will be staying. He is an excellent handyman, and we can certainly use that talent in Havenshold. But Harry Wartle is another matter."

She thought for a minute and then said, "But that's all I needed to know from you. Welcome back! You have been missed!"

They said good-bye, and Chloe headed over to the library. She was immediately greeted by Gregory, who seemed really pleased to see her. "The library hasn't been the same since you left," he remarked.

She thanked him and thought how wonderful it felt to be back in the library. Once Gregory went back to his office, Chloe headed to her alcove. She was thrilled to find a long note from Libby, welcoming her back, congratulating her on her progress, and inviting her to resume their morning chats over breakfast the next day.

Life settled into a very lovely routine for Chloe over the next couple of years. She always spent summers with Bertha and the rest of the year in the library. Chloe enjoyed watching the progress of Beulah at the animal clinic where she was now working most days. And Zelda worked really hard with great success; she had even been allowed to place an outfit or two in each of Marjorie's shows. The other apprentices were progressing rapidly as well. The length of time that an apprenticeship ran varied with each situation. Five to six years was about the average, and dragon riders studied for nine, not only because of the amount they had to learn but also because that was the rhythm of the hatching cycles, with a new set of apprentices every three years.

Bertha and Libby had both explained that her apprenticeship wasn't governed so much by time as by her achievements. She continued to improve with her farseeing. She could contact Amy from the library, for instance, without using the locket. That came in really handy when she was running late for dinner. She contacted her dad every evening. They'd set up a schedule, and they both really enjoyed the forging of a new, stronger relationship. She got to hear and see his latest toys, and she shared her struggles and triumphs.

Chloe still couldn't manage teleportation, except in emergencies, which she was thankful were infrequent. The last time she'd had any success was the camping trip with Bertha, and now that seemed ages ago.

Her conjuring was definitely improving, and that was a good thing. On the eve of her third anniversary as an apprentice mage, Emily called her into rider headquarters.

"Take a seat," said Emily. "I wanted to talk to you about the library."

Chloe shook her head and looked confused. She waited for Emily.

"Yes, you might well shake your head in confusion. The library is, as you know, better than most—the nicest building in the complex. I've been studying the few rider histories we have here, and I discovered that it was also the first official building that King Alfred had built. But it has never really been used. It is over five hundred years old and still looks brand new."

Chloe shrugged her shoulders and muttered, "It is a very nice building and very well built."

Emily laughed. "OK, I get it. You aren't going to say a thing. But Gregory has told me some fascinating stories. First, he loves his academy office, and he says that since he started the academy three years ago, it feels as if the library has awakened and blossomed. Now Gregory is a wonderful man, which I'd be the first, as his wife, to acknowledge. But he is not poetic or terribly imaginative. For him to say that is really something. Then he said that he finds occasional notes from someone named Libby, mostly during the summer when you are with Bertha. And then there was the whole lab thing where a fully equipped lab appeared overnight. Later, there was the observatory. This is magic, right?"

Chloe smiled and said, "Yes, the library is a very special place. That much I can say, and yes, there is magic involved."

"Right," continued Emily. "Well, I don't need to know more. But what Gregory is now asking is whether he can move his other office, the one where he works on volcanology, into the library. He says he just works better there."

There was a stunned look on Chloe's face. *Had Libby made that much of an impact on Gregory? How about on others? Now that she thought about it, there were certainly more people stopping by, not just academy students and not just on nights when the observatory was open.*

Emily interrupted Chloe's thoughts. "I have to admit that Gregory's office down the hall is really small and not very inviting, so I can see why he would want to move. He wants to move into the lab, now that it isn't really being used what with the telescope being finished. Would that be all right?"

Chloe thought hard and fast, but before she could answer, Emily went on, "And while we are at it, William wants to move in as well. He needs more space for his research on forms of communication, and I guess Jake is tired of having William's office in their home. Their caves have been joined and are spacious, but I can see having an office along with the two of them and their dragons would make things cramped. William also says that now that his work is expanding with both Lucy and Beulah, that some of his studies involve people who don't like being that close to a dragon if Thunder or Harmony happen to be napping."

"Wow," said Chloe. "So both Gregory and William want offices?"

"Yes, that's the long and short of it, and I agree because both of them are involved in research, and isn't the library the place for that?"

Chloe nodded and said, "Well, I'll go ask, I mean, I'll go see what can be done and get back to you."

Emily laughed as Chloe rushed out the door. "Mages!" Chloe heard her say as the door shut.

The next morning, Chloe shared Emily's request with Libby as they enjoyed their breakfast ritual. Chloe presented the plan and then ate while Libby pondered.

"They really like it here?" asked Libby.

"Yes, they do. You are a wonderful library, and you have brought a lot to everyone's lives, not just mine."

"I have to admit I feel more alive than I have in years—well, ages, really. King Alfred used to enjoy spending his evenings here, and he would talk with me, but no one else ever did. And after a lot of years, I just sort of drifted off, waking only occasionally. But now, I really feel useful and I love having people here. So what do you think?"

"I think it is a good idea. William and Gregory are also trailblazers, and Draconia has never really had any scientists or researchers because people were just making a living and beginning a society. But things have evolved beyond the point of struggles. Havens hold is growing, and the capital has attracted artisans from the other countries, so I think it is time to encourage the development of beneficial research. Gregory works diligently with Lucy and others to be sure our volcano is happy and that the energy is being used wisely and fairly. And William has really made a difference with communications between various species. Besides which, they are both really nice, quiet, gentle souls. I think they would be a good fit for the library."

Libby smiled. "I agree. I just wanted to hear your reasoning. Now what about space? What do you visualize there?"

"Emily is right that we don't need the large lab anymore, but I do think we should keep a lab in the library for tinkering on the telescope and whatever else comes up. I'd also like to encourage students to try to learn more about this world, and that means a lab. Michael mentioned the last time he was home that he'd like a place to store plant specimens. So I think the lab stays, and now that I'm thinking about it, I don't really want it to shrink either."

"Again, I agree, and your argument is well reasoned. We don't want to get rid of it only to find that we need it again. So what about the spaces for Gregory and William?"

"I've seen where each of them works. Gregory does have a very small office in Rider Headquarters, and he needs walls to hang maps on and a drafting table. A cabinet with map drawers would be nice as well as good lighting and a desk, chairs, file cabinet, and I don't know if there is anything else."

"Do you think he would want two offices or just one larger one?" asked Libby.

"He keeps saying that it is hard to remember which office he needs to be in, so I think he'd appreciate one larger office." Chloe thought for a minute before saying, "And it's not like we can't change it if he wants two. I'd just put a partition through it."

"What about William?" asked Libby.

"Anything we do for William will be a step up. Right now, he is using a corner in their cave where he has a small desk and two chairs. Papers are always spilling all over the place, and he stores notes in cardboard boxes stacked in the corner. I think William will be very happy with a well-lit office with filing cabinets, a desk, chairs, maybe a couch to relax on, and a big bulletin board to put notes and thoughts on."

"So can you see what each office will look like?" asked Libby.

"Yes, I think so. I'm just not quite sure how they will fit in the library," said Chloe with her forehead wrinkled in concentration.

"You let me worry about that. Folks don't seem ever to have noticed, but I can grow bigger on the inside without ever changing on the outside. Now, when we did the lab three years ago, you managed to shift one wall. Let's see what you can do now, apprentice mage."

Chloe took a deep breath and began. "I'll start by making Gregory's office larger." Closing her eyes so she could concentrate harder and see things more clearly, Chloe began by pushing the right-side wall, the one that wasn't next to the lab, farther away. *I wonder what was on the other side of that wall.* Once she had the room as large as she wanted, she added a large window on the outside wall and then put a glass wall with a door on the inside to match the one the lab had. She hung a holder for maps on the wall she had just moved and also a blackboard. Then she added all the furniture she had envisioned, hanging lights right over the drafting table. She even put retractable shades on all the windows in case privacy was needed. She enlarged the desk that Gregory was currently using and also gave him a nicer chair, since he would be spending much more time here. She put a small area in one corner with a coffee pot and a small cupboard above for coffee, tea, condiments, and the like.

She sat back in her chair and used farseeing to examine the room. "What do you think?" asked Chloe.

Laughing, Libby said, "I think your magic has really grown. Remember how tired you were after moving just one wall? This is a wonderful office, and I am sure Gregory will really enjoy it. Have another piece of toast. Are you ready to do William's?"

Munching on the toast, Chloe considered. "Yes, but I'm trying to decide just where to put it. Gregory is in the same spot, and after all, as head of Pathfinder Academy, he should be encouraging students, so the fact that people have to walk past the lab to reach his office isn't a big deal. But I'm not so sure about William's work. I think it would be better to have his office further in the front. Would it be all right to put it just to the right of the main doors as people enter?"

"Wherever you like," said Libby with a big grin on her face.

Closing her eyes again, Chloe formed the office just inside the main doors off to the right. She made the office large with plenty of light. She added a large desk so that William's papers wouldn't spill as quickly, with a comfy chair. Then she added a smaller table, a few more chairs, a couch against one wall, and a bulletin board and blackboard on another. William also got a small table with a coffeepot as Gregory had.

Finally, Chloe opened her eyes and looked over at Libby. "Is that all right with you? Have I changed you too much?"

"You have made an old library very happy! Your work is outstanding, fully worthy of the title of journeyman mage! Congratulations!"

Chloe looked dumbfounded. "But I can't teleport yet?"

"Don't argue with your mentor. You have demonstrated enormous talent, surpassing journeyman standards in farseeing and transformations. And you have shown that you can teleport when it counts. Both Bertha and I feel that you are ready for the next step."

"Thank you!" said Chloe.

"Consider the offices as your journeyman's exam. Emily now has a certificate on her desk proclaiming your new status! I'm sure that new status will also mean new duties, but for now, let all your friends know and celebrate!"

Chloe walked back into the library just as the doors were unlocked. Before long, Emily, Gregory, and shortly after that William and a whole host of folks arrived to admire the new offices and congratulate Chloe on her promotion.

Chloe really enjoyed watching both Gregory and William walking around their new spaces, checking everything out with wonder and amazement. They each gave her hugs and thanked her profusely. There was a big celebration at Amy and Todd's that night, and Chloe was glad to see that Zelda and her dad were there as well.

This has been a fantastic day with totally unexpected results, thought Chloe as she finally crawled into bed. *I'm a journeyman mage now,* and with that thought, she was fast asleep.

— 22 —
JOURNEYMAN MAGE

Chloe found out quickly that Libby was right about the added responsibilities. Emily called her into her office first thing the next morning, and after congratulating her and thanking her yet again for the offices, she said, "Clotilda would like to see you this afternoon."

Chloe stammered, "The Q-Queen? She wants to see me? Why?"

Emily just laughed. "As she'll tell you herself, just call her Clotilda. She used to have my job before she and Matilda took over for the former king Jacob. Believe me, she's not hard to talk to at all. She wants to congratulate you, and I suspect she also will want you to add some duties, but I'll definitely let her explain that."

"Oh, dear," said Chloe as she sank further into her chair.

"Now don't worry. It is all good, and you are a journeyman now after all." Emily took a drink from her coffee mug and then said, "Turns out, I also need to meet with Clotilda, so you'll be riding with me and Esmeralda. We'd like to leave now, if you can, as then we will be there in time for lunch! Palace lunches are not to be missed."

The flight was wonderful. Chloe really enjoyed flying on Esmeralda. And the lunch was everything Emily had promised, although Chloe was too nervous to eat a lot. Clotilda had told her just to call her Clotilda, again as Emily predicted, and she was very nice and not as daunting as Chloe had thought she would be.

Once the dishes were cleared away, Clotilda pulled out some paper and began. "First, let me congratulate you on your promotion. You are now the first ever journeyman mage in this world, and we are very proud to have you."

"Thank you," said Chloe softly.

"As I suspect you can guess, your promotion will also bring more work. That's always the way of it, I guess. Anyway, you are not just a local mage, but rather a mage for all the nations in our world. With that in mind, I would like to have you start traveling."

Chloe gasped and began wringing her hands.

Clotilda said, "Now, don't worry. We aren't throwing you to the lions or anything like that. Let me tell you what I had in mind. I know you still have a lot of studies ahead of you, and I know as the time for the prophecy fulfillment draws nearer, you will have more and more to do to accomplish that. At the same time, as you know, we've already needed you to act to protect our seer and indeed all the bears. There aren't many bears in our world, which is one reason why they are protected—that and of course their relationship with the dragons."

Clotilda went on, "It is important that you are seen as being available to help all four of our nations, not just Draconia. I know you know Hans. Well, he is now my ambassador-at-large. I send him wherever I need to, and at the moment, he is in Sanwight. But when he returns, I want the two of you to set up a schedule so that once a month, you visit the other three nations for brief meetings and then come here to report to me."

"But how long will that t-take?" stammered Chloe. "I still can't teleport, and oh, I have so much to learn."

Clotilda said, "Please don't worry. This will mean about five days a month away from your library, which, by the way, I am hearing astounding things about. If you two leave on a Monday morning, for instance, you would arrive in Sanwight in plenty of time to settle in, have dinner at their palace, and chitchat and then meet with Queen Priscilla and her advisors Tuesday morning. Leave there right after lunch and fly to Granvale. Same routine there and after meeting with Queen Penelope and her advisors, leave again after lunch and arrive in Forbury late on Wednesday. I suspect you will be staying at Baron Geldsmith's in Forbury because he loves to have visitors and King Alfred prefers more quiet, but you will meet with King Alfred and his advisors on Thursday morning, and that should get you back to Alfredsville and a meeting with me easily by Friday morning. Then you will be back to the library that afternoon and sleeping in your own bed Friday night."

"Well, I guess," said Chloe. "But I wouldn't know what to say to any of them."

Clotilda laughed. "Don't worry. You will be with Hans, and he is my official ambassador. For a while, these visits will just be more of a 'show off the mage' type thing. You will be there, but I'm guessing the monarchs will be doing more to show you their lands, and all you'll have to do is nod a lot. Hans will always take the lead.

"Now, that raises another question. Since you will be on display, so to speak, do you have any mage robes or whatever? You need to look impressive."

Chloe really did feel terrified now. "No, I don't have anything like that."

Clotilda turned to Emily and said, "Could you put your mom onto organizing something. I could give you about three weeks.

I'm planning on having 'the mage tour' cycle during the fourth week of each month. That is the week that will miss most of the festivals, et cetera."

Emily nodded. "I already have some ideas. We'll have something suitable by the fourth week in October."

"Great! And, Chloe, I deliberately arranged the tour as I did so that you would begin with Queen Priscilla. She is just the same age as Hannah and Rupert, and I know you will like her a lot. And we are ending the tour with the baron, whom I'm sure you've heard about."

Chloe nodded, and Clotilda went on, "Actually, you'll find that you and he have a great deal in common, so that should be a lovely way to end the tour. King Alfred is mellow and nice, and so is Queen Penelope. We are very fortunate that there are really good relations between all four nations. We just want to be sure it stays that way. Now, Emily, what did you have to discuss with me?"

Chloe wandered off to the windows as the other two discussed day-to-day matters. She barely saw the grounds outside, although they were very beautiful. All she could think about was "The Tour," which now loomed in her mind as fully worthy of capital letters and all-out terror.

Once Emily and Clotilda were done, Clotilda hugged them both and said again, "Please don't worry, Chloe. You'll be just fine."

With that, Emily and Chloe were again on Esmeralda and headed home.

That night, after dinner, Amy said, "Emily explained about the fact that you need mage robes and that you need them in three weeks. I had an idea that I wanted to run past you."

"OK," said Chloe with a bit of a tremor in her voice.

"Marjorie is the best designer in Havenshold, and of course, Zelda is her apprentice, so I think asking them to do the robes is the best plan."

"That would be wonderful!"

"Great, I thought you'd like that. What I also thought was that Marjorie could approach your mother to see if she'd like to help. The time frame is short, and that would be Marjorie's excuse, but if it worked, it might help your mother as well."

"But do you really think she would?"

"Well, we won't know if we don't ask. And I noticed at the last couple of Marjorie's shows that your mother was there—oh, she stands in the back and races right out. Zelda says that she has never stayed to talk to her, but I do think it is a good sign that she is coming out."

"I would be very happy if this proves to be a way to reach her, and she has always loved Marjorie's clothes. She has tried for years to get me to wear something more than comfortable slacks and a shirt."

"Excellent," said Amy. "I'll go see Marjorie first thing tomorrow."

"But, Amy, can you make sure they don't go overboard and that these robes are comfortable and something I can move in without falling over myself. I don't even wear skirts. Please!"

"Don't you worry. I'll be sure that they not only reflect your position but also who you are as a person."

The next three weeks went by way too fast for Chloe. Hans had stopped by a few days after Chloe had met with Clotilda, and he was very reassuring. She realized this was all old hat for him. She was certainly glad he was in her court.

Amy's idea for handling the robes worked out better than Chloe had dared hope. Her mother was very flattered when Marjorie asked her to help, and once she was in Marjorie's studio, she and Zelda began sewing together. Zelda told Chloe that their mother did make a lot of cracks about her daughter, the high and mighty mage, but that after a few days, once she had heard enough people talking about all the good Chloe was doing, she stopped with the putdowns.

By the time of the first fitting, her mother was definitely in a better place, and while she still criticized how Chloe stood and moved, she didn't raise her voice or use foul language.

Marjorie controlled the entire situation, and when she asked Chloe for her input and her mother started to say something, she just held her hand up and Hazel was quiet. Chloe said, "I really like purple or medium blue. And my favorite fabrics are really soft ones, like velvet. Also, could I have pockets?"

"Pockets!" exclaimed her mother, and then she turned to Marjorie and said, "See, I told you she would be impossible."

Zelda rolled her eyes, but Marjorie just said, "I think pockets are an excellent idea. I can make slash pockets, which won't be seen but will hold small items, such as handkerchiefs. After all, you will be traveling so I think that is an excellent suggestion. I also was thinking of velvet as it will hang well over any garments. Do you normally dress as you are today?"

Hazel started to say something, which Chloe was sure would have been derogatory, but Marjorie again held up her hand. Chloe said, "Yes, I'm afraid so. I have never liked clothes the way my mom and Zelda do. They always look so nice," she said, glancing at the two of them, and her mother had the grace to nod. "But it just isn't me. I only want practical and comfortable. And I love my boots just the way they are," she added as the thought of shoes filled her with horror.

Marjorie laughed in a good-natured way. "Don't worry. I have plenty of customers just like you, and I always manage to make them look nice while they feel comfortable. I think purple for the first robe. Eventually, you will want several, but let's start with that, and I was hoping, Hazel, that you might be able to do some embroidery on it."

Hazel looked surprised to be asked, but she smiled and said, "I would like that. What did you have in mind?"

Marjorie walked over to a nearby table and picked up some sketches. "Zelda has drawn some ideas here, centered around astronomy. Chloe, are these something you would feel comfortable with?"

"Yes," answered Chloe promptly. "Zelda brought those by the library yesterday, and she has totally captured me with them. I even noticed she put in some books and a bear. I really like the sketches, but isn't that a lot of embroidery to do in such a short time, Mom?" she concluded, turning to include her mother.

"Well, it is rather a lot," she said, but then she went on, "Your grandma can still do the finest embroidery, and our stitches match really well. Between the two of us, we will be able to do it."

Chloe gave her mother a big hug and then laughed at the startled expression on her face. She turned to face them all and said, "Thanks so much. I'm really anxious about this tour thing, but if I'm wearing a robe that contains my family, well, I know that will make me much more confident." And then to cover her mother's obvious embarrassment, Chloe asked Marjorie, "You will keep the length to something short enough so I won't trip on it if I have to go up stairs or anything, won't you?"

Her mother laughed, but this time, Chloe thought there was a bit less sting in it. "But a shorter robe will show your pant legs. Marjorie, do you have any purple pants that she would like?"

Marjorie smiled. "Of course. We'll have her outfitted like a proper mage. Thanks, Chloe, you can go, and meanwhile, the rest of us had better get to work."

That night, at dinner, Chloe couldn't stop thanking Amy. "You wouldn't believe the change in my mom. Oh, she still got in her digs, but Marjorie was wonderful and kept her from just dominating me. And Marjorie also seemed to understand what I want, even down to pockets, which horrified my mother. But my mom idolizes Marjorie, so she listened. Did I tell you that she and Grandma are going to do all the embroidery?"

"Yes!" Amy laughed.

Todd chimed in, "It is so wonderful to see her out again and working with you and Zelda. Who knows what will happen? One step at a time."

Chloe slipped into bed feeling happier than she could believe, even with the thoughts of the tour and the robes. *Well, if it weren't for them, I wouldn't have gotten to see my mom.* With that comforting thought, she was asleep.

— 23 —
THE TOUR

All of a sudden, it was the Monday morning when the tour would begin—but not until she had her morning chat and breakfast with Libby. Chloe picked at her breakfast, and Libby said, "Nervous?"

"Yes," she answered. "Until I met Clotilda, I'd never been out of Havenshold really, except Bertha's cave, but that's in a forest. And now, I'm traveling to all the other nations."

"You'll do great! Just be yourself. That's all anyone can ask. Now, let's see you in your robes, if you have eaten all you are going to, that is."

Chloe laughed and pushed her plate away. "I'm too nervous to eat. But wait till you see my robes! Marjorie got them finished yesterday just in time, and what was even more amazing is that both my mom and I thought they were great!"

Chloe slipped the robes on and then swirled a bit. The robes fell to her midcalf, so there was no danger of tripping, and they even had enough fullness with discreet slits in the side so that she wouldn't rip them when she was on Fire Dancer.

Libby gazed at her and said, "They are just perfect! And you have pockets as well! I'll be right here when you return, eager to hear about all your state visits."

Chloe laughed, and then all too soon, she was saying good-bye and heading to the courtyard in front of the library. She walked out the library doors and then just stopped and stared in amazement. It looked as if the entire town had turned out to send her off. She shook hands with or hugged nearly everyone—Beulah, Imogene, Clarissa, Amy, Todd, Gregory, and many more. They were all there to wish her well, but the ones who mattered the most were Zelda and her dad, and right next to her dad stood her mom and grandma! Chloe started to cry as she hugged both her mom and grandma. "Thank you both so much," she said.

"Well, you do us proud now," said Grandma.

"And don't forget to come to tea when you get back and tell us all about it. Watch your manners, and try not to trip," said her mother.

Chloe laughed and said, "Yes, Mom." She was just so happy to see her mother looking better.

Hans helped her up onto Fire Dancer, and Chloe was thrilled that she managed it with reasonable grace even with the robes. She caught Marjorie's eye and gave her a big thumbs-up. She mouthed, "Thanks."

And then they were in the air with everyone below shouting, cheering, and waving. Hans pointed out various points of interest along the way, and Chloe thoroughly enjoyed the flight. She gasped when she caught sight of the ocean just as they were coming into Dalzian, Sanwight's capital.

"That's Sprite Sea, and the area right in front of the city is called, fittingly enough, Dolphin Bay." Fire Dancer landed in the courtyard in front of the palace, and no sooner had they landed than a young woman came racing out. Chloe guessed she was the queen because she was wearing a tiara, but she was just as excited and easygoing as Hannah and Rupert.

Introductions were made, and Priscilla, as she insisted on being called, led them into the palace where they met her chief minister, Benjamin, who immediately asked about Rupert and a number of other riders. That was when Chloe remembered the history that had been drummed into her by both Gregory and Emily over the past three weeks. Benjamin was instrumental in getting Rupert released after the baron had kidnapped him in a power play for Draconia's throne.

Priscilla then took them on a tour of the palace, although it would be more accurate to say that she took them on a tour of the magnificent grotto beneath the palace. "All palaces are pretty much the same, and the ones in both Granvale and Forbury are older and finer than this one, but what we do have that is totally unique is the grotto."

After they went down a vast number of stairs, Chloe thanking her lucky stars that Marjorie had made her robes trip-proof, Priscilla stood to the side and let Chloe enter first.

Chloe was blown away. There was a large underground pool, which Priscilla said was connected to Dolphin Bay. The walls of the grotto were covered in handmade ceramic tiles, and the tiles told the history of the dolphin riders. The entire area was magnificently designed, and Chloe noticed that the sides of the pool sloped at a gentle angle so that the dolphins could slide nearly out of the water. As she was wondering why they would want to, she noticed Benjamin bending down to pet a dolphin who had just appeared.

"Chloe, this is Horace, my bond mate, and Horace, this is Chloe, our world's first ever mage," said Benjamin.

"And here comes Zenith, my bond mate," said Priscilla as another dolphin approached.

Chloe was allowed to touch each of the dolphins, and she was amazed at how smooth and soft they were, but when each of them greeted her telepathically, she was even more amazed. She decided to try to speak with them with her farseeing abilities even though they were right next to her, and she was thrilled to find that it worked.

Priscilla then took them back into the palace where they had a lovely dinner before being shown to their quarters.

The tour progressed just as Clotilda had assured her it would. There was a meeting after breakfast with Priscilla, Benjamin, and some other dignitaries. Hans did most of the talking. Since she'd already chatted with Priscilla and Benjamin about her life as a mage, they had no questions, but several of the other ministers did. They mostly wanted to know what she would do for them. Chloe was thankful when both Hans and Priscilla stepped in to explain that this was just a tour to show the mage the other worlds, but Hans did explain in deliberately vague terms about the prophecy and the building of the telescope.

Chloe could tell by the looks on their faces that they didn't believe a word he said, but she really didn't care. She realized that she would be the most successful if no one ever found out about a danger she averted.

After the meeting and lunch, it was time to leave for Granvale. Once they were in the air, Hans said, "You handled that like a pro."

"But I didn't do anything," protested Chloe.

"You didn't have to. Your calmness and your presence were superb. Clotilda was right to insist on the robes. The most important people to get to know are Priscilla and Benjamin, and the fact that you could speak to Horace and Zenith won them over right there. I knew that you weren't telepathic, but this farseeing of yours seems to be nearly the same."

"Yes, it is, but I didn't realize it would work close up. Farsee is meant to contact people who are at a distance, and it allows for both speaking and seeing. But I was really happy to see it could also work at close range."

Hans went on to show her more points of interest. "Granvale has the best farming land in this world with the fewest mountains. Sanwight as a lot but not as much. Draconia really depends on both of them for a lot of our food and all of our fish. Draconia, in return, supplies some beef, but mostly energy from our volcano. We have ranches and farms, but the ground isn't as fertile."

Hans handed her a sandwich and then took one for himself as they flew. Soon, he pointed down to a city below and said, "There is Stargan, Granvale's capital."

The visit was a repeat of the first one. As they landed in the courtyard, Queen Penelope came out, walking in a much more stately fashion, but then she looked to be at least twenty years older than Clotilda. After the introductions, Queen Penelope took them around the unicorn complex and introduced her to several riders and their unicorns and then to her own unicorn, Bright Star. Chloe was then introduced to Elizabeth, Queen Penelope's head of state, and her unicorn, Jerome.

Hans joked with Elizabeth, saying, "Blown anything up lately?"

Elizabeth just laughed. "You're never going to let me forget that, are you?"

"I should say not. You rather saved the day and allowed us to have a war with no casualties."

Queen Penelope smiled at that and said, "Yes, if you have to have a war, that's the kind to have, but I'm grateful for the current situation with peaceful relations all around."

Chloe thought the unicorns were magnificent, but they didn't speak to her. She remembered her training and did not try to speak to or indeed even pet them. She immediately noticed the riders weren't constantly petting their bond mates, as both dragon riders and dolphin riders did. They just seemed more regal and distant.

Queen Penelope and Elizabeth took them in to dinner after they had seen the rider complex briefly and from a distance. The dinner was much more formal, and Chloe concentrated on remembering all she had been taught about which fork to use and so forth. She was very glad that Hans did all the talking. Neither Queen Penelope nor Elizabeth seemed the slightest bit interested in her, and that was just fine by her.

She and Hans were then shown to their quarters, and she had the most luxurious room she had ever seen. She was afraid to touch anything, and in fact, she ended up sleeping in an overstuffed chair, covering herself in her robes, which she was sure would have horrified her mother.

The next morning, breakfast was served to Hans and Chloe alone, and then they were escorted to the queen's receiving chambers. As before, there were more dignitaries along with Queen Penelope and Elizabeth, but this time, all that occurred was introductions. Then Queen Penelope thanked them for their visit, and they were led back to the courtyard where Fire Dancer waited.

Once in the air, Hans asked her for her thoughts. "Well, I'm sure glad we started with Sanwight."

Hans laughed. "Queen Penelope and her people are very good people, and they help us out a lot. But they are very formal and reserved. I was surprised Elizabeth let me get away with that one crack, but she really was instrumental in arranging things so we could bring the baron to a discussion. And it was Emily's plan, so Elizabeth was only following directions, but her knowledge of explosives was critical. I do like them both to know how much we value their assistance."

"Well, we've had the casual and the ultra-formal. What will Forbury be like?" Chloe asked.

"Just wait and see," teased Hans.

Chloe noticed that the terrain changed dramatically as they crossed into Forbury. There were some mountains along the coast, and Hans told her that both Granvale and Forbury were bordered by Ercesa Ocean, but most of Forbury was forest.

"We get a lot of gems and minerals from the mines in Forbury, and the baron is now, no surprise, the richest mine owner in the nation. But you'll like him," Hans continued. "He is both friendly and generous. And wait until you meet Oswald. I'm sure you will fall in love with him just as everyone else does."

And with that comment, Fire Dancer banked and came in for a perfect landing in a small open area in front of a very large two-story home. As Hans helped Chloe down, the baron came out and gave them each a hug, saying, "I'm so glad you are here and earlier than I'd thought. Bet the meeting in Granvale didn't take long." He chuckled.

"You're right there," said Hans.

Just then, a gryphon came barreling around the corner, sending telepathic thoughts to everyone. *"You haven't started without me, have you?"*

The baron laughed and patted Oswald. "Never, my friend. We wouldn't dare."

Chloe was amazed when Oswald went right up to Fire Dancer and rubbed his face on her wing. Chloe wasn't sure if that would feel good, but Fire Dancer gave as close to a hug as a dragon could do by swinging his wing around Oswald. Oswald then greeted Hans and finally, Chloe. *"You must be the famous mage I've heard so much about,"* thought Oswald.

Chloe laughed and then tried her farseeing again by saying, *"I don't know how famous, but yes, and you must be the famous and utterly adorable Oswald!"*

Oswald seemed to blush, and everyone laughed. The baron invited them into the house, and the four of them, because of course Oswald wasn't going to be left out, had a marvelous evening. The baron surprised Chloe by being an excellent chef, but when she commented on it, he said, "Well, when you live alone away from any towns, you learn to fend for yourself."

He then showed them to their rooms, and Chloe noticed that there were two very large guest rooms on the main floor. Unlike those of Queen Penelope's palace, these rooms were furnished tastefully but very comfortably. Chloe knew that tonight, she would sleep well in what appeared to be a very cozy bed.

"These rooms are rather large," Chloe remarked before she could think better of it.

"They are indeed. They are designed that way intentionally so that when needed, gryphons or dragons can sleep in here with their partners. Just ask Lucy about that some time, right, Hans?"

Hans nodded, and the baron went on, "I'll never forget that time. She was brought here right after her father had wounded her so badly that her bad arm had to be amputated. She was really brave; her only fear was that someone would try to take Harriet away from her. She had to keep her good arm touching Harriet all the time, so Harriet slept in here with her. And we soon straightened her out. After all she'd been through. No one ever breaks a dragon bond, or a gryphon bone, eh, Oswald? What's a missing arm or a couple wings among friends, right?"

Chloe could swear that Oswald purred. Then she remembered that gryphons were related to both lions and eagles, with the body of the first and the head and wings of the second, so they probably could purr.

"Well, you are in here, and, Hans, you are across the hall. I'll get you up early enough in the morning so you can have some of my pancakes before you leave," said the baron.

"Chloe, you are in for a real treat. Thanks, Baron. Thanks, Oswald," said Hans, and everyone headed to bed.

No one had to wake Chloe, as the smell of the fresh coffee did that just fine. After washing and dressing, she headed for the kitchen where she found Hans and the baron already chatting as the latter cooked. The breakfast lived up to everything Hans had promised and more. And Chloe found herself really liking the baron. She knew his story and that he had been through a lot, but obviously, he had a pure heart and soul at his core or Oswald wouldn't have bonded with him.

And Oswald was so cute and friendly. Hans was right there also. She loved Oswald from the moment she first saw him. After giving the baron a hug as they left, she reached over and gave Oswald a really big hug and rubbed noses with him. She had been right earlier. He did purr!

It didn't take long to reach Forzia, the capital of Forbury, and Hans pointed out the mines, which were barely visible through the dense forest. The palace was built entirely of stone, and King Alfred (no relation to Draconia's first king) came out to welcome them. Chloe thought he, like Queen Penelope, was much older than Clotilda. He used a cane and obviously had badly injured his leg at some time in his life, but he was very pleasant, if rather shy. He brought them into a large conference room and introduced them to his advisors.

Again, Hans did most of the talking, explaining about Chloe and in very general terms what a mage was. Then there were a few questions, but nothing very serious. Chloe was worried when one advisor said, "So can you tell us where the biggest diamonds are?" But then he quickly smiled and laughed, so that she knew he was just teasing her.

After the meeting, King Alfred saw them out to the courtyard and waved as they flew away.

"See, that wasn't really so bad, was it?" asked Hans.

"I guess not, but I was sure glad to have you there. Thanks so much, Hans."

"My pleasure, and it is my job, remember. Now just relax, and we'll be with Clotilda in no time."

As they flew, Hans again pointed out landmarks, most notably the site of the massive earthquake where Cliffside, Lucy and Gretchen's home, had once been. And then they were landing in the palace courtyard.

Clotilda didn't keep them waiting, and after bringing them to her sitting room and being sure they had whatever food and drink they wanted, she said, "Now, Chloe, aren't those robes worth it all?"

Chloe laughed and said, "Oh, if only you knew. My sister designed all the embroidery, and my mother and grandmother sewed it."

Clotilda, who of course had been informed of Chloe's history, said, "Oh, I am so happy for you. That is the best news! But now, I don't want to keep you any longer than necessary. Hans, you can give me your report after you take Chloe back to Havenshold, but, Chloe, what did you think?"

Chloe shared what she'd already talked with Hans about and then concluded, "The three other nations are very different from us and very different from each other. But I felt welcomed in all, well, maybe most of all in Sanwight and at the baron's, but still, everyone was friendly. I don't think anyone really believes in mages or prophesies, but that's OK too. I have seen a lot, and it is going to take a while for me to process it, but I think it is good for me to get to know more about this world."

"Excellent, and that is enough to be getting on with. If you wouldn't mind sharing your thoughts in writing sometime over the next few days, I'd be grateful. Just give it to Emily, and she'll see that I get it. Now I know you are anxious to get home, so off you go," and she gave them each a hug.

As they were flying back to Havenshold, Chloe asked, "Do you miss being at Havens hold?"

"Sometimes," admitted Hans. "But it is good for Emily not to have me so close and good for the other riders as well, so that she becomes their true leader. She's pretty well done that now in just three years, so I may be around more, but honestly, I really do enjoy this roving-ambassador gig. I don't have a spouse or kids, and I doubt that I ever will. But that means I'm free to travel wherever Clotilda wants me to. And Fire Dancer and I love to travel and meet new people. My years as leader of the riders have given me a wealth of diplomatic skills, so I'm suited to the position. So, yes, in answer to your question, I do miss it at times, but I also love what I'm doing now."

"I get it," said Chloe just as Fire Dancer circled over the complex and into the courtyard.

Chloe was grateful there weren't as many people there this time to greet her as there were on Monday for her send-off, but there were still a lot of them. After shaking hands, hugging, and saying a number of times that the trip was wonderful, she was finally allowed to head home. She was glad to see that Amy and Todd were there to walk with her, and she was surprised when Zelda and her father caught up as well.

They all had a wonderful dinner, and Amy took her mage robes for cleaning and pressing. Zelda was very pleased to see how well the robes had held up and promised to let Marjorie and her mom know.

Finally, Chloe was able to head to bed, and after thanking everyone and saying good night, she crawled into her wonderful bed and was asleep before she could think a single thought.

— 24 —

OSWALD

The next year flew by, and before Chloe knew it, she'd been a mage for four years and a journeyman mage for a year. Her skills in everything except the teleporting grew noticeably, and she was wondering now if she ever was supposed to be able to teleport. Maybe she never would be a fully qualified mage, but she was happy.

She'd started teaching classes in astronomy, something she was finding she really enjoyed. She only taught small classes, with six or fewer students, and the classes were completely voluntary, so she only had students who really wanted to be there. She discovered that while she was very nervous at first, as she gained experience, she also gained confidence. And the confidence she gained helped her with her monthly tours.

She had suggested some changes in the tours to Clotilda so that now, when she and Hans went to each nation, they would stop in different towns or villages so she could really get to know the people. She always visited with Priscilla and the baron and Oswald. She just wasn't going to give those stops up because they were coming to mean so much to her.

Chloe was sitting in her alcove after breakfast on a cold, wintry Tuesday morning. She was reviewing her notes for her evening class and enjoying a mug of coffee when Gregory came running over. She looked up immediately because he didn't run and certainly didn't run in the library.

As he stopped practically on top of her, she said, "What's wrong?"

"It's my father—or rather Oswald. You've got to help!" he said.

Just then, Emily walked in. While she wasn't running, she was obviously moving faster than normal, and there was a deep frown on her face. "Let me explain," she said. "We just heard from Drake, a gryphon in Forbury, that there has been a mine cave-in. Drake was able to reach Matilda telepathically, and then the message was passed to Esmeralda and me. We don't have all the details, but apparently, the baron and Oswald, along with Bartholemew, Drake's bond mate, were inspecting a mine to see if they could use explosives to go any deeper. Bartholemew had just exited the mine when the baron came running out, nearly knocking him over. I guess there had been a weakening of one of the walls inside, and Oswald stayed behind to support the side beam while the baron got out. Oswald was then supposed to follow, but before he could, the front of the mine collapsed, and Oswald is now trapped. That's all I know."

"Well, how can I help?" asked Chloe. "Can someone fly me to the mine?"

"That's the problem—" Emily began.

Gregory interrupted. "There isn't time," he moaned. "Oswald's air will run out before any rider, even Hans in the capital, could reach them. You are our only hope. Can you do anything? My father will be devastated if he loses Oswald."

Emily nodded and confirmed, "It is never easy when one member of a bonded pair dies."

"And I love Oswald too," said Chloe. "I don't know what I can do, but let me see if I can reach Oswald with my farseeing. Is he in the mine closest to your father's house?" she asked, looking at Gregory.

Gregory nodded. "That's a good thing because I've at least seen that mine and remember the location. Thank heavens for the monthly tours. Here goes," she said as she closed her eyes and concentrated on trying to farsee Oswald.

"Oswald, can you hear me?" said Chloe, and she was relieved when he answered back to her in her head.

"Yes, I can. Are you nearby?"

"Unfortunately not. I'm in the library in Havenshold. Can you see me?"

"Yes! That is amazing. Is that farseeing?"

"It is, but now can you look around your enclosed space so I can see it too. And what can you tell me about your situation?"

As he looked around the space he was trapped in, he continued, *"This wall..."* He indicated the one he was leaning against. *"...started to bulge as we were leaving the mine. I pushed right up against the side beam and told the baron to get out first. I figured I'd just follow after him, running as fast as I could, but before that could happen, a wall of rock dropped down in front of me. At least the baron got out."*

"Do you know what he is doing?" Chloe asked.

"Yes, thank heavens for telepathy. He sounds pretty distraught, but he said that Bartholemew and Henry were trying to figure out a safe way to dig me out. I'm sure they will, as Bartholemew is the best explosive expert in the country and Henry understands mine engineering. It will be fine."

All of a sudden, Chloe could hear the baron's telepathy to Oswald as the baron wailed, *"They say they can't do anything without risking further collapse. They can't even get an air pipe through as the rocks and debris are packed too tightly!"*

Chloe felt like an eavesdropper as she heard their communication through Oswald.

"Hang on, Baron. I'm sure it will be fine and remember, we've had a good run that neither of us expected ever, so no matter what the outcome, please remember that. Remember our time together and our love. Nothing can ever change that."

Chloe then heard the baron sobbing, and she realized she had tears coursing down her cheeks as well. *I need to be there. I can't do a thing from here. I need to be at the mine. I can't let Oswald die without trying.*

Chloe concentrated just as hard as she could, totally oblivious to anything else. She didn't even notice her own sobbing or that Emily had her arms around her. She focused as hard as she could on the front of the mine. She could see the baron, Bartholemew, and Henry, along with other miners, all staring helplessly at the spot where the mine entrance used to be. *I have to be there. Maybe I can do something.*

Suddenly, she felt a jerking in the pit of her stomach, and before she could even figure out what was happening, she sensed that she was being pulled like a piece of string. The next thing she knew, she was standing next to the baron. His mouth was gaping wide open, as he was obviously as surprised as she was. *I teleported!* she thought, and then her knees started to buckle.

The baron caught her and eased her over to a nearby rock so she could sit. Just as he was going to holler for food and coffee, Henry appeared at her side with both. He had a steaming mug of coffee and a large chocolate bar. Nodding her thanks, she took a big gulp of the coffee, not even caring that it burned her tongue. Henry had opened the chocolate bar's wrapper, and she took a bite of that as well before looking up at the baron.

"I'm so sorry," she said to him.

"But now that you're here, you can save him, right?" said the baron.

"I don't know," she said, and she started to pace. Then she looked at Henry and said, "What is between us and Oswald? Is it mostly debris and small stuff, or is it solid rock?"

Henry said in a somber voice, "I'm afraid it is pretty nearly solid rock. That's why we couldn't get the air pipe through to buy us more time."

"How much time do we have?" she asked.

"Not much more than twenty minutes. Oswald already reports that the air is bad."

Chloe thought for a minute and said, "If Oswald moves away from the side beam, how long before it all collapses?"

Henry pondered a bit and said, "Well, once he moves, the beam will break and then everything will collapse. My best guess is that it will take less than a minute and possibly only a few seconds."

The baron buried his head in his hands and sobbed.

Chloe reached out to Oswald again with her farseeing. *"I don't know if I can pull you free,"* she said.

"I know," answered Oswald. *"But look at it this way, I don't have anything to lose by your trying. There are no other options."*

"Right," said Chloe to him. *"Then here's what I am going to try to do. I am going to try sending an energy tendril out to you, wrapping it around your body just behind your front legs. And then I will pull. I have no idea what will happen. I might be able to get you only partway and leave you caught in the rocks. Do you understand?"*

"I do," said Oswald, and then he brought the baron into the link before he said, *"Both the baron and I trust you to do the best that you can, and neither of us will blame you if it doesn't work. And, Baron, I love you."*

The baron sobbed as he said, *"I love you too. You are the best part of me."*

Chloe wanted to cry as well but realized that she had to stay strong and focused. She had everyone move away as she stood in front of the former opening but several feet back, as she had no idea what the collapse would do. She finished both the coffee and the chocolate and then drew all her strength together into the core of her body. She focused on Oswald and saw him standing with his back quarters pushing on the side beam. She gathered her energies and sent a tendril of energy as she had explained to Oswald. When it reached him, she wrapped it around his body. Then, taking a deep breath and centering her thoughts, she imagined Oswald moving through the rock and out in the open. For just an instant, she thought she felt both Bertha and Libby, but she kept her focus until suddenly, everything went black.

And then she felt a wet tongue licking her face. She opened her eyes to see Oswald standing over her, the baron at his side hugging him. She was flat on the ground. Then she heard in her head, *"Congratulations, Mage!"* and *"Well done, Mage!"* from voices that could only be Libby and Bertha. She shook her head, and they vanished.

Oswald moved back a bit, and Henry helped her to sit up. The baron looked at her with tears streaming down his face and just said, "Thank you!" before burying his head in Oswald's neck.

Chloe looked at the mine and saw that the entire hill had collapsed, leaving a major divot in the landscape. She didn't even want to think what would have happened to Oswald if she'd failed.

"But you didn't," said Oswald in her head.

The baron pulled himself together and said, "We need to get you back to my home. Drake, will you send a message to Matilda to let everyone know that Chloe saved Oswald!"

Oswald insisted that Chloe ride on him, which Chloe knew was a real honor, as gryphons only allowed their bond mate to ride them. Soon she was tucked up on a couch in front of a warm fire in the baron's living room, wrapped in a lovely quilt.

Oswald said to both the baron and Chloe, *"Queen Clotilda sends her congratulations as does Emily. Rest well, and Hans and Fire Dancer will arrive in the morning to take you home."*

Chloe thanked him and then wondered, *"How come I can hear Oswald telepathically now?"*

"I sure don't know," answered Oswald to Chloe's great amazement. They practiced back and forth and with the baron as well before he burst out laughing.

"It seems this has been quite a day for you!" he said when he'd stopped laughing. "Your first real teleport, and now you're telepathic also. And all I have to say is, I couldn't be happier for you and for all of us!"

Chloe laughed as well and said, "I guess the magic decides when powers are awakened, but I too am thrilled at the timing."

They enjoyed a lovely quiet dinner, and Chloe slept wonderfully well in the baron's guest room.

Hans and Fire Dancer arrived earlier than she'd expected, but all Hans said was, "I wasn't missing one of the baron's famous breakfasts!"

After the indisputably fantastic breakfast, Hans helped Chloe onto Fire Dancer, and soon, they were away. As they were flying back, Chloe heard Oswald saying, *"Thank you so much!"*

She answered, *"I love you, Oswald. Take good care of the baron."* For the rest of her flight to the Havenshold, she pondered the changes within her. She thought, *I'll sure have a lot to ask Libby about!*

As soon as they landed in the courtyard, Chloe was swamped with hugs and questions. Not only were Emily and Gregory there, but so were Amy and Todd, and to her great surprise, Clotilda as well.

Once everyone had gotten to hug and congratulate Chloe, Clotilda called for silence before saying, "Emily and I each received a certificate on our respective desks saying that you are now a fully qualified mage."

Chloe's jaw dropped. Clotilda continued, "Congratulations, and our heartiest congratulations and thanks for your rescue of Oswald. He is very special to us all."

Chloe said, "Thanks, and yes, I too love Oswald."

Just then, Chloe noticed that her father and Zelda had arrived in the courtyard, but she didn't have a chance to greet them, as Clotilda went on, "You know that you were warned with your last promotion that with recognition comes responsibility. Well, now, Honorable Mage, rest and relax because as news of your achievements spreads, you can expect to be called on even more. And furthermore, a fully qualified mage needs robes suitable to her new exalted rank!"

Chloe let out a loud groan, and everyone laughed! They knew how little Chloe cared for all the trappings.

Zelda hollered out, "I'll get to work on the sketches right away, and I know Mom and Grandma will be sharpening their embroidery needles."

Everyone headed into the library where Chloe was amazed to see tables laden with food and drinks. As the celebrations got into full swing, Chloe managed to sneak away to her favorite alcove with a plate of food and a mug of hot cider. She enjoyed just watching everyone. Emily came over to sit by her and then said, "Do you know how weird it was to be hugging you and then have you disappear?"

Chloe laughed. "Well, if it is any comfort, it felt really weird to me also. I think I'm going to have to practice the takeoffs and landings more."

— 25 —

EXPLANATIONS

After a good night's sleep in her own bed, Chloe was up early and headed to the library. She had a million questions for Libby.

As she walked into Libby's sitting room, Libby said, "Wonderful job! Congratulations!"

Chloe thanked her and sat down to a lovely breakfast, every bit as good as the baron's, she thought, but she'd never tell him. After she finished eating, she began to sort her questions. Just as she was going to begin, Libby said, "I bet you have a ton of questions in that head of yours. I can see your brain swirling from here!"

Chloe laughed and said, "Yes, I certainly do! I'm not even sure just where to start."

"Why don't we start with the powers you awakened yesterday?" suggested Libby.

"For sure! First off, what is the relationship between farseeing and telepathy, or is there one? I've been able to use my farseeing even close up, as when I was able to communicate with Horace and Zenith in Sanwight. But I've never been able to communicate with more than one other at a time—never until yesterday, that is."

Libby thought for a minute and then replied, "Farseeing is first and foremost a visual ability. You picture a place, and then you are able to tune it in. Those who become truly adept at farseeing, as you have, are also able to tune into the sounds of the place and hence are able to talk with anyone who is there. Does that make sense?"

"Yes," said Chloe, "but how does telepathy fit into the picture? I know that the riders and their dragons can communicate telepathically, but they don't see each other. And I know that some people, like Gregory, can communicate telepathically with some dragons, for instance, but not with other people. Argh! This is complicated."

Libby laughed. "It isn't as complicated as you might think. Telepathy is a gift of the bonding process. And those who can communicate with their own bonded mate are also, sometimes, able to communicate with others who are also telepathic. So that is why some riders can communicate with more than just their bonded mate and why some people, who have the innate ability, are able to receive telepathic communications. In Gregory's case, for instance, I suspect that he has a latent ability inherited from his father and that is why he is able to hear Esmeralda."

"OK, so I get that, I think. But I'm not bonded and I have never had telepathic gifts before. However, two days ago at the mine, I swear I heard both you and Bertha. And then later, I could 'talk' with Oswald as easily as we are now chatting. Why?"

Libby laughed. "First, you did hear both Bertha and me, but we'll get to that in a moment. Some mages do have the gift of telepathy as part of their magical gifts. You didn't seem to. And it appeared that you lacked the gift for teleporting also, except in a few isolated incidents. Yesterday, your gifts blossomed. I'm guessing that the teleporting finally clicked into place as a result of all your practicing, no matter how unsuccessfully. I think it clicked at that moment because of the need and more importantly because of your love for Oswald."

"Really?" said Chloe, reaching for another piece of toast.

"Yes, and while we thankfully won't have to prove it, I believe that if someone else whom you didn't know and had no relationship with had been trapped, that you would never have moved out of the library alcove."

"Oh," said Chloe. After a few minutes, she said, "Does that mean I will only be able to teleport in circumstances similar to that?"

"I don't think so," said Libby. "I think that now, having awakened the talent, that you will be able to use it when you want. Remember, the first time you used the farseeing ability, you needed my locket, and you also could only farsee with those you knew and loved. But now you can farsee with anyone you want, even dolphins you have just met. I believe the same will be true with the teleporting."

"If I practice, you mean."

"Yes, so why don't you try to teleport to your alcove and then back again?" suggested Libby.

"OK," said Chloe with obvious doubt in her voice.

She concentrated on her favorite chair, and before she realized it, she was sitting in it. Then she thought about the comfy couch in Libby's sitting room, and bingo, she was back again, sitting across from Libby.

"Wow, that was amazing!" Chloe said.

"Remember, now, magic takes energy, and new talents take more than established magic, so make your teleports short and not really frequent as you build confidence and ability," cautioned Libby.

"Got it, but that still doesn't answer my question about telepathy."

"Again, this is just a guess, but as far as Bertha and I can figure—and by the way, we both are telepaths as well—you have always had that latent talent, probably inherited through your mother and grandmother and all the riders that went before them in your family. You are like Gregory in that way, but you also have magic. We think the magic and your natural latent ability have combined so that you now have complete telepathic abilities. I am guessing that you will be able to sense what non-telepaths, such as your father, for example, are thinking. I'd be interested to know if this proves true, but remember to let anyone know before you attempt it."

"Certainly," said Chloe, "but that is exciting!"

"Yes, and that is why Bertha and I agreed that you were now a fully qualified if still rather inexperienced mage."

"Thanks, but what about my hearing you in my head when I was rescuing Oswald? Did you help me?"

"Not exactly," said Libby. "I was aware of your teleportation as you left the library, and I used my farseeing to confirm that you were successful in getting to the mine site. Then I contacted Bertha, and we chatted. As I said earlier, we are both telepaths, a legacy from King Alfred, and so we talked. We knew that your first teleportation, especially since it was such a long trip, would drain your energies. Neither of us would have been able to rescue Oswald, and frankly, we also decided that it wasn't our place to try. This was your mission, and we felt that it would be an excellent test of your progress and abilities."

"Thanks, I guess," said Chloe.

"At the same time, we knew that your energies would have been seriously depleted and no chocolate bar or coffee would bring them back to the point where you'd be able to move a gryphon through solid rock. So what we did do was send you energy, pure energy. Think of it in the same way as the baron's chocolate. It didn't free Oswald. It just gave you the resources so that you could perform the teleporting of Oswald using your own formidable skills."

"And I blacked out right after. I didn't even see Oswald appear."

"That's just how close your energies were to total depletion even with what we were able to send you! A lesser mage wouldn't have succeeded. And it is a good thing that Oswald doesn't have wings, or they probably would have been ripped off. Sometimes we discover unexpected benefits to what otherwise might seem like tragedies."

"I'll never forget waking up to find Oswald licking my face!" Chloe chuckled.

"And with practice, you won't require quite so much energy, although I doubt that it will ever be easy to move someone that large through solid rock. But we are thrilled that you have progressed so far so fast. Bertha thinks that before long you will discover what the prophecy means, and then you will need every bit of strength and then some. So keep practicing all your skills. And keep watching the stars."

"I will; I promise." As she stood, she added, with a wink, "The library should be opening now, so I'd better get out of here. Thanks and please thank Bertha also."

"I will, but remember, now you can link with her or me anytime you want. You won't have to wait for our morning chat, although I hope you still will keep coming."

"You better believe it! See you tomorrow," and with that, she left Libby's sitting room.

Chloe walked into the main reading room of the library and noted that both Gregory and William were already there, each in his own office. Gregory looked up when she walked past, and he hurried out to see her.

"I just wanted to thank you again for what you did for my father," said Gregory.

"And Oswald too," Chloe said with a smile.

"For sure! I love that guy too, but my father hasn't felt close to anyone since my mother died, until that is, he met Oswald. Oswald has really made a tremendous difference to him, and yes, he to Oswald also."

"Your father has always had a heart filled with love and goodness. He just lost sight of that for a while. Oswald was able to reconnect your father with his true self. And I am both thrilled and not a little humbled by the fact that I was able to do what I did. Anyway, I obviously missed my class two nights ago, but I think I have a good excuse, don't I, oh leader of the academy?"

Gregory burst out laughing. "Yes, and no worries there. When you vanished on us, I canceled the class. I tentatively rescheduled it for tonight. Does that work for you?"

"Perfectly," Chloe answered. "I've already planned the lecture. I'll just brush up on my notes."

That evening, she took the four students from the current class up to the observatory. It was a cold winter night, but the observatory was heated. She went over to the blackboard and drew the diagrams she needed for tonight's talk before beginning.

"Tonight, we will be looking at the stars in the northeastern quadrant of the sky. We are taking advantage of the fact that the moon won't rise for about six hours. The darkness provided by the moon's absence should allow us to see more stars in this quadrant."

The students took their turns looking through the telescope, and then after they all had gotten as many looks as they wanted, Chloe asked if there were any questions. Once their questions were answered, she escorted the students back down and out of the library, making sure that the doors were locked behind them, and then she returned to the observatory.

She looked up at the heavens and wondered where she would search tonight. She was noticing more and more meteor showers, and she wasn't sure if they were related to the catastrophe mentioned in the prophecy, but she was hoping to find a meteor that was headed toward the planet. She didn't want a big one, and she knew that small meteor hits weren't all that uncommon. *If I could spot one approaching and then change its course or move it away or do something to it, that might give me an idea of what I am supposed to be doing to save this planet.*

She watched for nearly an hour but then decided that she was too tired to continue. Libby was right. Her energies were at a low ebb. She walked back to Amy and Todd's, and after sharing a cup of hot chocolate with them, she headed up to bed.

— 26 —
DISCOVERIES

Chloe spent the better part of the next year practicing her magical skills and watching the heavens. The biggest personal difference in the year was the change in her relationship with her mother. Hazel had started doing embroidery piecework for Marjorie, and Zelda said that her mom really enjoyed it. Marjorie and Zelda participated in some shows in the summer, and people flocked to the ones with Hazel's embroidery. Soon, people were asking Hazel to put embroidered designs on garments they already had, just to give them a new look. Before long, she had so many requests that she and her mom could barely keep up.

What amazed Chloe most though was the way her mother seemed to be thriving, basking in the compliments and taking on every request that was made of her, even some that Chloe thought she would stick her nose up at. Schoolgirls were asking her to embroider their artwork onto pants, shirts, jackets, and even backpacks, and Hazel loved it.

Zelda still had a couple of years left as Marjorie's apprentice, but she and their mom were already talking about maybe setting up their own shop. Marjorie was really encouraging Hazel, and the two had become good friends.

When Marjorie, Zelda, and Hazel were working on Chloe's new robes, Chloe was amazed by the warm, happy atmosphere in the room, and her mom didn't once needle her as Chloe groaned and fidgeted. Oh, all three of them teased her, but there was no bitterness from her mother.

Best of all, she was now having dinner occasionally with her mom and her grandmother, and the meals were becoming increasingly pleasant and enjoyable. Chloe noticed that her mother was bragging about both her daughters, but she was also taking the credit for Zelda's designing talents and Chloe's magic. Chloe laughed the first time she heard her mother, but she was not laughing at her at all, rather enjoying the joy of realizing that her mother had found a much better path.

Her dad was fast becoming the most famous toymaker in not only Havenshold but Draconia as well. He loved his cottage, and he'd earned enough with his business to buy it and also build a bigger workshop. Things were looking up for everyone. *Now if I can only figure out what my part in all this is,* Chloe thought as she headed back up to the observatory after she had celebrated her fifth year as a mage with Libby. The solstice had been quiet this year, as it was not a hatching year, and Chloe liked the slower pace.

Her dad had made her a swivel chair at just the right height so she could sit and watch through the telescope in comfort. She picked tonight's quadrant and began her viewing. She'd gotten quite proficient at combining the telescope with her far-seeing abilities so that the net result was a magnification about three times what the telescope alone could manage.

She was beginning to tire when suddenly, she saw what she'd hoped to find, a meteor headed straight for her—well, the planet actually—but it did seem to be coming at her. It wasn't really big, and it was moving at a reasonable pace. As she tracked it, she tried sending out an energy tendril, but she came nowhere near it. Was it just too far away? How close would it need to be, and what could she actually do?

There was an asteroid belt nearly beyond the range of her telescope, but she'd never seen anything there to alarm her. She figured the prophecy had to be talking about a meteor. She kept tracking this one and realized it would be several weeks, maybe even a month, before it got really close.

She finally called it a night and headed home, but she planned a new schedule so that she would be in the observatory every clear night to watch the meteor's progress.

The next morning, Chloe explained her plan to Libby over breakfast. Libby said, "I like the idea, and it certainly would be nice if you could try stopping something small before you have to do something really big. Did Bertha tell you that she thinks the prophecy will be fulfilled before the summer solstice?"

Chloe nodded and said, "Yes, the time frame she gave me when I first became a mage seemed so long. What does a fifteen-year-old think of five to six years after all? But now, all of a sudden, it seems to be on top of me, and I still don't have a clue what it is or how to stop it."

"Well, if you can spot and stop a meteor or two as test cases, that should help. But as you are tracking this particular meteor, don't lose track of the rest of the heavens," Libby cautioned.

"I won't," Chloe promised. "I keep thinking that if it is something big enough to cause catastrophic damage, then maybe it will come from the asteroid belt. But everything there looks so stable. I just have no clue. Why can't prophesies be more specific?"

Libby laughed and said, "Not to mention seers! Anytime before the summer solstice. That's six months! How helpful is that?"

Chloe smiled and said, "Well, when she first started talking with me, she said five to six years, so I guess we are narrowing the window down."

"True," said Libby, "and we shouldn't tease. Bertha is a fantastic seer, and without her, we wouldn't have any warning at all."

Chloe kept her watch through into January, but then they had a major snowstorm that lasted for over a week and cloudy skies for the week after that. By the time Chloe could see the meteor again, it was approaching the atmosphere. Again, she stretched out a tendril of energy and tried to grab it—again to no avail. Then she tried to put up a shield just outside the planet's atmosphere. The shield seemed to be holding, but she had no idea what would happen when the meteor hit it.

Two nights later, she found out what would happen. The meteor passed through her shield as if it were butter, slowing slightly but not stopping or—as she'd really hoped—bouncing off.

But then she had an idea. What if she just slowed it down to a speed where the impact would be almost nonexistent. She sent her energy toward it much as she figured she'd done unconsciously when Zelda fell out of the tree all those years ago.

The meteor was slowing; there was no doubt about that. But was it enough, and where would it hit? She looked at its trajectory. It seemed to be headed for the northwest corner of Forbury. *I don't want it landing there,* she thought. *The land is heavily forested, and the impact could start a fire.*

With that incentive, she shifted energies slightly so that she was still slowing it but also pushing it southwest, out over the Ercesa Ocean. There was a large island she had to miss. She didn't know if it was inhabited, but she couldn't take the chance.

Sweat poured down her face, and she realized just how much energy she was using. *"Libby, Bertha, can you send me some energy? I'm losing this meteor."*

Even before she heard Bertha's cheery, *"Coming your way now!"* Chloe could feel the extra energy. She managed to change the trajectory so that the meteor would land in the ocean just barely off the coast, but the trade-off was that it hit harder than she'd hoped. Once the meteor was out of sight, she collapsed in her chair, thanking both Bertha and Libby.

She packed up her things and headed home. As she climbed into bed, she thought, *Well, that didn't make a lot of difference, and meanwhile, it was only a meteor. What more can I do?*

The next morning, she received a message from Emily asking her to come to her office as soon as she could.

When Chloe got there, Emily motioned her to a chair and said, "We received a report out of Forbury. They experienced exceptionally high waves along their western shores. Thankfully, those shores are very mountainous, so there was no damage, but they were curious if you had any idea what caused the waves."

"Actually I do," said Chloe, and she proceeded to explain what she had done. "Even with the added energy from Bertha and the library, I could only move it a short way. I couldn't get it slowed enough to prevent the high waves. And that was only a small meteor," concluded Chloe, who was obviously very discouraged.

Emily smiled at Chloe and said, "You have done something really amazing, something no one else would even have thought of. And you prevented major damage in Forbury, damage that would have struck close to the baron's house, I might add."

"But it wasn't enough, and it won't be nearly enough if something bigger comes at us," moaned Chloe.

"Maybe not, but the fact that you could channel extra energy from Bertha is amazing. And just what is the library?"

Emily held up her hand as Chloe was about to speak. "I know, you can't say anything, but it doesn't take a genius to realize that the library is magical. Let's just leave it at that. My question now is can you only channel energy or do you get recharged, so to speak, from those two sources? And are they the only possible sources?"

Chloe blinked and tipped her head up in excitement. "I don't know. They are the only two other sources of magic that I know of." She stopped for a minute and then went on, "But there is a connection between my magic and the telepathy shared by bonded pairs. I was never telepathic until I rescued Oswald, and Lib—I mean the *library* has shown me the connection. Do you think maybe dragons and riders could help?"

Emily laughed and said, "I am sure I don't know, but it sounds as if that possibility ought to be explored and explored fast, if Bertha is right about the time table. Why don't you start by seeing if William could boost your energy? This sounds like just the sort of experiment he would like, and he knows more about telepathy than anyone else on the planet. Let him help figure this out. And let me know right away when you find out one way or another, because if it works with dragons and riders, it should also work with other bonded pairs. I can then get the word out."

"Sure," said Chloe, feeling much more hopeful than she had when she arrived.

"Oh, and if you and William meet with any kind of success, try to figure out how far away the person or being can be and still send power. My guess is that the baron and Oswald would love to help with that."

"Right," said Chloe, and she ran out of the office.

Chloe was still running when she burst into William's office. He looked up from his papers, startled, and said, "What can I do for you?"

Chloe took a minute to catch her breath, and then she told him what had happened the previous night and how the power channeling had worked and then about Emily's idea. Chloe could see the excitement growing in William's eyes as she spoke, and as soon as she was done, he jumped right in.

"You know, there have been documented accounts of times when a rider was facing exhaustion, especially if they'd been hurt, and their dragon kept them going. The accounts mention feelings of renewed energies. And it has also worked the other way around when a dragon has been flying through a storm, for instance, and doesn't have the strength to stay aloft, but then the rider pours power into the dragon. Of course, the reports don't call it that. They talk about how love can manage unusual powers, but it sounds an awful lot like what you say Bertha and the library," he added with a question in his voice, but Chloe merely nodded, "what they were able to do for you."

"So you think it might work? How can we test it? We need to know soon because if it does, we'll have to figure out how to combine energies once we know whatever the threat is and when it is coming."

"And Bertha says it will be before the summer solstice?" asked William.

Chloe nodded and said, "Bertha's window keeps narrowing. When she first told me, it was five to six years out, and now it is within the next six months, which is still indefinite and also not a lot of time if we are going to try something totally new."

"Right. Well, let's start first with me and Thunder. Can you feel the surge of energy even when you aren't calling upon it?" asked William.

"Your guess is as good as mine. Hmm. Let me ask the library for some energy now, and I'll see."

"Libby, did you hear any of this?"

"Yes, my dear. When you came running, I figured you'd want me to listen, and after all, you both were speaking aloud, so I could always hear."

"That's fine! I'm glad. So could you try sending me an energy boost now?"

"Did you feel that?"

"Maybe a little," answered Chloe.

"How about now?" asked Libby as Chloe bounced out of her chair.

"Yep, thanks. I felt that."

Chloe sat back down and said to a very puzzled-looking William, "Yes, it does work. I suspect the flow would be better if I were using the power, but I could feel it."

Chloe, William, and Thunder worked all afternoon. Chloe was really glad she had made William's office so big, because even curled up, Thunder took up a lot of space. They discovered that William and Thunder could channel energy back and forth, which William found very exciting. He was all ready to race off and test other riders when Chloe pointed out that as nice as that was, and undoubtedly helpful, it didn't really solve their problem.

"Well, what if we tried it when you were in need of energy?" said William. "Can you do something that you need a lot of energy for?"

Chloe thought for a moment, and then she said, "What if I tried to teleport someone else? I know, what if I brought Gregory here from his office? I'll go ask him."

William got a twinkle in his eye and said, "No, let's just do it."

"But that's not part of the mage code. You can't just invade someone's world."

"However, we don't intend any harm, and isn't it true that Gregory has telepathic abilities? Well, we want to see what Thunder and I can do, and if he knows, he might inadvertently help."

Chloe thought the logic was definitely spurious, but she also believed that Gregory would enjoy the joke if it did work, so she agreed. She concentrated on teleporting Gregory and also on drawing the necessary energy from William and Thunder. It was challenging not to use her own resources, but she thought she'd managed it. Suddenly, Gregory was standing on William's desk.

"What the heck is going on?" he demanded, and then, looking at William, he added, "And wipe that smirk off your face!"

As he climbed carefully off the desk so as not to disturb Thunder, Chloe explained what they were doing and why they were trying it. Gregory caught on really fast and said, "Well, did it work?"

Chloe started to say, "I'm not sure—"

But William interrupted. "Both Thunder and I felt as if our energy was draining out of us, and I'm glad it didn't last any longer."

"So it worked!" exclaimed Chloe.

"We're going to need a lot more practice, though. We need to be able to monitor our own energies so that we give you what you need without draining ourselves and so that the flow is steady, because I would imagine you'd need that."

Chloe said, "You are right. But first, Emily wanted to know about distances. Gregory, are you game to be teleported a bit more, now that you know why?"

"Definitely," answered Gregory. "I am finding this fascinating."

"OK, thanks," said Chloe, "but remember, since you also have some telepathic powers, don't do anything to help."

"Right," said Gregory.

Chloe contacted Emily telepathically and updated her on the situation and then asked if she would let Chloe draw on her to send Gregory back to his office. Emily readily agreed, and Chloe concentrated again. In the blink of an eye, Gregory was back in his office, smiling and waving.

Emily reported, *"It felt as if my energy was just draining away."*

"I know, we have to work on that part for sure, but still, it works at that distance. I'll keep you posted."

Chloe turned back to William, and they decided to try it again with Hans and Fire Dancer in the capital. Once again, Gregory was whisked into William's office, and once again, Hans reported the energy drain.

The last test of the day was with Oswald and the baron. This time, Chloe asked William and Thunder to boost her telepathic powers, and she found that she could then reach all the way to the baron's home! The effort was made again, and Chloe was really surprised to find that it worked. She had to draw a bit on William and Thunder, but she got most of the power from Oswald and the baron.

The baron reported the same energy drain, but he and Oswald were really thrilled to have helped. Chloe thanked them and promised they'd be hearing more.

Gregory walked into William's office this time and said, "I could get used to this teleporting thing, you know. It was rather fun."

Chloe laughed, and William told Thunder he could go. Chloe thanked Thunder, and he said, *"My pleasure,"* as he carefully maneuvered himself out of William's office and the library.

William couldn't wait to make his observations. "Do you realize what this means? We'll be able to communicate over much longer distances, and we'll even be able to teleport people using bonded pairs!"

Gregory laughed and reminded him, "And Chloe! You do need her. Without our mage, this wouldn't have happened."

"Well, yes," said William, and he paused before going on, "But it is still amazing."

Gregory and William agreed, and then Gregory said, "What now?"

"Well," said Chloe and William at the same time, and then William went red in the face and motioned to Chloe to continue.

"I want to check with my sources on this. We need to find a way to make sure that no matter how much power I need, I don't drain anyone too far. After all, it will do no good to save the planet and not have any riders left."

"I noticed that when you called on Thunder and me to supplement what the baron and Oswald were sending that we didn't feel near the same drain, and we were even able to regulate the flow."

"That's the key," said Chloe. "We will need lots of linked pairs, and we should also have a monitor. But for now, what do you say to my asking Emily to notify all riders about this plan and to see if we can work with them in small groups?"

"And we can check with the baron to see if the Forbury gryphon riders want to participate. Hans can ask both Granvale and Sanwight—I'm sure Sanwight will," said Chloe, "and then we can set up a master schedule for tests."

William said, "I'll start drawing up a template for the schedule. Say, Gregory, do you want to be our resident traveler?"

Gregory leaned over and rumpled his brother-in-law's hair. "Of course, little bro."

The meeting broke up with everyone laughing. Chloe headed back to her alcove to write up a detailed report for Emily, and then she went home, feeling much more optimistic than she had in a while.

— 27 —

EXPERIMENTS

The next morning, work began in earnest. William set up his spreadsheet to use for assignments. He started by putting in all the active riders and their dragons. He then moved to the retired dragons and riders, such as his in-laws. And finally, he penciled in the apprentice dragons and riders, starting with the ones who would graduate next year and working down to the most recent apprentices.

"Do you think we will have to use apprentices?" asked Chloe.

"Maybe not, but I do think we need to devise a system so that if needed, we can keep calling on energy for as long as you require it," answered William.

"I agree, but let's space things out a bit more and spread our tests to both Forbury and Sanwight, who have now agreed to help us. What about testing all the active riders from all three nations first, then moving to the retired pairs in each nation, and finally the apprentices. That will mean that we have the most experienced and hopefully the most powerful sorted out first, and it will also give the apprentices more time to learn."

"Excellent idea," agreed William. "And I'll encourage all three nations to increase their apprentices' training, both to strengthen their bonds and increase their telepathic skills."

The next two months flew by with every day involving a number of testing sessions. It was most gratifying to discover that the dolphins and riders could send energy just fine, as long as they were in the grotto under the palace. The gryphons were equally powerful, and Chloe was sure that none of them would want to show themselves to be less powerful than the baron and Oswald. Competitions were actually developing, and Chloe encouraged that as long as they stayed friendly. Various prizes were awarded and the entire experiment started to take on the air of a contest.

Gregory quickly tired of being the pawn in this game, and so Chloe and William asked for volunteers. They were swamped with people who wanted to be teleported. Many who had never thought to become riders now thought that it would be fun to see what teleportation felt like.

Chloe also wanted to try teleporting people farther than just across the library, so again, William set up a spreadsheet for volunteers, taking down their names and ages, and then he added a column for destination. Chloe had some in mind, but they decided to let the volunteer pick where he or she wanted to go.

The results were amazing. People who had never been outside Havenshold suddenly wanted to see the ocean, visit a mine, or even go to visit family or friends in neighboring villages. Chloe set things up so that people were transported out of the library during the morning and then retrieved during the late afternoon and early evening.

These day trips, as they came to be called, became incredibly popular, so popular that Chloe and William had more volunteers to travel than they had bonded pairs to test. Chloe suggested sending two at a time. Her abilities were growing rapidly, and she knew she had to strengthen her own skills as quickly as possible.

The atmosphere in Havenshold was very festive indeed, but that ended in early April. Chloe was in the observatory watching for any sign of trouble. It was getting closer to the solstice, and Bertha, now awakened from her winter hibernation, could not pinpoint things any more closely. She kept most of her watch on the asteroid belt as she just felt that any trouble would come from there. She'd also been watching an approaching comet, which hadn't yet entered the asteroid belt.

Suddenly, she saw the comet hit an asteroid, sending it spinning out of the belt. She watched carefully, using her farseeing ability to its fullest and was horrified to see the asteroid falling away from the belt, tagging along for a bit with the comet that had hit it before taking on a new trajectory.

She grabbed paper and pencil and went to her charts. Plotting the asteroid's new trajectory, she realized that Bertha was right. The asteroid was headed straight for her planet. And it was a lot larger than the meteor she had sort of moved last February. By her calculations, unless something happened, the asteroid would hit in early June, just two months from now.

Chloe notified everyone she could think of the next morning, and she could feel the somber tone filtering through the entire community. Many people had forgotten in the fun of the experiment just why they were doing all this.

Talking telepathically with Clotilda, Chloe had explained her calculations, promising that she would check them again and again. Clotilda replied, *"I definitely want daily updates, first thing each morning. And I am going to contact all the other monarchs. I know Sanwight and Forbury are prepared, but maybe now Granvale will realize we weren't just making things up."*

"I could only see this by using both my telescope and my farseeing abilities," said Chloe. *"But within the next month, everyone should be able to see the asteroid in the sky with their own*

*eyes, if they know where to look. And of course it will keep get-
ting bigger."*

"I understand. Good luck!"

The testing was nearly done, and Chloe and William had
compiled lists of pairs and their strengths and who worked best
with whom. They weren't the least surprised that bonded pairs
worked best with their spouses, and Amy and Todd, with Fern
and Jupiter, proved to be at the top of the strength lists.

They were now testing the apprentices and, also no surprise,
their strengths were directly proportional to the length of time
they had been bonded. Today, they would be testing Chloe's
friends, Patty and her green dragon, Emerald; Steven and his
red dragon, Winifred: and George with Egbert the blue one.

Just as they were getting ready to start, Hazel walked in. "I
want to know if you would use me as a test subject."

Chloe looked at her mother in surprise. "You want to do
this? Are you sure?"

"Yes," said her mother with a strong but not demanding
voice. "I really want to help. The entire community is pulling
together on this, riders and non-riders alike, and now that the
threat has been confirmed, I want to be sure I do my bit also."
She paused for a minute before saying, "I haven't always felt
as if I belonged here, but now I'm starting to, so please, may I
help?"

Chloe looked at William, who nodded. Then Chloe looked at
the next volunteer who had been planning to be sent, and the
young woman shrugged her shoulders, nodded, and stepped
back into the line of volunteers.

"OK, Mom," said Chloe with a smile. "Looks as if you are
next. Where do you want to go for the day?"

Hazel looked down at her feet, and her cheeks reddened
before she finally looked at Chloe and said, "I'd like to go visit
Bertha, and I'd like to stay for three days, if I can."

"Bertha?" said Chloe. "Why do you want to see her?"

"She's made such a difference in your life, and you really seem to blossom more over each summer. I just thought... maybe...she could help me," Hazel concluded.

Chloe was dumbfounded. Her mother really was changing. After a minute, she said, "OK, let me check with Bertha first."

"Bertha, would you like some company? My mother wants to visit you and not just for a day but for three days."

"Wonderful," said Bertha. *"I could use a visit after the long winter. Send her along."*

"Thanks, and, Bertha, you'll let me know she made it OK, won't you?"

"Of course, now send her over."

Chloe went over to her mother and gave her a big hug. "Bertha says it is OK, so here goes. We are using apprentices for today's test, and it is Patty and Emerald's turn."

Both women turned toward Patty and Emerald, who definitely looked nervous, as Patty was wringing her hands and Emerald kept pawing at the rug in William's office.

Chloe said, "William, will you and Thunder stand by, in case we need you?"

William nodded, and Chloe said, "Ready, Mom?"

Hazel stood up straight and tall and said, "Ready!"

Chloe concentrated on Bertha's cave and also on Patty and Emerald. She could feel their power, and using only that, she started the teleportation. Partway there, she could feel William add a little bit of his own power, and her mother was gone.

"Got her," said Bertha before Chloe could even wonder. *"Now don't worry about a thing. We're going to have a nice visit, and you can take her back on Friday evening."*

"Thanks, Bertha."

Chloe then looked at Patty and Emerald. "How did that feel?"

Patty gave the answer that was so familiar now, "I thought all our energy was draining away."

Chloe then looked at William, "I felt you give an added boost."

William nodded and said, "I could feel them weakening. I think we will find that the apprentices will need to be in larger clusters. Let's try with these three." He pointed at Patty, Steven, and George. "As a team. We'll go into the main reading room so that Steven and George can bring Winifred and Egbert in as well."

Chloe looked at the young woman who had agreed to let her mother cut in line and said, "Aster, thank you for letting my mother through. Now where would you like to go?"

Aster really surprised her. "I want to go to one of the islands in the Sprite Sea. I'll be finishing school this spring, and I haven't decided what I want to do afterward, but I do know I want to see somewhere that I've never seen before."

Chloe thought for a minute before turning to William, "Do we know anything about those islands?"

"I bet Benjamin and Horace do," he answered quickly. "Why don't we ask them? It would be a wonderful test for you to teleport her somewhere you have never been."

"Yeah," said Chloe, "if it works." As William communicated with Benjamin, Chloe looked at Aster and said, "Do you realize just how risky this is?"

"Yes," Aster said firmly. "And face it, if you aren't able to stop the asteroid, none of us will be around anyway, right? William said this would really help you also, so please."

Chloe looked at William, who said, "Benjamin and Horace have visited the largest of the islands, and he says he is sure he can guide you. We'll use all three apprentice pairs, and Benjamin and Horace will lend support there as well."

"But how will we know if she reaches the island safely?" said Chloe with a very worried tone in her voice.

"Sometimes you just have to trust," said Aster with a wisdom beyond her years. And then she smiled. "You'll know when you bring me back tonight!"

"Aster, you are incredibly brave! William, grab some of those protein bars and a water bottle for her to take."

After a few minutes, they had a backpack outfitted for Aster. Benjamin had let William know that the island was uninhabited, and there were no known dangers, which eased some of Chloe's fears.

Finally, they were ready. Aster looked excited, and Patty, Steven, and George looked nervous. "OK, let's give it a try," said Chloe. She received the visual picture from Benjamin showing the island in as much detail as he knew, primarily a beach he'd taken a nap on once ages ago. Gathering the energy from the three apprentices and their bonded mates, she concentrated on the view of that beach and sent Aster on her way.

"Well, wherever she went," said William, "she left here."

"This is going to be a very long day," said Chloe.

The two of them worked through the day with the last of the apprentices, the ones who had just been bonded for a little over two years. Chloe found that while they did have some energy to give, they would definitely need to be in clusters, possibly with more experienced pairs.

"I agree," said William as the last of the pairs to be tested left. "But we do want to know about absolutely all the energy we have available to us."

"You are right. That asteroid is huge. Now I can't wait any longer. Let's bring Aster back."

"Benjamin and Horace are waiting. I thought we'd just use them, in case there are any problems."

"Thanks, William."

Chloe connected with Benjamin and Horace and then brought the vision of the beach into focus. She reached out to grab Aster. At first, she couldn't find her, but then all of a sudden, she had her.

Chloe opened her eyes when she heard William say, "Hi, Aster!"

Chloe ran and hugged her and then thanked Benjamin and Horace. Benjamin signed off after asking if he could get a full report on what Aster found.

"Aster, how was your day?" asked Chloe.

"It was absolutely fantastic. The island is wonderful! There are beaches and then forests. Oh, I'd love to explore more. I nearly didn't get back to the beach in time. I had to run the last bit to be sure I was there when you said to be."

"That explains why I couldn't find you at first," said Chloe with relief in her voice. "Well, we are all tired now. You go home, but I want a full, detailed report from you soon. We can work something out with Miss Murphy to give you extra credit. And if you can, drawings or a map would be a nice addition."

Aster promised, and after giving Chloe a hug and saying, "Thank you so much," she headed out of the library.

"Whew," said Chloe. "I don't know about you, but I'm all done in. I'm going to go home for dinner and a bit of quiet time before coming back to track that horrible asteroid."

William agreed, and they both left for their homes.

— 28 —
A STRATEGY

The next morning, Chloe and William met to discuss what to do next. Every bonded pair—active, retired, apprenticed—from all three nations had now been tested and their strengths measured.

Just as they were starting to formulate their next step, Emily stopped by. "Just heard from Clotilda, and now, since they can actually see the approaching asteroid in the sky, Granvale has offered their strength as well."

"Finally!" said William.

"That is wonderful news," said Chloe.

Emily continued, "You are to communicate through Elizabeth and Jerome. They will connect you with Granvale's bonded pairs. Can you start with them today?"

"Certainly," said William. "I've worked with Elizabeth and Jerome, and they are a bit standoffish, but nowhere near as prickly as Queen Penelope and Bright Star!"

"Well, I'll leave you to it then. Good luck," said Emily as she departed.

Chloe and William resumed their meeting, and Chloe said, "I wonder how my mom is doing with Bertha?"

"I'm sure they are both fine, and she will be back in two days. If there were any problems, Bertha would have contacted you."

"I know. I'm worrying needlessly. Now what shall we do next? I know we want to test the Granvale pairs, but we also have to develop some overall strategies," said Chloe.

"What if we contact Elizabeth now and see what she is thinking and then try to set it up so that we only test for half a day and spend the other half of the day sorting our data and making plans."

"Sounds like a plan. Would you contact Elizabeth? You know her much better than I."

"Sure," said William.

Once William was in contact with Elizabeth, he brought Chloe into the discussion so that they could have a three-way conference.

"Sure glad Granvale is willing to help," said William.

"Yes, thanks," said Chloe before adding, *"I think we are going to need everyone's help."*

"I really don't think that you are going to be able to do any-thing. That asteroid is large and heading straight for us. But Queen Penelope wanted us to offer whatever assistance we can. At least it will give us the illusion of doing something before we are all blown to smithereens," said Elizabeth, sounding very resigned to the inevitable.

Chloe could feel William's anger rising, so she put a hand on his arm and replied to Elizabeth, *"Your help is most appreciated."*

"Well, neither the queen nor I has the time or frankly the patience for this. We've heard all about the frivolity of your experiments. But on the off chance that this might save the world, I'm delegating Heather and her unicorn, Helena, to be your contact from now on. I suggest that you draw on me and Jerome and teleport Heather to your office. When you are done with whatever it is you are going to do, let me know, and we'll

bring her back. That will give you a reading on me and Jerome. Rest assured, we are a bit stronger than Queen Penelope and Bright Star, so that will take care of testing for the four of us."

"Certainly," said Chloe with her hand still on William's arm. *"Whenever you are ready."*

With no further ado, Chloe teleported Heather into William's office. Then she contacted Elizabeth. *"Can you tell me how that felt on your end?"*

Elizabeth didn't answer at first and then said, *"Honestly, I didn't really expect to feel anything, but both Jerome and I felt a tremendous loss in energy. Is that usual?"*

"Yes, that is what everyone reports. What we are working on now is a plan to link bonded pairs together in compatible groups and then set up something like a chained link or branched tree so the energy flows evenly to me, but without anyone being unduly drained and hopefully with enough power for me to move and/or slow the asteroid."

Again, there was a pause before Elizabeth finally said, *"I'm beginning to see what you are driving at. I have to admit I've always felt all this mage hype was a bit much and honestly, even with your robes, you're not very impressive. You haven't been flashing any power around on your visits."*

Now it was Chloe's turn to watch her anger. *"I have had no need to, as you say, flash power. But if you need a reference, I suggest you check in with Baron Geldsmith and Oswald. Now we will discuss everything with Heather, and we'll let you know when we are ready for her to return."*

Heather, who had been privy to all that, burst out laughing as soon as Chloe broke contact. "You are amazing, Chloe, and I am so glad that Elizabeth is a snob. Otherwise, she wouldn't have foisted the assignment onto me since she considered it to be a pointless waste of time. And that traveling by teleportation is awesome! How can I help?"

Chloe and William quickly brought her up-to-date and showed her the results so far. Then Chloe pulled out a sheet of paper with the names of all the bonded pairs listed on it. They worked out a schedule to test all the Granvale pairs over the next two weeks, but that would bring them to the third week in May.

"That is cutting it close," said Chloe. "I can't be exactly sure, of course, but from what I have been able to figure out based on the asteroid's current speed and trajectory, it will be entering our atmosphere by the second week in June."

"That soon?" said Heather.

"I'm afraid so," said Chloe. "What you will need to do in addition to supervising the testing is to talk to your riders and work out some grouping for us of those you think will work well together. We are finding that married bonded pairs, such as William's in-laws and their two dragons, work really well together and that the combined strength is more than double, in fact in some cases quadruple, what it is separately."

"That would really make a difference," said Heather, "but how will I know?"

William said, "We've found that bonded pairs with the strongest telepathic links work best. For example, as Chloe has mentioned, my in-laws are able to communicate telepathically with each other and with both dragons. And they can communicate with the other one's dragon nearly as easily as with their actual bonded mate. I think the telepathic abilities are tied closely to the amount of energy a given pair can provide."

"Got it," said Heather. "But should we be putting strong with strong, or trying for a balance with strong helping the weaker?"

"That is a very good question, and we are going to be testing things out both ways on our end. If you can just be noting who seems most compatible, then we can form the actual groups."

The three of them worked for a bit longer on the schedule, and then William copied off the relevant dates and times on a paper for Heather to take back. "This has us starting right away, this afternoon, if that works for you. The more we've talked, the more I've come to realize that we really need to get the testing all done and have a list of all participants and their strength levels before we can move forward. So if your riders and unicorns are willing, I'd like to test as many as possible each day. I'm afraid we can't give them the luxury of day trips as we did earlier because we are simply running out of time," concluded William.

"I understand, and after all, if the queen and Elizabeth hadn't been such snobs and if they'd checked into things earlier, well, we could have had the day trips. Oh well," she said, and then she grinned. "But maybe after you save the world, I could go to see the dolphins!"

Chloe laughed. She really liked this young woman and her spunky can-do attitude. She'd make sure she looked her up once her tours resumed, always assuming they did, of course. "I'd be happy to," she answered. "Now, shall we send you home?"

When they contacted Elizabeth, they got a major surprise. It seemed that after their last conversation Queen Penelope had contacted both King Alfred and the baron and what she'd heard, especially about Oswald's remarkable rescue, made her rethink her attitude. Elizabeth said, *"Queen Penelope and Bright Star would like to be your energy source for the return trip. She was most impressed with what she's heard about you and your powers."*

Chloe refrained from giving back a sharp retort or even reminding them that it wasn't smart to judge people on looks alone. Instead, she said, *"We'd be honored, Your Majesty, and that way, we can get an accurate reading on your powers rather than having to guess."*

The teleportation went swiftly and easily, and as before, Chloe asked what sensations the queen noticed. The queen replied, *"I have never felt anything like it before, and neither has Bright Star. Our power just seemed to drain away. It was almost frightening."*

Chloe was quick to reassure her and to let her know that her reaction was typical and that they would be combining pairs so that no one would be injured.

"Honestly, at first, I thought you were making this all up. And then when I could actually see this horrible thing headed right for us, I felt our world was doomed and that you and your experiments were just providing a false hope. But now, after what Elizabeth and I have learned, I actually believe that maybe you will be able to pull off another miraculous rescue. Granvale will help in any way we can."

"Thank you, Your Majesty, and I certainly hope I can do it also, but I know for sure that I can't do it alone."

After they broke off the conversation with Granvale, William said, "How about that for a turnabout."

"I think the queen is very old school and that she thinks the way my mother and grandmother and, truth be known, many people do—that the way you dress tells the whole story. I hate that, although I can see how even with my lovely robes, I might not inspire a lot of confidence."

"You sure will after you save the world," said William confidently.

They started testing the Granvale pairs that very afternoon and discovered that the testing went really easily and quickly. Chloe suspected that the queen and Elizabeth had something to do with that, and she was very grateful. They had finished gathering all the data by the middle of May. That was the good news. The bad news was that the asteroid seemed to be picking up speed, so now Chloe's best guess was early June.

They had been so caught up in the new testing that they nearly forgot to bring Hazel back from Bertha's. Chloe was very glad when Bertha contacted her to let her know that Hazel was ready. *"I nearly forgot!"* Chloe said, and Bertha laughed.

Chloe and William decided to bring Hazel back using the next pair from Granvale as a way to confirm information about distance and directions. The teleportation worked easily and smoothly, once again letting them know that the distances didn't affect the power availability in any significant way.

Once Hazel arrived, she gave Chloe a big hug. Chloe was amazed at the radiant glow in her mother's face. "I don't really need to ask, but did you have a good time?" said Chloe.

"Oh yes, and I will have so much to share with you once you have taken care of that pesky asteroid!" exclaimed her mother.

Pesky asteroid! Is that my mother talking? She must have picked that up from Bertha! Chloe kept her thoughts to herself; she just hugged her mother and said, "I am so glad you had a good trip. I'll look forward to hearing all about it," and she walked her mother out of the library.

The next two weeks were a bit frantic as plans were made. Everyone had ideas, and pulling it all together required a lot of skill on Chloe's part. Emily, the baron, Heather, and Benjamin had each grouped their bonded pairs into different configurations of varying sizes. For instance, Amy and Todd were paired together with their dragons as a foursome. But they were also listed with Emily, Esmeralda, and surprisingly, Gregory as another possibility, and so it went.

Then the next stage was arranging these groups into some sort of branchlike configuration so that Chloe could draw power as needed without weakening the entire structure. The larger configurations contained groups from each of the nations so that the power was spread out over the entire planet. Chloe did this in case she had to raise a shield for part or, heaven forbid, all of the planet.

Her mother showed up at one of the meetings with an idea of her own. "You folks are all concentrating on the power from the bonded pairs and that is obviously the most important thing. But have you thought about support for the pairs or groups or whatever? Chloe, if you, for instance, draw on Amy and Todd and then move on to another, Amy, Todd, Fern, and Jupiter will need sustenance so that they could be called on again. Am I making any sense? I'm not entirely sure I understand all this, but I do know that a lot of non-riders are asking how they can help, so I thought of this."

Chloe looked at William and then back at her mother. "You are brilliant! What do you think, William?"

"I think your mother has provided me with a new way to organize this. If the network keeps up a constant stream of power to you, but the network itself keeps taking that power from groups in rotation, then with your plan, Hazel, we could, in theory, have an infinite source of power for Chloe to work with," William concluded.

"So it's a good idea?" asked Hazel, a bit confused by William's response.

"It is an absolutely marvelous idea, Mom," said Chloe. "But can you organize it in time?"

"Of course I can," said her mother. "I will need a coordinator though from each of the other nations."

"We'll get that for you. I know Bernard would love to do it in Forbury, and I have some other ideas for Granvale and Sanwight. I've met some wonderful folks during my tours. I'll get you the names right away."

Hazel looked happier than Chloe could remember ever seeing her as she said, "Right, well, I'd better get cracking!"

As the first of June rolled around, Chloe and William reviewed all their plans. "Each of the clusters in the network has been notified, and the order for the power to circulate has been confirmed," began William.

"The clusters have also been working on strengthening their telepathic links," continued Chloe.

"Your mother has done an incredible job of organizing the relief forces. She and her fellow leaders in the other three nations were right about having all the bonded pairs located in a central point in each nation. Granvale and Sanwight will be using their capitals; Forbury will be at the baron's, and then the dragon riders will all be here in Havenshold," said William.

"I can't believe that King Alfred and Fredrick were willing to leave their castle, but the baron pointed out that he had a lot more resources for Bernard to use for the support crew. And can you believe Bertha is coming to Havenshold with her twins? My mother has even provided for minders for the twins. I think Sylvester will get that honor." Chloe chuckled.

"Everyone is gathering, and now we just need to see what that asteroid will do," said William.

"I'll be watching each night, and all I have to say is that I am sure glad it is nearly summer and that the skies are clear," said Chloe.

"Well, you get all the rest you can. The rest of us are well taken care of, so you just need to be sure you are in peak condition."

"Yes, sir," she said, giving him a mock salute.

— 29 —

THE PROPHECY

Everything that could be done had been done. Everyone was on standby, alert for the final message calling them to action. The asteroid was close enough now that Chloe decided she had to try something. She talked with Bertha and Libby and then said, "Tonight, let's see just what our possibilities are. Would you two be willing to back me up as I try to reach out to the asteroid? We only have a few days left."

Libby said, "I think that is a really good idea. You are much stronger than you were with the meteor, and we can certainly lend you our magic as well."

Bertha and Chloe climbed up into the astronomy tower, and Libby resumed her natural amorphous shape, in which her magic was stronger. Chloe opened the dome and focused the telescope on the asteroid. "It looks gigantic!" she moaned. "What if I can't stop it?"

"Of course you can," said Bertha. "That's what the prophecy said."

"Not exactly," said Chloe. "It only says that a mage will appear in time of great peril. It never says that the mage will succeed."

"Then why would the prophecy have been written? There would have been no need to say that the mage would come if the mage was going to fail."

"Maybe," said Chloe doubtfully, "and maybe I'm just not the right mage."

"Don't be silly, and don't start doubting yourself now! It is time to get to work. What did you have in mind?" answered Bertha in a no-nonsense voice that would brook no dissent.

Chloe laughed, shook herself, and said, "Right! I want to try reaching out tendrils of energy to the asteroid. If we can reach that far, then I want to try to drag it or slow it down."

"Excellent idea," chimed in Libby. "Let's give it a try."

Chloe reached out using her farseeing abilities and managed to get a tendril to touch the asteroid all on her own. "Wow, I'm here!" exclaimed Chloe.

"Nice work," said Libby. "We will feed you our magic as you need."

With that assurance, Chloe sent the tendril around the asteroid, or at least around one projection on it. *Thank heavens it is really bumpy,* she thought. Then she focused all her energies on the asteroid, very glad that she had Bertha and Libby backing her. She wouldn't have to give a thought to taking energy from them because unlike the bonded pairs, they knew how to send energy. Once she was fully focused, she tried to move the asteroid to the north. Its current trajectory was heading for an impact on Draconia's border with Granvale, so the shortest distance to get it to miss the planet was to the north.

She used all her own energies and then added the inpouring of much more energy from Bertha and Libby. Sweat was running down her face, but the asteroid wasn't shifting at all, not even a tremor. She stopped and said, "That isn't working. Let me try a shield and see if I can slow the speed with the drag of the shield.

Chloe tried again but could only manage a dish shield in front of the asteroid before all three of them were totally exhausted. Bertha collapsed on the floor, and Chloe slumped in the chair next to her. Libby seemed to recover first because after a few minutes, some sandwiches and tea appeared next to both Bertha and Chloe.

Once she had eaten, Chloe returned to the telescope to see if she had accomplished anything. "Look at that beast. Even with the shield, it is still barreling straight for us. Nothing I did made the slightest difference."

"That's not good," said Libby, "because face it, what Bertha and I can give you in the way of energy is more than half what you can get from the energy network. The network has the advantage of not running out of steam, thanks to the way William has designed it and your mother is supporting it, but their power isn't magical and hence nowhere nearly as strong as what Bertha and I can provide."

"On top of that," added Chloe. "I realized tonight that with the two of you, I don't have to focus on drawing the power from you. You simply feed it to me as I need it. That means that whenever we try the network, you two will have to monitor it and take the power so that you can feed it to me without my having to think about it. So we did learn that tonight."

"I admit that I hadn't realized that either," said Bertha. "That is useful information, but what now?"

"Now we are stopping for tonight. I need Robert, as he has a lot more knowledge of physics and structures. If he can tell me how to change the trajectory, maybe I can be more efficient."

"We need to just hit it out of the sky," said Bertha waving her right paw as if she were going to smack it.

"That's it!" exclaimed Chloe. "I need to send something a lot bigger than an energy tendril. There needs to be impact. After all, that is what the comet did to knock the asteroid loose in the first place."

Libby said, "That is fine and dandy as far as it goes, but how are you going to hit it? And with what? And where?"

"I know," said Chloe, sinking back into her chair. "I have no idea. But we do need Robert. Even if I figured out how to throw something at it—and that is a pretty big if—I'd still need to know where to hit it to get it off of its path toward us."

And with those not-very-encouraging thoughts, they called it a night.

The next morning, Chloe contacted Clotilda and asked if she would talk to Robert and see if he would come to Havenshold.

"If you need him, he will be there," said Clotilda. "I'll send someone for him, and once he is here, then we can teleport him to you."

"Oh thanks so much!" responded Chloe.

True to her word, Clotilda found Robert, and he was in the library by late morning. "This teleportation is pretty darned cool," said Robert. "Now how can I help?"

Chloe explained her idea, and Robert thought on it and then dragged out paper and began sketching and figuring. After about a half hour, he said, "You would need something large, moving fast, so that is the first problem, and then you would need to hit the asteroid right here," he concluded pointing to his diagram. "And then, with a lot of luck, its trajectory would alter enough so that it would go past us toward the sun instead of hitting us."

"Can you think of any other way to change the trajectory?" Chloe asked, suddenly overwhelmed by the magnitude of her task.

"No, honestly, I can't. If you hadn't thought of hitting it, then that is just what I would have suggested as the only hope."

"So what should we do?" asked Chloe.

"My suggestion would be that you take a practice shot or two. I think you should get the mechanism down first. That asteroid isn't going to get angry if you swat it a few times. So start with, say, a twenty-five-pound rock and see if you are able to get it to hit the asteroid in the right spot."

"That's just what we need to do," said Chloe, suddenly feeling better at having a plan. "I'll need lots of target practice, and I know Bertha and the library can help with the smaller target practice. But what do you think we will have to use for the real shot?"

"Honestly, I'm not sure we have anything that would be big enough. Hey, didn't I hear about a meteor hitting near the coast of Forbury? How big was that?"

"Bigger than any rock we could quarry here on the planet," she said, "but I dropped it into the ocean."

"Well, I say that we send the gryphons and their riders to find out just where it is and then figure out how to get it onto the land, if that is even possible."

"They sure know more about rocks than any of us," said Chloe. "OK, during the day, we work on raising the meteor, and at night, I'll take target practice."

"I'll watch your target practices to see if I need to adjust my figures, and we'll know more once we find out if the meteor can be retrieved."

Chloe immediately contacted the baron. *"Do you think your people can find the meteor?"*

"We'll get right on it, and as soon as I know anything, I'll contact you. How much time do we have?"

"Not more than five days," answered Chloe.

Next on her list was to get help locating suitable practice rocks. Bertha joined them, and she, Chloe, Robert, and William planned. "It doesn't make sense to lug the rocks up to the observatory," Bertha noted. "For sure, that meteor will never get up there. I think you'd better come up with a long-distance solution."

"You're right," said Chloe. "I'll need to be on the telescope so I can use it enhanced by my farseeing. Then I think it makes the most sense to have you next to whatever I am going to throw, as our magical connection is nearly seamless."

"Let's start with that," agreed Bertha.

Robert said, "How about for the initial practice, we have rocks in the courtyard outside the library?"

Soon, their plans were formed, and they asked Emily to arrange for the rocks. "I can give that task to the apprentices! It will be excellent practice for them." She chuckled.

The baron then contacted Chloe. *"The good news is that we found the meteor and it isn't really deep. Thankfully, it just missed an ocean trench, or we never would be able to manage. Bernard is rigging some equipment, but he says that he'll need some of your magic as well. Lifting something that size out of water is hard."*

"I understand. Let me know when you are ready, and I'll use farseeing so that I can both see and hear you. And thanks! That is good news."

Chloe shared the baron's information. "I'm hoping that they will be ready to lift the meteor by morning, as we are running out of time."

"Right, then," said Bertha. "One step at a time. Let's get ready for target practice tonight."

Everyone laughed, and Chloe thought just how lucky they were to have Bertha, not only for her talents and her magic, but for her determination and her humor.

That evening, as soon as it was dark enough to see the asteroid, Robert and Chloe went up to the observatory while Bertha and William, along with a group of supporters, waited in the courtyard. Robert looked through the telescope once Chloe had it positioned and said, "You want to hit it on the right-hand edge near the middle of the asteroid."

"OK, here goes!" First, she sent a tendril of energy to the spot Robert had indicated. Then she called to Bertha, *"Can you pick up one of the smaller rocks for our first try?"*

As Bertha held the rock, Chloe latched onto it, bringing it up outside the observatory until it was in line with her energy tendril. *Now or never,* she thought as she summoned all her energy, backed by both Bertha and Libby, and started shoving the rock, increasing the speed as she went, following along the tendril. She stepped away from the telescope when she was in a place where she could use her farseeing, and Robert watched using the telescope. She kept accelerating as hard as she could and finally *thunk*! She actually felt the impact.

"Perfect," confirmed Robert. "You hit right were you needed to. It was too small to have any effect," he went on, "but for target practice, it was a bull's-eye!"

They practiced several more times that night and decided that tomorrow night, they would need to have the rocks located in Forbury at the site where they hoped the meteor would be so that Chloe could practice again in a situation closer to the real one.

They all headed off to bed with not only a much better idea of what still had to be done, but also more hope that provided Chloe could increase her skills quickly enough, there was a solution.

The next day, Chloe used farseeing to connect with the baron and Bernard.

"Bernard has everything ready," said the baron, and Chloe could see various types of equipment behind him.

Bernard stepped into view. "I have managed to get ropes around the meteor, and believe me, that wasn't easy. Thankfully, it isn't as deep as we'd feared. The ropes are then strung over a pulley, as you can see." He pointed behind him. "The men and gryphons are harnessed and ready to pull in a team, but they will need help."

Chloe made a quick check that Libby and Bertha were standing by, and then she said, "We're ready. On your signal."

Bernard did a countdown, and then on his signal, everyone—men, gryphons, and mage—aided by Bertha and Libby, pulled. When it looked as if they wouldn't be able to get it over the edge of the cliff, Bertha quickly called in the power of various dragon rider pairs to boost the energy, and at last, after nearly an hour of effort, the enormous meteor rolled up over the cliff edge onto a flat spot that had been specially prepared.

"Well done!" shouted Chloe as the men and gryphons cheered. She called Robert over to let him know that the next phase in Operation Asteroid Move was completed. "Do you need to see the meteor?" she asked him. "I could send you to Forbury."

"No, I don't. It is certainly the biggest consolidated mass we have on this planet. Either it will work or it won't."

"It has to work," she said, and then she returned to Bernard and the baron. "That is excellent work on your end. Getting the meteor positioned was the second hardest part of this plan. Now, we were wondering if you could arrange to have some smaller boulders in that same location by tonight, as I need to test whether I can sling the rock if it is farther away than the library courtyard."

The baron laughed and said, "You'd better be able to because there is no way this meteor is going to be moved to Havenshold, especially not in four days!"

"You're right! So if you can put some practice boulders there, say midsize up to the largest you can get, I'll practice tonight and tomorrow night. Then we'll arrange everything for the third night."

"We'll be ready on this end," concluded the baron, and he turned to Bernard as Chloe ended her farseeing.

The next two nights were filled with very hard work. Chloe was getting better and better with sending the energy tendril to just the right spot, and she was able, with just Bertha and Libby's help, to move all the midsized boulders. She thought it would be harder when she had to use her farseeing to locate the boulders and then send the energy tendril from the boulder to the spot on the asteroid, but after a few misses, that became almost second nature. The three of them managed all the midsized boulders, but then, as the boulders became larger, they started tapping into the bonded-pair network.

It turned out to be a good thing that they were testing the network early because there were a few minor glitches, and William wanted to shuffle several of the groups around for greater efficiency, but overall, everyone was pleased. Of course, even the biggest boulders were still much smaller than the meteor, but everyone was confident because so far only about five percent of the energy network had been tapped into for any single launch.

"Congratulations, everyone!" said Chloe, using telepathy to be sure that she was including the entire network. "We are as ready as we will ever be. So please, get a good night's sleep and have an easy day tomorrow. It will be dark enough to see this asteroid by nine, so be sure you are comfortable and properly situated by then. The support staff will be in full swing, and William has worked out all the kinks in the rotation so that the energy will keep right on flowing, but each of you will get short breaks. Any questions?"

There were none, so Chloe ended with, "Good night then, and just know that without each and every one of you, we would have no chance at all."

The next evening, all the bonded pairs in Draconia found their assigned places in the courtyard and library. In the other three nations, their pairs were also gathering in their capitals or, in the case of Forbury, in the baron's home and yard.

Chloe addressed them all telepathically. *"We've practiced, and we know what we are doing. You all know how the network works, and Bertha will be pulling the actual energies, funneling them to me so that I can focus only on moving the meteor. Are there any last-minute questions?*

When everyone was set, Chloe sent out an energy tendril to the asteroid, locking in the same place as before. Then she fastened the other end to the meteor. The tendril would not support anything, but it served as her guide so that the impact would be at the spot Robert felt gave them the best chance.

Chloe took a deep breath and calmed herself. Her whole life had been leading up to this moment, even if she hadn't always realized it. She began lifting the meteor. Robert was watching through the telescope, but fortunately—or unfortunately—the asteroid was close enough now that it could be seen with the naked eye. Chloe did activate her farseeing though for both the meteor and the asteroid.

"Remember," said Robert, "you have to keep pushing even after impact."

Chloe nodded and then focused entirely on her task, totally unaware of anything else. Slowly, the meteor rose, and she positioned it on the energy tendril before beginning to push it in earnest.

Bertha kept feeding her energy from the network, and Libby fed her energy directly. Getting the meteor moving and then getting it out of the planet's atmosphere were the hardest parts. Once it was free of the planet, they could pick up the acceleration. She kept right on accelerating just as much as she could. She was only vaguely aware of Libby's stepping out of the energy loop from time to time and then returning after recharging herself. Bertha's energy remained constant because she was only channeling the network's energy. They were keeping Bertha's own magical energy in reserve.

After what seemed like eons, but in fact was about an hour, Chloe later learned, she felt the impact as the meteor hit the asteroid, and she was pleased, if shaken, to realize that it hit hard.

"The asteroid shifted slightly," said Robert. "Keep it moving. Don't stop. Remember all the physics I taught you. A body in motion will stay in motion, so let's keep that asteroid moving."

Chloe did as he said without saying anything; she needed every bit of focus she could bring to the task. She was starting to feel tired even with the channeling of energy. But they had to move the asteroid past the break-even point, as Robert had termed it, the point at which the asteroid would snap back to its original trajectory or one so close as to make no difference. Once past the break-even point, even if the asteroid fell back, it would fall past the planet. And if they could push it even further, the asteroid would make a new trajectory and head for the sun.

Robert kept her up-to-date with the asteroid's progress. "Great," he said after a while. "It is past the break-even point, so we're good there, but if you can keep it up to get it further, then when the meteor falls away, it won't return here."

That gave Chloe the incentive she needed, as she was really flagging now. She didn't want to have to deal with either the asteroid or that meteor ever again. And just when she thought she could shove no longer, Chloe felt Bertha's magical energy surging through her. *We can do this,* she thought and shoved even harder.

"You did it!" yelled Robert sometime later. "You can stop now. The asteroid will fall to the sun now and the meteor with it."

Chloe collapsed back into her chair, and then she heard all the cheers, both telepathic and real. Her mother was in the observatory within minutes with food and a hot mug of tea. After Chloe got some food into her and drank her tea, she felt much better. She went down to the courtyard with her mother and Robert, and the crushing of hugs was immense.

Todd had brought fireworks, because, as he said, he knew she would do it. He shot off the fireworks, and everyone celebrated. Chloe received a ton of telepathic congratulations as well. The party lasted all night, as no one wanted to leave.

Clotilda came up to her at one point and after hugging her again, said, "This year's summer solstice celebration is going to be really huge. We are going to invite the other three nations to participate if they wish, and just so you know now, you'll be making a speech."

Chloe started to shake her head, but Clotilda said, "Yes, you will. You have two weeks to prepare. Now get some rest! And again, there just aren't words to thank you."

Chloe headed back into the library while the party was still going on. She found her cozy alcove and fashioned herself a comfy spot to sleep in. *A speech!* she thought as she fell into a deep sleep.

— 30 —
WHAT NEXT?

The next two weeks were a blur in Chloe's mind. Her mother and sister were determined to make a special set of robes, so they were very busy, and she was glad that they'd made so many for her that she didn't have to put up with a lot of fittings.

Gregory asked her into his office about a week after the War of the Asteroid, as it had been named. "Have a seat," he said.

Once she was settled, he began, "You know, I started this academy because there was a real need for it. Those who finish the required schooling but haven't yet decided on an apprenticeship need a safe place to explore their options. I was lucky, as I loved to study and teach myself. But that doesn't work for everyone."

Chloe nodded, wondering where this was going. "And I think the first five years of Pathfinder Academy have been wonderful. All seven of our students from your class are nearly finished or finished with their training and are ready to embark on their chosen paths. I am very happy with how the academy has developed."

Chloe nodded again, still very puzzled. Gregory continued, "But I think it is time for some changes. When I took this on, it was in addition to my full-time job as a volcanologist. My work has expanded to the point where I now want an apprentice or two of my own. And Emily makes a wonderful leader for the dragon riders, but that is also a big job. Adding the running of Pathfinder Academy is just too much, especially since we hope to start our own family."

Chloe looked up at that and said, "That's wonderful!"

"Thanks, but it means that I need to find someone else to take charge of the academy. As our most illustrious and certainly our most capable graduate, would you be my successor?"

"Me! You think I could do this?" said Chloe, stunned.

Gregory laughed. "You could do it with your hands tied behind your back. Look at how popular your astronomy classes are. And Aster keeps coming in to talk with you about coming here next year. Yes, you would be wonderful, if you are willing."

Chloe looked at him before saying, "Could I have a few days to think about it?"

"Of course," said Gregory with a smile.

The summer solstice celebrations were even bigger than Chloe imagined. Havenshold was overflowing with not only dignitaries from the other three nations, but many of the bonded pairs who had been part of the energy network and a good portion of the support crews that her mother and others had run. And all these were in addition to the regular solstice crowds. There were booths with arts and crafts and of course a ton of food booths. As Chloe walked through the arts and crafts section, she was thrilled to see that her father's booth was crowded with people wanting his toys. She waved as she passed, thinking that the new shop he was planning to open in the fall would definitely be a success.

Next, she passed Imogene's weaving and Clarissa's art booths, which were also nicely attended. One of the largest booths was Marjorie's, which had a section set aside for Zelda and another for her mother. That booth was also swamped with people, not only buying but placing orders. Again, she waved at them as she passed, and she thought that she had never seen her mother so happy.

Finally, it was time for the official ceremony, and again, Todd and her father had built the platform, and again, Chloe was seated on it, this time right next to Clotilda. Chloe fidgeted with a handkerchief she'd taken out of her pocket as Clotilda gave a considerable speech acknowledging her achievement. Then she had Chloe stand as she presented her with a large plaque commemorating her defeat of the asteroid.

Then it was Chloe's turn. "Thank you, Queen Clotilda, and thank you, everyone. Yes, I am the one who guided the meteor, but the reality is that you all should have a plaque just like this. Each and every one of you, whether you were part of the energy network or whether you were one of my mother's support team..." Here, she nodded to her mother, who was also on the platform and who seemed to be glowing from the recognition. "You all made this world safe again. I thank each and every one of you from the bottom of my heart."

She bowed and started to turn when someone shouted out, "What will you do now?"

Chloe turned back to the audience as she thought, *What indeed?* but she couldn't say that, so instead, she chose a lighthearted tone and shouted back, "I think a vacation is in order! Thanks."

There was lots of cheering, and she had many people who wanted to congratulate her. Then there were the fireworks, which were absolutely the best ever, as was said at every firework display. But this time, Chloe really did think that Todd had truly exceeded all expectations. Finally, Chloe slipped away to the library, seeking some quiet and solitude.

The next morning, she had breakfast with Bertha and Libby. She was feeling definitely unsettled. Libby finally asked her what she was thinking.

"Remember last night when someone asked, 'What's next?' Well, that's what I'm thinking. So there was a prophecy, and therefore, I became a mage, and then, thankfully, I was able to move the asteroid, with a lot of help from nearly everyone on the planet. But now what? I ran away from the hatching nearly six years ago because I hadn't any idea what to do next. Well, the last years have been productive and interesting and at times a lot of fun. I am so glad I've gotten to know you two, for instance. But now what do I do?"

"What would you like to do?" asked Libby.

"That's just it! I don't have a clue. My sister and mother are nearly ready to open their own shop, and now my mother and even my grandmother are wonderfully happy, something that I am certainly very glad about. They had both been living such horrible, bitter lives that I'm thrilled they have found a new path. And Zelda will be a great designer. Then my father has his own place, which even as nice as my mother now is, I think is still a very good idea because he can't really be himself with her. His toys were selling like hot cakes yesterday, so I know his new shop will be a success as well. Beulah is already a fully qualified veterinary assistant, and Sylvester is now training her to be the second vet in the clinic. Ultimately, when he retires, the clinic will be hers. Bruce is nearly a fully qualified blacksmith, and he is also making decorative ironworks, so he's set. Imogene and Clarissa are nearly done with their very successful apprenticeships, and they know where they are going. Patty, Stephen, and George will be senior apprentices this year and in three years, fully qualified dragon riders, and so on. But what about the mage who fulfilled the prophecy? I'm at a dead end!" Chloe wailed.

Bertha wrapped Chloe in her paws, and both she and Libby waited until Chloe calmed down. Then Bertha said, "As both Libby and I know, since we are the only ones of our kinds also, being the trailblazer is never an easy or comfortable path. Libby has been totally alone for most of her over five hundred years. You have a lot of friends and family, which will continue to be a big source of comfort for you."

"Yeah, but—" started Chloe.

Libby held up a hand. "No buts about it. When Bertha isn't off being our ursine seer, she has Boris and Berla to care for and train. I know that helps her a lot. And now, thanks entirely to you, I too have people enjoying my space. I can't tell you what that means."

"OK, but what am I supposed to do now?"

"What about accepting Gregory's offer? Especially since you are still trying to figure out what a mage does and what that path means, I think you are suited perfectly for the job of helping others, like Aster, find their paths. You've already done that for your family."

"Yeah," said Chloe a bit hesitantly.

"And you love teaching. What about teaching more? You knew nothing about astronomy five years ago, and now you are the planet's expert. You seemed to enjoy the physics that Robert taught you. I know it was basic and he isn't a physicist, but you sure could be if you wanted, and then you could encourage others. We have lots of manuscripts in this library, but face it, Draconia doesn't seem to value education beyond the basics. Maybe you could change that and bring real life to me."

"Maybe," said Chloe with less hesitancy. "But how could I run the academy if I have to keep on with these tours of mine?"

This time, Bertha answered. "I suspect you will be able to fashion those tours however you want, and now that you can teleport, you could, for instance, pop up to Granvale and visit with Heather and Heidi and see what is happening there and then pop back all in the same day. You could similarly visit the baron and Oswald, and so forth, staying longer if you wished and it worked with your schedule or making a quick visit. And I'm sure Gregory would stand in for you if you needed him to. And you will, I hope, keep coming to see me for visits, especially in the summer."

"Of course! Yes, he did say he would be my substitute," agreed Chloe.

"So that seems to be a lot of 'What now,'" said Bertha.

"And," continued Libby, "isn't it time that you had your own place? It was wonderful that Amy and Todd were willing to foster you, but you are twenty now."

"But where would I go?" asked Chloe, twisting her hands.

"I would love it," said Libby, "if you made a small apartment, whatever you wanted, right here in the library. Maybe even with a magical door into my sitting room so that we could spend evenings together if we wanted and you could come to breakfast in your pj's if you wanted."

Chloe brightened up considerably. "Oh, could I? I love it here."

Both Bertha and Libby laughed. "We'd noticed," said Bertha. "You seem to spend as many nights here now as at Amy and Todd's."

"So why don't you do that right now! Make an apartment, and we'll watch," said Libby.

"And put in our two cents worth as well," said Bertha. "I want to see this before I head home."

So that is what Chloe did. She made a small, one-bedroom apartment right next to Libby's sitting room at the very back of the library. She decorated it all in pink and purple, but she didn't worry much about decorative items like wall hangings or pillows because she was quite sure her friends would all be eager to help with that. She did make a closet in her bedroom suitable for hanging her robes, but she didn't make it much bigger than what she actually needed, as she didn't want to encourage her mom and Zelda too much. Then she fixed up her living room with a comfy couch long enough to nap in and with a foot-stool for when she was reading. She made a small alcove with a table and a couple of chairs in case she had someone over who wanted to share a meal. She didn't bother with a kitchen, since she didn't cook and had no desire to. Her living room had a glass door looking out over the library but with drapes, which could be closed for privacy. She also put a few windows on the outside of the building as well as two skylights, one in the living room and one over her bed. The wall that adjoined Libby's sit-ting room had an invisible magic door. Then she finished off her apartment with a door to the outside, so that if the library were closed, she could come and go through her own apartment.

She sat back on Libby's couch and said, "How's that?"

"Why don't we walk through it!" exclaimed Bertha. The three of them went through Chloe's magic door and looked at what Chloe had done. They pronounced it absolutely perfect. Then Libby said, "I've heard that Sage has had kittens, and Lucy says there is one sweet female, white with a few tan spots, who seems to have Sage's telepathic abilities. Don't you think the library could use a mascot and you could use the company?"

"Oh, that would be nice," said Chloe. "We were never allowed to have pets when I was growing up. I'll go see Lucy today!"

Lucy was very happy to have found a home for the small white kitten, especially after Chloe had enough sense to ask the kitten what her name was. That made for an instant bond, and the kitten answered, *"Calliope."* After receiving all the instruc-tions for the care and feeding of a kitten, Chloe hugged Calliope and the two of them left, promising Sage, Lucy, and Gretchen that they could visit whenever they wanted.

Chloe and Calliope settled into a new routine. Clotilda had agreed to let Chloe have the summer off after all she had done, so Chloe relaxed, read, and studied some. She met with Gregory to learn about her job there and visited Amy and Todd to thank them yet again for all they had done for her, and she and Calliope even spent two weeks with Bertha and the twins.

A month after she had moved, she had an open house, and as she had figured, she received a lot of house-warming gifts to brighten and decorate her new home. The small apartment was jammed by the time all of her friends and family arrived, but no one seemed to mind. Everyone was happy about Chloe's new role as principal, librarian, and teacher.

Once everyone had left, Chloe sat on the couch with Calliope, put her feet up on the footstool, and said, "I think I've finally figured out what's next, at least for now." Calliope purred.

ABOUT THE AUTHOR

Daphne Ashling Purpus has long loved the written word—as a reader, writer, and teacher. Currently soaking up the beauty of Vashon Island in the Pacific Northwest, she is a retired librarian and teacher who still volunteers as a tutor at the local alternative high school, Student Link.

Purpus is both a poet and a fiction writer. She has published *A Year of Haiku* as well as three fantasy novels: *Dragon Rider*, *The Egg That Wouldn't Hatch*, and now *Dragon Magic*.

When she's not tutoring, writing, or reading, you can find Purpus quilting lap quilts, which she calls "portable hugs" and donates to anyone in need of such cheer, or caring for her three dogs and three cats.